WHERE THE MEMORIES LIE

ALSO BY SIBEL HODGE

WHERE THE MEMORIES LIE

SIBEL HODGE

THOMAS & MERCER

Text copyright © 2015 Sibel Hodge

Published by Thomas & Mercer, Seattle

www.apub.com

Amazon, the Amazon logo, and Thomas & Mercer are trademarks of Amazon.com, Inc., or its affiliates.

ISBN-13: 9781503947467
ISBN-10: 1503947467

33614056436743

Cover design by bürosüd° München, www.buerosued.de

Printed in the United States of America

Prologue

'What lies have you told recently, Mum?' Anna walks into the kitchen and slaps some textbooks down on the table.

In the middle of cutting up some peppers on a chopping board, I swing around with fear, my heart banging.

What does she know? She can't have found out the truth, surely.

'Mum, you've cut yourself!' She points to my finger.

I glance down. 'Oh.' I turn on the cold tap and run my finger under the flow of water. It's only superficial. 'What do you mean?' I swallow and lick my lips, aware that my voice is shaky. 'What lies are you talking about?' I inhale a sharp breath and brace myself for the worst.

'It's for my Religion and Ethics homework.' Anna sits down at the kitchen table, picks up a notebook from on top of the pile of books and taps it with a pen.

The relief hits me like a cold rush of air to my skin, sudden and hard. *Thank God.* I even manage a small laugh, although where I summon that up from, I don't know.

'Well, we all tell lies, don't we?' I say, forcing myself to sound casual.

She thinks about that for a moment, chewing on her lip. 'Even religious people? I mean, what about . . .' She waves the pen in the air. 'Priests and vicars, for example?'

I think about the horrific stories that have come to light over the years in the Catholic orphanages. About vicars sexually abusing their choirboys. Nuns physically abusing their charges. 'Especially them.'

'But that's hypocritical.'

I know all about being a hypocrite.

'Religion isn't supposed to be about lying, is it?' she asks.

'Absolutely right.' In fact, I'm a staunch atheist. I don't believe in something that tries to oppress people – women in particular – and control the masses. I don't particularly like the idea of religion being a compulsory subject at school, either, but Anna loves the ethics side of things, and she's good at debating. Maybe she'll become a lawyer.

Her smooth forehead scrunches up in a frown as she scribbles something down. 'But there could also be some good reasons for lying.'

If only she knew just how good.

I turn off the tap and pat the small cut with kitchen roll before wrapping it around my finger and squeezing.

'I have to examine the pros and cons, you see.' She scribbles something in her book with neat, precise handwriting. 'So, what lies have you told lately?'

'I think I should ask you that instead.' I try to grin but my mouth won't cooperate properly and probably makes me look as if I have severe constipation. Luckily Anna doesn't seem to notice.

She gives me a cheeky grin. 'Maybe we should do hypothetical lies.'

I raise my eyebrows. 'Wow! Is it that bad, then? What did you lie about?' I'm sure it will only be something ridiculously small. Anna is a good girl.

She blushes. 'No, it wasn't anything, really.'

'OK, hypothetically.' I turn my back to her and carry on with the peppers. 'This is your homework so you tell me.'

'Um . . . What about when you're planning a surprise party for someone and you lie about it because you don't want to ruin the surprise? That would be a good thing. A pro.'

'Yes.'

'And a white lie could also be a pro. To spare someone's feelings and stop them getting upset.'

White lies. I've tried to convince myself this is just a white lie I'm carrying around inside.

'Very good. We might tell lies with good intentions in mind.' My voice cracks slightly. I scrape the peppers from the chopping board into a frying pan and grab some mushrooms and an onion from the fridge.

'Does that make them acceptable, though?' Anna asks

I hesitate, going over the same things I've been asking myself. 'I think if you're trying to spare people's feelings – trying to protect them – then that's OK.'

'But what if the person you're trying to protect should know the truth? What if they would *want* to know whatever you're trying to spare them from?'

'Well, take you, for example. I would want to protect you from harm. If I knew something that could potentially upset you or have a negative impact on your life, as your mother, it's my job to protect you. I would think of it as a necessary good in some situations.' I peel the onion and begin chopping, glad for once that it's making my eyes stream. I want to cry again as I think about the enormity of everything that's happened, and the onion will mask it. I sniff. Wipe my eyes with the back of my hand. 'What else can you think of?'

'Don't women lie about their age?'

'Some men do, too. Let's not be sexist here.'

'Is that good or bad, then?'

'Probably pretty inconsequential, unless it affects someone else.'

'So, there are harmless lies.' She writes that down and underlines it a few times. 'And politicians lie, don't they?'

'Probably every time they open their mouths.'

'Well, that's definitely a con.' I hear her scribbling furiously behind me. 'They're supposed to be working for the benefit of their people and they're lying about a lot of things. That is *so* hypocritical, too!'

My daughter has strong ethics. She's intelligent and inquisitive. Old and wise beyond her years. I was glad we'd moved on from the Capital Punishment homework she'd had recently because Anna becomes a little obsessed about things sometimes. She works hard at school. Reads a lot of books that are probably beyond her years, but if she feels strongly about something, she'll go on and on about it. Read about it. Research it on the Internet morning, noon and night. I'd been forced to watch documentaries and films about prisoners on death row for weeks on end. I can now envision being bombarded with research about lying, and I don't need to be reminded, thanks all the same.

'Don't people lie on their tax returns?'

I smile, despite myself. 'Yes. And their CVs.'

'That could be an offence, though, couldn't it? The tax return, I mean.'

'It's actually how they caught Al Capone in the end.'

'Who's he?'

I wave the knife around. 'It doesn't matter.'

'OK, so, that's actually a bad one, then. If you know your lie is covering up a crime?'

My stomach twists. I transfer the onion to the frying pan, put the lid on and wipe my eyes again with my knuckles.

'Isn't it?' Anna prompts me again, jerking me out of the thoughts I'm lost in about her. About what happened. How it only takes one split second. One wrong move to make everything implode.

I think again about how far I'd go to protect my daughter, my family. The lies I'd tell. And I convince myself again that not all lies are the same.

And when the memories lie, sometimes it's best to let the truth stay hidden.

Chapter One

B y the time they found her remains, I hadn't thought about her for years. I'd been too busy getting on with my life. A life I thought was normal.

Normal for me that week was trying to get out of the house on time in the mornings. I'd been expressly forbidden by Anna to walk her to the bus stop now she was twelve. I'd tried to tell her that I wasn't really walking her to the bus stop at all, that I was just meeting Nadia there so we could walk the dogs together, but she wasn't having it. I knew that Anna could quite easily go down our path, out of the gates, and walk two hundred metres to the bus stop without anything happening to her, but it didn't stop me worrying. Luckily, Anna hadn't turned into the usual pre-pubescent, difficult monster yet, despite being twelve years old and nearly at the end of her second year of secondary school. And we still had a very close and loving relationship. When we were at home she still followed me everywhere most of the time, as if she could never bear to be that far away from me. She even followed me to the toilet sometimes, chatting on about stuff! I jokingly called her my little Klingon. Maybe I was too overprotective, but I'm a mother: it's my job. Plus, Anna nearly didn't arrive in the world. After six miscarriages, it was touch and go whether she'd make it to full term. She was my little miracle baby, and you don't go taking miracles for granted. You appreciate them every day. Take that extra effort to make sure nothing happens to them.

Our house was set back from the road, with a big front garden and a tiny rear one. I didn't mind having all the space at the front as it was completely private from prying eyes with the seven-foot-tall laurel hedges. Plus, the views at the back were amazing, looking out onto the woods behind that led onto sprawling hills of green Dorset countryside.

I unlatched one of the six-foot wooden gates and pushed it open. Poppy, our crazy golden retriever, escaped out first, dribbling with excitement at the prospect of a walk. I headed the short distance up the road, past the Kings' Arms pub towards the bus stop on the opposite side. Anna was chatting with a few of the other village kids already waiting for the bus to drive them the nine miles to their school in Dorchester. No Nadia or Charlotte yet, which was strange. My sister-in-law Nadia was an organised control freak who was always on time. Some might even call her anal. For once, I'd beaten her. Go, Olivia!

I carried on walking, scanning the road, looking for them. Hopefully Charlotte wasn't sick again. She'd had some kind of virus a few months ago that she couldn't seem to shake, and she always looked tired lately. Mind you, she was studying really hard for her GCSEs. All twelve of them. Yes, twelve! I thought they worked the kids much too hard these days. Charlotte barely had any spare time with the amount of homework she'd been given in the last few years.

And then I saw them both, hurrying towards me as the school bus pulled up at the kerb. I waved. Charlotte waved back, her fine long hair fanning out over her shoulders as she ran towards us. She looked pale still, with dark rings under her eyes.

The other kids and Anna climbed aboard. I wanted to kiss her goodbye but even though she's still a model child and not a terrible, hormonal teenager, I know public displays of affection are definitely 'uncool'.

I settled for a wave instead. 'Have a good day.'

'Hi, Aunty Olivia. Bye, Aunty Olivia.' Charlotte rushed past and swung herself aboard.

With a whooshing sound the bus doors closed and they were off.

I turned in Nadia's direction and waited for her to catch up with her chocolate brown Labrador, Minstrel. She looked wrong. Usually, she's immaculately turned out. She doesn't even go to the corner shop without her full makeup on and her wavy blonde hair perfectly straightened and hanging down her back like a sheet of smooth, shimmering metal. This morning, her hair was pulled on top of her head in a messy bun. She wore old tracksuit bottoms that she normally wouldn't be seen out dead in. Her face was as pale as Charlotte's. Her eyes puffy and red. She had a lump of mascara caked in the corner of one of them.

Poppy tugged on the lead as they got closer, and then the dogs were involved in full-on sniffs and licks of fur.

'Are you OK?' I put a hand on Nadia's arm. 'Aren't you feeling well, either?'

She closed her eyes for a brief moment, as if steeling herself for what she was about to say. When she opened them again they were wet.

'Not here. Let's talk on the path.' Nadia walked ahead of me, back along the direction I'd just come from.

My house is the last one at the edge of the village. It's an old barn that my father-in-law Tom beautifully renovated and converted twenty-five years ago into a family home. Nadia, Ethan and Chris had all lived in it with their Dad until they left home. Then when

Tom got Alzheimer's, Ethan and I bought the house from him. I'd always loved it, you see, so I jumped at the chance. It was rustic and country with exposed brick walls, original quarry-tiled floors, thick wooden beams and trusses, oak-framed windows, earthy tones and bags of cosy charm. Nadia and Lucas prefer new, modern spaces, not something rustic and quirky, so they didn't want to buy it, and it was far too big for Chris on his own, so that was that. Tom lived with us there for a while before things became . . . well, let's just say difficult. Unsafe, actually. And upsetting. None of us wanted to see him in a nursing home. It was an awful thought. But I had Anna to consider, and Tom almost blew the house up one day by leaving the gas hob on and lighting his pipe in the kitchen when Anna was upstairs. Nadia did a lot of research to find the nicest nursing home with the best reputation, and that's how Tom ended up at Mountain View Nursing Home. Not entirely sure why it was called Mountain View – there are no mountains in Dorset – but anyway, we couldn't ask for somewhere nicer, really. The staff were so good with him.

Along the side of Tate Barn is a public footpath that takes you through a canopy of trees onto woods. On the other side of the woods are sprawling hills and fields that eventually lead to the next village of Abbotsbury.

'So, what's wrong?' I asked again as I let Poppy off the lead. She bounded off, then realised her playmate wasn't with her and bounded back again, tongue lolling to one side.

Minstrel, named by Charlotte after the chocolates she loved, barked back at her as Nadia stood there, staring off into space.

I put my hand on her shoulder. 'Nadia?'

She let Minstrel off her lead and the dogs ran away together, ears flapping.

'It's Lucas. He's having an affair.' Her eyes welled up again. She closed them and pressed her fingertips against the lids.

I gasped. 'No. No way. Why do you think that? Has he told you?'

'No, but I found some texts. To this *woman*!' She spat the word out as her eyes flew open.

'What woman?'

She started walking along the path. Marching, actually. I marched alongside her.

'She works with him. She's an air steward.'

Lucas was a long-haul pilot and was often away for a few days at a time.

'No! Are you sure? What did the texts say?'

'That she was missing him. That she couldn't wait to fuck him. That she was looking forward to a night together in Jamaica.'

'Where is he now, then?'

She wiped her eyes. 'Jamaica.'

'Oh.' For once I didn't know what to say.

'I thought he'd been acting a bit weird lately. Secretive. Whenever a text comes through he's fiddling with his phone for ages so I thought I'd check it, but he's started deleting his texts as soon as they come in, which he never used to do. Then yesterday, when he was in the shower, I heard a text arrive so I looked at it. Her name's Patty.' She snorted. 'God, Patty sounds like a bloody dog, or a hamster or something.' She stopped and turned to me, looking like a shell of herself.

I pulled her towards me in a hug. She was taller than me, nearly six foot, and my head rested on her shoulder, her collarbone digging into my cheek.

'I'm so sorry. What are you going to do?'

She didn't say anything for a long time. We just stayed like that, holding each other. Then she pulled back.

'He's my life. I love him more than anything. So I'm not going to do anything. I can't. I can't lose him.'

I gave her what I hoped was a supportive smile.

'What? Do you think that's weak of me?' She sniffed.

'I . . .' I didn't know what it was. I was in shock. I couldn't imagine Lucas having an affair. They always seemed so perfect for each other. They'd been together a year longer than Ethan and I, so that would make it twenty-seven years now. That's no mean feat these days, when people change their partners as often as their mobile phones. 'Maybe it's not what you think. Maybe there's some explanation for it.'

'No, there's no mistake.' She stared out into the thick mature oaks and beech trees. Then she shook her head. 'But I've decided. I've really decided I'm not going to do anything about it.'

'Are you sure?'

'Yes. It will just blow over, I'm positive. I can't lose him, Olivia. I just can't. I'm not going to make him choose. I need him. Charlotte needs him. We're his family.'

I thought about what I'd do if I found out Ethan was having an affair. I couldn't just do nothing and let him carry on. I couldn't handle knowing he was sleeping with someone else, thinking of someone else. Maybe even falling in love with someone else. It would always be there, wouldn't it? The elephant in the room. Hanging over what you did and what you thought, until jealousy and suspicion sucked the life out of anything you had left. Because everything that you thought you knew – that you trusted, believed in – would be a lie, and I had a big thing about honesty. Ethan and I had never had any secrets. How can you have a relationship based on deception? And what about Anna? It would rock her world, too, but I would have to think about what was best for her.

'I think it will just blow over,' Nadia said again, but I didn't know who she was trying to convince – me or herself.

'Yes, of course it will,' I said, going for supportive instead of judgemental. I suppose a lot of us don't know what we'd do until we're in that situation. I knew, though. I'd cut Ethan's balls off and shove them down his throat. 'Is Lucas coming back for the picnic this weekend?'

'Yes.' She glanced over at me and forced a slight smile. 'Promise you won't say anything to anyone. Not even Ethan.'

'Oh, God, Nadia, you know we don't have any secrets.'

'Please.' She gripped my arm tight, making me stop. 'I don't want Lucas finding out I know. They're best mates, and if you tell Ethan, he'll want to get involved.'

'He won't say anything to Lucas if I ask him not to.'

'He'd probably punch him! No. This is private. This is my secret, not yours.'

I groaned, looking skyward. 'OK.' I just hoped she knew what she was doing, though.

'Can you do me a favour?'

Poppy trotted back towards us with a stick in her mouth, closely followed by Minstrel, who was trying to jump on her back. She slobbered on my walking boot, keeping us company as we headed through the woods.

'Of course. What?'

'I was going to see Dad later, but I don't feel up to it today. Is there any chance you can go instead?'

Since Lucas and Ethan were away such a lot with work, it was usually Nadia and I who took turns to visit Tom every few days. Chris went, too, of course, when he was working locally. Most of the time I didn't mind seeing my father-in-law so much. I loved him, after all, and I wanted to make sure he was as happy as he could be, but sometimes it was tiring and frustrating and became more of a chore or duty than a pleasure.

'I'm on the late shift today, but I'll go in and see him when we've finished our walk.' I worked part time as a practice nurse at the village doctor's surgery, job sharing with another part-time nurse called Elaine. 'I was going to go to the supermarket soon, but that will have to wait, I suppose. I got tied up with taking Anna clothes shopping yesterday and forgot to go. Just about managed to rustle up some stale toast for Anna's breakfast. I'm such a bad mother.'

'You're not. Anyway, thank you.' She turned around. 'Let's head back now. I've got accounts coming out of my ears. I don't know how I'm going to be able to concentrate.'

Nadia worked as an accountant and office administrator from home, pretty much single-handedly running Tate Construction, the building firm Tom had started forty years ago. It was a family effort, with Ethan as the company's architect and Chris as the project manager. She also did the accounts for several local children's charities for free, and organised fund raisers for them. I don't know how she juggled it all with Charlotte as well. I found it enough juggling five hours of work a day and looking after the house and Anna. Then again, I wasn't a super-efficient organiser like Nadia, although sometimes I wished I was more like her. She always got the job done, whereas I was often late, forgot to organise Anna's packed lunches in advance and missed appointments. Nadia was the complete opposite. Always early and had a week's worth of dinner menus worked out in advance. She was three years older than me, so I'd never had much to do with her at school, but when I'd started going out with her brother, and then married him, we'd naturally become close over the years. She was like the big sister I'd always wanted. A natural nurturer, she organised all the family get-togethers and was the first one to step in and offer help if any of us needed it. The strong one. If she was an elephant, she'd be the matriarch, which was not surprising, really: Eve, her mum, had died of a sudden brain aneurism when Nadia was nine years old. Ethan was six at the time and Chris was three, so Nadia had naturally stepped into the role of caretaker, looking after her brothers, learning to cook – she's an amazing cook, unlike me! – and generally helping her dad out in any way she could. I asked Nadia once how she'd kept it all together with such a huge responsibility from an early age, but she'd just said it was easier to be strong when other people needed her. Her craving to help others stopped her falling apart. Eve's death eventually brought the Tates closer together, and they had a bond that went deeper than just being family. They were part of one another, and I was a part of them.

We said goodbye at the end of the path and I gave her another hug.

'Will you be all right?'

'I'll have to be, won't I?'

'Oh, Nadia, I'm so sorry this is happening. I just—'

She shook her head to cut me off. 'Don't say anything. It'll be fine. You'll see. I'm glad I've got you to talk to, though. What would I do without you?' She let me go and walked away, leaving me standing on the path, watching as her shoulders shook with the tears she was holding inside.

After settling Poppy in her basket in the kitchen, I drove into the nearby town of Dorchester. Mountain View nursing home was on the outskirts, set in three acres of lush, well-tended gardens. Tom had always loved working in his own garden at Tate Barn when he had any spare time, and he missed it now he was unable to. He had to settle for walks in the grounds these days instead. When I moved into my first house and got a garden of my own, I always wondered how he'd ever found the time, what with bringing up Chris, Ethan and Nadia single-handedly, running a busy construction business and looking after his own home. But he said gardening relaxed him. In a busy, chaotic world, it was his little haven where he could empty his mind of the stress and not have to think about any problems for a while.

As I stopped at a set of traffic lights, I glanced out the window and caught sight of a woman walking up the street. She was slim and busty, her clothes showing off her best assets. Her long hair bounced on her shoulders as she walked in very high – and very uncomfortable-looking – stilettos that defied the laws of gravity. She looked so much like my childhood friend Katie, who'd left the village ages ago, that the breath caught in my throat for a moment. Was that her? I hadn't seen her in years. I craned my neck, trying to get a proper look as she hurried past on the opposite side of the road, just the back of her now visible on the busy street. The traffic lights changed and someone sounded their horn behind me. By the time I'd driven along, she'd disappeared. I shook my head. No, it couldn't have been her.

My Mini crunched to a stop on the gravel car parking area at Mountain View, and I got out and walked up the steps to the reception.

'Hi, Mrs Tate.' Kelly, the very perky receptionist, smiled at me.

'Hi, how are you?' I smiled back and wrote in the visitors' book, recording the same things as usual: my name and address, who I was there to see, my vehicle registration number and the time I'd arrived.

'I'm pretty good, thanks. Just counting the days until my holiday now.'

'How exciting. Where are you off to?'

'Portugal. Have you ever been?'

'No, but I hear it's nice.' I put the pen back on top of the book as her phone rang.

The smell of disinfectant, laced with pine, vomit, boiled carrots and a hint of lavender, hit my nostrils as I headed up the corridor to the nurses' station in Tom's wing. Eau de Nursing Home.

'Hi, Mary. How is he?' I asked the head nurse, who was looking down at a folder of notes on her desk.

She gave me a half smile and I immediately knew something was wrong.

'What is it? Is Tom OK?' I didn't want any more bad news today.

'Yes, he's OK, it's just . . . I wanted to talk to you before you pop in and see him.'

I leaned my hip against the desk.

'For the last few days he's been very agitated. More than usual, I mean. He says he's having bad dreams, about a woman called Georgia.'

'Well, as you know, he's suffered from nightmares for years.'

'Yes, but these seem different. When he wakes up afterwards, it takes us a long time to calm him down again, and he keeps saying Georgia is haunting him.'

'Georgia?' I frowned. 'As far as I know, he doesn't know anyone called Georgia.'

'Ah, well, that's what I wanted to ask. He said she'd gone missing.'

'Missing?' I pursed my lips, thinking. 'No, it doesn't ring any bells.'

'I'm sure it's just the usual confusion, but when he said she was missing, I wanted to check with you.'

I shook my head. 'No, I've never heard him mention anything like that before. Did he say anything else about her?'

'Not really.'

'You know what he's like. Sometimes when he watches TV, he thinks the characters are people he knows. Sometimes he doesn't recognise the family anymore, or thinks Nadia is his wife and Ethan is his brother. I'm sure it's nothing.'

'The other day, he was convinced I was someone he went to school with.' She nodded and rolled her eyes good-naturedly.

'I'll let you know if he says anything else, though.' I headed past her desk to his room at the end of the corridor.

Every time I saw Tom, he seemed to shrink inside himself more. Once a tall, solidly built, active man, he was now stooped and colourless and bony. It broke my heart to see the changes this ravaging disease had forced upon him. I was a nurse, so I knew what death and illness looked like, but when it was someone you loved, it didn't make you hardened to it. The worst thing was the slow, steady and relentless progression of a disease that would eventually be fatal. From the initial stages of attacking the part of the brain where memories are formed, over years it makes new memories harder to form. Then it spreads to different regions of the brain, killing cells and compromising function. The damage to the areas where emotions are processed then makes it harder for patients to control moods and feelings. Next it wreaks havoc on the senses, even causing hallucinations and delusions, and erasing the oldest and most precious memories of a person. In the last stages it destroys the area of the brain responsible for regulating breathing and the heart. For family members it can be horrific to watch the person you once knew literally change into someone else. Someone who was kind and compassionate can become vicious and bitter. Someone who was calm and happy can become angry and spiteful. Sometimes patients have no idea of their surroundings or loved ones. They can't identify everyday items. They have trouble understanding what is being said or going on around them. They gradually lose their ability to walk, become incontinent, or exhibit unusual behaviour. The symptoms are heartbreaking.

Nowadays Tom's lucid moments were outnumbered by the confusion, although he usually still recognised me. He was asleep, sitting in a comfy foam-padded high-backed chair in front of the window, overlooking the gardens. The newspaper was strewn messily over the surface of the small table in front of him, as if he'd become frustrated with it and flung it down in anger. Next to the paper was an intricately carved wooden box that Tom had made for Eve. It was designed with a secret compartment that could only be opened by sliding out and pushing in certain hidden parts of the design in a unique combination. Tom called it a magic box, and Anna had loved playing with it when she was a kid. I could never manage to open it but Anna always could.

'Hi, Tom.' I sat in an identical chair next to him and patted his hand. Loose skin hung from his fingers.

His eyelids fluttered open and it took him a moment to familiarise himself with his surroundings.

'Olivia.' He smiled warmly. 'Nice to see you. You haven't been here for ages.'

'I came in two days ago, Tom.' I patted his hand again and he gripped mine.

His eyes narrowed, as if he didn't believe me. 'Was that when you—' He stopped mid-sentence.

I waited for a moment. He often forgot what he was talking about in the middle of a conversation, or forgot words. Sometimes he liked to be prompted; sometimes it made him angry.

When he didn't carry on, I said, 'When what, Tom?'

He picked at his trousers with a fingernail, rubbing the same spot over and over. 'Fucking bastard.' He stared down angrily at them.

Before the disease, I'd never heard Tom swear. Never seen him lose his temper, either. He was the most laid-back person I'd ever known. He never seemed to get stressed about anything. Not anymore, though.

'That fucking bastard stole my trousers.'

I stroked his hand. 'It's OK, Tom. Don't worry. I'm here, OK? I won't let them take your trousers.'

He turned to me. 'You sure? Because they sneak in here at night. No one thinks I know, but I bloody know. I'm not stupid.'

'Of course you're not stupid.' I pointed out of the window to a rhododendron bush in full bloom, trying to distract him. 'What's the name of that bush, Tom?' I knew it, but I wanted to try and calm him down.

'That one?' His face softened as he pointed a shaky finger towards it. 'It's a *Rhododendron arborescens*. I planted one in our garden once for Nadia. I took all the kids to the garden centre and got them to each pick out a cocktail they liked.'

I knew he didn't really mean cocktail. He obviously meant plant.

'Then we named the cocktail after them. Every birthday, I'd hide a present under their cocktail for them when they came back from school.' He chuckled gently. 'They used to love it.'

'I bet they did. And do you remember doing your yearly Easter egg hunt for Anna and Charlotte? Hiding all that chocolate in the garden for them to find?' Tom had enjoyed watching the girls screeching and giggling all round the garden so much, he'd done it right up until he sold the house to us, and even though they were nearly thirteen and seventeen now and a bit too old for it, Ethan and I still carried on the tradition Tom had started.

He smiled and nodded, but I didn't know if my words had registered. 'How's Ryan?'

'Who's Ryan?'

He looked at me quizzically. 'You know.'

'No, Tom. Is he an old friend?'

'He's your son.'

'I have a daughter. Anna – remember? She's doing really well at school, although they're breaking up for the summer holidays in a few days.'

'I hope he calls you. It's not nice when your children don't keep in touch. You worry about them, don't you?'

I always thought it was best not to dwell on the memories he now got wrong, so I steered him in another direction. 'Charlotte's studying hard for her exams. Next term she'll be going to sixth form college. I can't believe how fast the time goes.'

'Fast,' he repeated, nodding softly.

'Mary said you'd mentioned someone called Georgia. Who's she? I haven't heard you talk about her before.'

He gripped my hand hard. 'You have to find her. She's haunting me.'

'What do you mean?'

He jerked forward, eyes wide. 'She won't leave me alone.'

I rubbed his arm soothingly. 'It's OK, Tom. She's not really here. It's just me.'

'No!' He pushed my hand away.

'Who is she, then? Why is she haunting you?'

'When I go to sleep.'

'It's just a dream, that's all. A recurring dream. I used to have one about—' I stopped abruptly. I used to have one when I was eighteen, about people who wanted to kill me, chasing me through an abandoned hotel somewhere abroad. It had gone on for about two years in the end. But it was probably best not to mention something so miserable to him in case he fixated on it. 'Anna's been having one about finding a horse in the garden,' I said instead. Yes, much more pleasant.

His brown eyes flashed dark with hatred, making him look nothing like the gentle giant of a man I once knew.

'She knows.'

'Knows what?'

He gripped the arms of the chair, lifting himself up. 'I want to get out! You can't keep me in here!'

'OK. It's OK. Let me help you with your slippers, though.' I worked his feet into a pair of moccasins with hard soles that Ethan and I had bought before he came into the home. 'Do you want to go for a walk in the grounds? Get some fresh air?'

'Can we go to Durdle Door?'

Durdle Door was a natural limestone arch formed on a beach near Lulworth, about a thirty-minute drive from Mountain View. It had always been one of Tom's favourite places to walk his dogs in his younger years, but it seemed to take on greater significance for him in the later stages of his Alzheimer's, and driving him for a trip out there always seemed to lift his mood. He couldn't manage to go all the way down from the top to the beach these days, but he was content to walk along the chalky white path on the cliffs above, where he could still enjoy the amazing views and refreshing, salty sea air.

'I don't have time to go there and back today, Tom. Next time I visit, I'll take you out along the cliffs. I promise.'

He nodded slowly. 'Let's go in the garden, then.'

'Do you want a wheelchair?'

'No. I want to walk. I'm not dead yet.'

I smiled.

Tom shuffled slowly along the corridor that led to the communal lounge/TV room and then through the large glass doors onto the patio.

I hooked my arm through his to steady him and we took a tour of the grounds.

'Ethan sends his love.'

'Ethan?'

'Your son.'

'Ethan,' he repeated. 'I don't think I know him.'

'He'll come and see you at the weekend. He's working in York again this week.'

'I don't want him here. *She'll* be here.'

'Who?'

'Georgia. She doesn't leave me alone. I want to be left in peace.' He stopped walking, turned to me and clutched my forearm with his bony hand. 'It's my fault.'

'I don't understand, Tom. What's your fault?'

His eyes watered and he averted them from mine, staring into the distance blankly as if in some kind of trance. 'I killed her, Olivia. I killed her.'

Chapter Two

I drove home with Tom's words echoing in my head.

I killed her.

After he'd uttered them, he became so agitated I couldn't get anything else out of him. It took half an hour to get him back inside. He'd thought I was trying to take him to an abattoir to chop his head off. Eventually, with the help of one of the male nurses, a wheelchair and a strong sedative, he was resting back in bed again.

What the hell did he mean he'd killed her? Killed who? Who was Georgia?

It couldn't be true, though. Absolutely not. Confusion was a perfectly normal symptom of the disease. Maybe he'd seen a TV programme about someone called Georgia who was killed, although quite frankly, I didn't think they should be letting the residents watch stuff like that. Or maybe he'd been chatting to one of the other patients whose daughter called Georgia had gone missing.

Yes, that was it. That was absolutely it. I'd never heard Tom mention anyone called Georgia before.

When I got home I made myself lunch and turned on the TV, flicking through the channels to find something to distract me. I ate a cheese and ham sandwich that I didn't even taste, swallowing it down with water to get it past my dry throat. I couldn't even tell you what programme I watched.

After letting Poppy out into the garden to do her business, I walked the ten minutes to work.

I was chock-a-block with patients from 1 p.m. until 6 p.m. when the nurses' appointments finished. I thought maybe dressing changes and assisting with smear tests and blood pressure checks would keep me occupied. Usually, I would have a great time chatting with the patients, putting them at ease, finding out what they'd been up to – I've always been pretty nosy and love talking – except I couldn't get it out of my mind: the look of guilt on Tom's face. The desperation in his eyes. The fear.

When I walked back in the front door, Poppy greeted me, wagging her tail so hard with excitement her whole backside shook. I praised her, flapped her ears a bit, which she loved, and kicked off my shoes by the bottom of the stairs next to Anna's.

'You OK, darling?' I called out.

'Yeah,' Anna said. 'I'm in the kitchen.'

I walked up the hallway and found Anna sitting on a stool at the island in the centre of our large farmhouse-style kitchen, which oozed sunlight and was the heart of the house. Her school books were placed in neat rows over practically the whole surface. Pens of various colours were lined up horizontally in front of her. She was so precise about certain things I sometimes wondered if she had OCD, but I always pushed that thought to the back of my mind. We all had it to varying degrees, didn't we? We all had routines, things that we liked just so. I'd seen far too many labels placed on kids these days. I wasn't about to put one on my precious girl.

I kissed the top of her head. 'How was school?'

'Good. But I've got some maths homework I might need help with. When's Dad back?'

Ethan was the maths genius and always helped Anna out with it. I could only add up with a calculator. I think I had number dyslexia, or something. When I looked at numbers on a page they all swam together.

'He'll be back Friday.'

'But he's always working away at the moment,' she whined.

'He's overseeing a big project in York and he needs to be on site. He can't commute from there to Dorset every day; it's too far.' I stroked her hair then peered in the fridge. My appetite still hadn't returned, and I didn't fancy cooking. What I fancied was a big glass of wine. 'He's going to call later so you can have a chat, though.'

'OK.' She bent over her notebook and underlined something neatly with a red marker pen and a ruler. 'I've got to do a project on capital punishment for Religion and Ethics.'

'Oh, how nice,' I drawled. I'd had a meeting with the school recently about them wanting to fast-track Anna through some of her subjects because they'd classified her as 'gifted'. Ethan and I had debated this for a while. I didn't think the school should be bandying about those kinds of terms. What about the other kids who weren't gifted? How would it make them feel? Still, Anna was very intelligent, and we'd decided in the end to go ahead with it. It meant she was learning some of the curriculum a lot earlier than she should've been, but she was clearly enjoying it, and from her reports she was doing really well.

'It's really interesting, actually,' she said. 'What do you think about the death penalty?'

What a cheery pre-dinner conversation. 'We don't have the death penalty in the UK.'

'Yes, I know, but I don't think I can put that excuse on my homework as to why I haven't done it. We've got to consider the ethics behind it.'

'Um . . . well, let me see.' I shut the door on the pretty much empty fridge. Unless I could make something out of a lone cheese triangle, some dried-up flat leaf parsley, a wrinkly mushroom and a potato with sprouty bits on it, then dinner would be of the takeaway variety. 'I think if you're guilty of committing a crime – and presumably to get the death penalty we're talking terrible types of murder – then I think you'd probably deserve it. I mean, take Myra Hindley, for example. What if she'd ever been let out of prison before she died? Or Peter Sutcliffe? People wouldn't be safe, would they?' I explained who they were. 'So the death penalty could be for the protection of the public to make sure it doesn't ever happen again. Plus, it would hopefully put people off doing such crimes in the first place and the crime rate might go down.'

'Actually, from the research I've been doing so far, about 90 percent of top criminologists in America think that the death penalty doesn't act as a deterrent to reduce murder or violent crimes. And . . .' she lifted her pen in the air and pointed it at me, 'doesn't it actually make you as bad as the criminal if you kill them?'

'No.'

'Why? It violates their human rights.'

I rolled my eyes. I hated these in-depth ethics homework debates. Sometimes you just know things, don't you? You know things are right or wrong, but you don't want to spend all night analyzing *why* you know it. 'Because people who kill and rape and torture shouldn't have any human rights. They gave them up when they did whatever heinous crime they committed. And if a bunch of psychos were allowed to wreak havoc and do whatever they wanted without consequences, then we'd be living in a world of anarchy and chaos, wouldn't we?' Although I sometimes thought we already *were* living in such a world, anyway, but we were calling the psychos 'governments'. 'Every action has a reaction. Every deed has a consequence. There's always a price to pay. And people have to think about that before they commit crimes.'

'Yes, but two wrongs don't make a right.'

'Sometimes they do.'

'You could make the criminal pay back to society by serving their time in prison instead. That would also give them punishment for what they'd done and would still protect the public.'

'Not if they got let out again, which happens a lot now due to overcrowding. Most of the time they only serve piddly little sentences these days. And I wonder how many prisoners actually reoffend. Have you researched that yet?'

'No, but that's a good point, Mum.' She scribbled that down.

'Yes, I make them occasionally.'

'Shouldn't they have a second chance to become educated in prison and change so they could start a new life when they're released?'

'Not everyone deserves a second chance.'

'What if the person was innocent, though, and they got the death penalty and were executed? Then you would've killed an innocent person.' She sat back smugly and crossed her arms. 'That wouldn't be justice, would it? We'd be as bad as they were for supposedly murdering someone.'

'Do you want a delivery pizza for dinner?' I changed the subject, not really wanting to talk about death anymore. It made me think of what Tom had said again, and I wanted to get it out of my head because there was no way it could possibly be true.

The guilt of not providing a healthy, home-cooked meal like Nadia would be doing right now was cancelled out by the excitement on Anna's face.

'Yeah!' Her eyes lit up. 'Ham and mushroom?'

'If you like.'

I ordered the pizza, fed Poppy and poured myself a large glass of something Australian, fruity and red. Ethan knew all about different kinds of wine. I just knew about drinking it. Pulling up a stool, I sat next to Anna and stared into space.

'What do you think?' she asked a few minutes later, popping the cap back on her marker pen.

'Pardon?'

'Weren't you listening?'

'Um . . . sorry, I was miles away.'

'About penicillin?'

'I know all about penicillin. What about it?' I said, thinking back to my medical training.

'No, it's OK. That would be cheating if I asked you. I'm going to do some research on the Internet about it.' She slid off the stool, tidying her books into a neat pile. 'I've just started doing the history of medicine.'

Conscientious to a fault, my daughter. I wondered how long it would be before it all went wrong. Before she locked herself in her room and only came out to eat. Before the only response I'd get from her would be a monosyllabic grunt. When she wouldn't want to be seen dead in public with me or Ethan, and would take the advice of her friends over her parents. Before she stayed up all night partying and slept all day. I dreaded the thought of when it would all change. I didn't like change.

Later, I was on my third glass of wine, staring through the window of the kitchen into the dark woods behind, when the phone rang.

'I'll get it!' Anna shouted from the lounge and picked up the wireless phone. 'Dad!'

I heard her chatting and laughing with Ethan but I couldn't make out what they were saying. I was too busy deciding how to broach the subject of what Tom had said. In between swigs of wine I chewed on the skin at the side of my thumbnail until I drew blood.

Fifteen minutes later, Anna padded gracefully into the kitchen like a dancer, all skinny long limbs and perfect posture. Not like some of the kids in her class who slouched all over the place. I wanted to tell them they'd end up with neck and shoulder problems later in life. She handed me the phone and padded out again.

'Hi, sexy,' I said to him, watching Anna's retreating back.

Anna glanced over her shoulder and pulled a face at the word 'sexy', miming sticking her fingers down her throat.

'Hi, darling. How's everything going?'

'I'm going to take this upstairs.' I slid off the stool, picked up my wine and went up to our bedroom, shutting the door firmly.

'Oh, sounds ominous. What's Anna been up to that you don't want her to hear? Did she get caught shoplifting? Or try to get served at the Kings' Arms with a fake ID?'

I laughed but it sounded flat. 'No, it's nothing to do with Anna. It's Tom.'

'Dad? Why? What's happened?' His voice rose with concern.

I lay on my side on our king-sized bed, head propped up with one hand. 'I don't know how to say this, but when I got to the nursing home today, Mary said he'd been having some bad dreams and acting agitated afterwards.'

'I thought you were going tomorrow, not today.'

By then, I'd completely forgotten what Nadia had told me before about Lucas and his possible affair. I wanted to tell Ethan about that, too, ask his opinion, but I'd promised to keep her secret. 'Well, Nadia was tied up with some stuff so I said I'd go. Anyway, Tom's been acting strange after these dreams, they said.'

'He's got Alzheimer's. He's been acting strange for years. And he's had bad dreams for a long time. What do you mean by strange?'

I stared up at the ceiling and took a breath.

'Liv?'

There was no easy way to repeat what Tom had told me so I just blurted it out. 'He said he'd killed someone called Georgia.'

Silence on the other end. Then, 'What do you mean? Killed someone?'

'Just what I said. Tom's been dreaming about someone called Georgia. Afterwards, he gets very upset and agitated, so much so that Mary asked if I knew anyone called Georgia because Tom told her she'd disappeared.'

'Disappeared? Well, who is this Georgia?'

'I don't know. That's what I'm trying to explain. I asked him about her and he said she was haunting him. That she wouldn't leave him alone. And then, when I took him outside for a walk and some fresh air, he told me he'd killed her.' My head throbbed. Probably with the wine, but maybe from anxiety, too.

'Don't be ridiculous, Liv!'

'I'm not being ridiculous. I'm not being anything. I'm just repeating something Tom told me and the staff.'

'Well, it doesn't make sense. He doesn't even know anyone called Georgia. Neither do I. He's just confused. I mean, last week he came out with a really obscure story about walking along the Great Wall of China, and he's never even been there!'

I rubbed my forehead. 'I know, I know. I've been thinking of all the strange things he's talked about lately that either didn't happen or didn't happen like he's remembering them. It's just . . .'

'Just what?'

'The look on his face. He really believed it, I'm sure. He believed he'd killed her.'

'Liv! This is Dad you're talking about. The man who traps field mice in humane traps so he can relocate them back outside and not have to kill them. The man who gets dogs from the rescue centre because he can't bear to see them alone and unloved. The man who spent six months doing volunteer work in India when he retired so he could help build schools and houses for poverty-stricken villages! He wouldn't hurt a fly. He's just confusing some story from another resident or a newspaper article he's read, and thinks he's done something when he hasn't. Or he's made it up. You know yourself that Alzheimer's is capable of producing hallucinations and delusions.' He paused for a second. 'I'll go and see him at the weekend with you, but, honestly, we've been here before with him talking about stuff that's never happened.'

'Yes, I know all that, but still, he . . .' I trailed off, feeling ridiculous then for even bringing it up. Ethan's voice sounded reassuring and confident and comforting, and he was absolutely right. Of course he was. 'Yes, I agree. You're right. He's just confused.'

'I'm always right.' He laughed.

'Hey, you're living in a house full of women. The women are always right here. You're only right when you're asleep.' I laughed back and changed the subject. 'So, how's the hotel project going?'

He groaned. 'The directors keep changing their minds at the last minute, which results in yet more headaches and delays. And at night I'm sick of seeing the inside of this hotel room where I'm staying. The food isn't as good as yours.'

I laughed again. 'OK, so now I know you're lying.' I was an average cook at best, with a tendency to overcook. Well, I called it 'overcook'. Someone else might say 'burn'.

His voice softened. 'I miss you, darling. And Anna. I wish this project was already over. Weekends with my favourite girls just aren't cutting it at the moment.'

I smiled. 'Miss you, too.' Even though we'd been together twenty-six years, since we were seventeen, the love we shared was still strong. And the passion. I still fancied the pants off him. I knew we were lucky in that respect. I'd known lots of childhood sweethearts who had broken up after they grew up and grew apart.

It hadn't happened with us, and I was really grateful for that. It hadn't happened with Lucas or Nadia yet, either, although who knew what would go on after Nadia's revelation. Was he really having an affair? How do you throw away all those years of history?

We chatted some more about the building project and Anna and what food we were going to take on the family picnic that weekend, and by the time I hung up it was just after 9 p.m.

'Bedtime!' I called down to Anna from the landing.

'Yeah, coming.' She trudged up the stairs and gave me a hug. 'Night, Mum.'

She was as tall as me now. When had that happened? I snuggled into her, sniffing in the scent of the strawberry body spray she liked. It was only recently that I'd had to stop moaning to get her to have a shower every day. Overnight, it was like she went from a smelly, dirty kid to a super clean freak. It would be makeup next, and bras, and boys. Oh, God.

'Night, darling. Love you.'

'Love you, too.'

I patted her back. 'See you in the morning.'

I went downstairs into the lounge. Anna had left the TV on and the news was playing. I didn't usually watch it; it was too depressing. Why didn't they ever report anything good? Imagine the state of the world if every news channel broadcasted only happy news? The media manipulated everything, anyway, as far as I was concerned. Ethan didn't agree. He liked to end his day watching the news. I couldn't think of anything more nightmare-inducing. No wonder people had insomnia.

I flicked the TV off and something Ethan said sparked in my head.

Newspaper article.

Tom didn't watch the news but he'd always loved reading it. Judging from the newspapers still regularly left in a messy heap in his room, he still did, or at least tried to. He must've remembered this Georgia from a story he'd seen.

Maybe it's not a good trait, but I am pretty nosy. And that was what spurred on my curiosity about what could've been in the papers to do with this missing woman that would make Tom 'remember' it so well and become so agitated by it.

Anna had also left the laptop on. It was the family laptop, although really it belonged to me and her. Ethan had his own. I was still worried about her having complete freedom to trawl the web for anything. Still worried about paedophiles grooming innocent girls. Even though I'd had to cave in recently and let her have her own Facebook, Instagram and Snapchat accounts, at least sharing a laptop meant I could monitor her online usage and make sure she was safe.

I opened it up and sat on the sofa, knees tucked to the side, resting it on my thighs. I supposed Georgia wasn't a very common name, but I didn't have a surname to go on so I wasn't expecting much, but I at least had to look.

I typed in *Georgia* and *missing person.* I got pages and pages of hits. Of course. Most of them had no relation to what I was looking for. There had to be millions of missing people in the world. I needed to narrow it down somehow.

Georgia, missing person, Dorset.

That still resulted in several pages and I started scrolling through. There was a missing persons page on Dorset Police's website, asking if the public knew the whereabouts of certain people. I checked each name but there was no Georgia. There was a story on the *Dorset Chronicle*'s website dated ten years ago about the body of a murdered young woman called Georgia Preston found in some woodlands, and her boyfriend had been convicted of the crime. How awful. Was that what Tom remembered? Had there been something in the paper recently giving an update on the case? Yes, that was the most likely scenario.

I chewed on my bottom lip, searching for any more recent articles about the case but couldn't find any. The rest of the pages didn't relate to anything relevant so I called Nadia.

She answered on the second ring, as if she'd been waiting for the phone. 'Lucas?'

'Sorry to disappoint you. It's just me.'

'I was expecting him to call hours ago. I hope he's not *otherwise engaged*!' Her voice rose with a bitter edge.

'Are you sure you can handle this without confronting him about it? I mean, you're going to be a nervous wreck every time he's late or misses a phone call or gets a text. If I was in the same situation, I'd *want* to know for certain.'

'Well, I don't want to know,' she said, slightly offishly.

'OK, I'm sorry. It's your marriage, your decision.'

'Yes.'

'I'm not going to mention it again, but if you want to talk, you can call anytime. You know that, right?'

'Thanks.' She warmed up. I couldn't even begin to imagine how worrying and hurtful this was for her to deal with. 'Well, I'm waiting for him to call so . . .'

'Oh, yes. Um . . . has Tom mentioned anything to you recently about someone called Georgia Preston?'

'No. Never heard of her. Why?'

I paused for a moment. There was nothing to tell her, after all. I didn't even know now why I'd called her. It was perfectly obvious that the story I'd read must've been what Tom was getting confused about.

'I think there's a Georgia in Charlotte's class, though,' she added.

My heart rate kicked up a notch. 'Is there? Is she still up? Can I talk to her for a minute?'

'Hang on a sec. She'll never hear me over that racket!' I could hear bouncy music in the background. 'Why are you asking, anyway?'

'Oh, no reason, really. Just being nosy – you know me.'

'Don't keep her long. I want her in bed soon. She's been so busy cramming for her exams, and what with that virus thing she still can't seem to shake, she's wiped out.'

'I thought she looked exhausted and pale.'

'Her friend Trish has had it for weeks and can't get rid of it.'

'I know. It's been doing the rounds at the surgery for months. Why don't you pop in for a blood test, though? Just to be on the safe side?'

'Yeah. I think I will when we get a minute.' The music got louder the closer she got to Charlotte's room. 'Turn that off now,' Nadia said to her. 'Here she is, Liv. Don't keep her on the phone long.'

'OK. I won't see you in the morning, though. I'm on an eight till one shift so we can't walk the dogs together.'

'OK. Night.'

'Hi, Aunty Olivia,' Charlotte came on the phone.

At sixteen, she was too old to call me Aunty, I thought. Or maybe I was too young to be called Aunty. Weren't your forties supposed to be the new thirties these days? I'd told her just to call me Liv or Olivia, but she still insisted, saying she thought it sounded rude otherwise.

'Hey, Charlotte. Who was that you were listening to?'

'Macklemore.'

'Cool.'

She laughed. 'It's not cool to say cool, anymore.'

'Whatever. Talk to the hand.' Yes, I'd picked up a few things from those annoying kids' shows Anna watched.

She laughed again.

'I just wanted to ask you about the Georgia who's in your class.'

'There isn't a Georgia in my class. She's called Georgina. Why?'

'Oh, nothing. Just me being stupid. Thanks for your help. Night, sweetie. I'll see you tomorrow.'

'Night.'

So that was that, then. There was no missing girl called Georgia that Tom knew. It was completely crazy to ever think there would be. He'd just come across the same story I had and it had become distorted in his mind.

Chapter Three

The Portesham Doctor's Surgery was in a purpose built modern and bright building in the village. When I discovered I was pregnant for the seventh time with Anna I'd given up my nursing job at Dorchester County Hospital in the A&E department. I'd passed my twelve-week danger time and wasn't going to jeopardise the pregnancy in any way, not after all the miscarriages. I took it easy, ate healthy food, got plenty of rest. But when Anna started primary school and a practice nurse job had come up in the village, it was the ideal solution. Half a day was perfect for me.

I sat in the nurses' examination room with a cup of steaming coffee, scrolling through my appointments.

Rose Quinn, the mother of my old friend Katie, was due in at 11.30 a.m. She was an alcoholic, rarely venturing out of the house unless it was to buy booze at the little village shop. I couldn't remember the last time I saw her. Katie's dad Jack, also an alcoholic, had died a couple of years ago from liver failure. Their drinking had been going on for a long time, since Katie and I were both kids, but even though we were best friends, she never really talked about her home life to me. She said it was depressing and embarrassing having them as parents. Katie learned to cover up the fact that she looked after herself and the house single-handedly most of the time. A job no child should have to do. In fact, she was so good at hiding and covering things up I didn't even realise what had been going on until much later.

The morning passed in a flurry of new patient health checks, assessing and treating minor injuries and giving advice for the diabetic clinic. When Rose entered the room I realised just how much weight she'd lost since the last time I'd seen her. Her eyes were dark hollow sockets, her cheekbones sharp and jutting. She wore leggings with holes in them, her legs skinnier than Anna's, and a big baggy dark green jumper, even though we were actually being treated to a full-blown summer this year – lucky us – and it was about twenty-eight degrees Celsius outside.

I gave her a warm smile. 'Hi, Rose. How are you?'

She hesitated in the doorway for a moment before walking slowly into the room and sitting down gingerly, as if it was painful for her to move. The reek of alcohol came off her in overpowering waves, and I tried to breathe through my mouth. During her infrequent appointments over the years, the doctors and I had all tried to get her into an AA programme and give support to help her quit the drink, but she wasn't interested. Unfortunately, some people you just can't help. As a nurse, it's a lesson that took me a long time to learn. I could patch her up and give her advice until I was blue in the face, the same as I would for anyone else, but I couldn't really help her.

'I'm here for a dressing change. I cut myself.' Her voice was now raspy and hoarse. I didn't remember that from childhood and was pretty sure it was a side effect of the booze. Or cigarettes.

'OK, just pop yourself up onto the examination couch and let me take a look.' I read her notes on the screen while she lay down and lifted up her jumper. She'd told Elaine originally she'd cut herself falling onto a glass coffee table a few weeks ago, which broke as she landed on it. Elaine had removed some embedded fragments of glass from a wound that stretched under her ribs and along her abdomen. Considering she would've been drunk at the time, she was lucky it hadn't turned out worse. It could've quite easily been a fatal injury if she'd caught an artery or vein. Because she hadn't come in to get the glass removed quickly, the wound had become infected, and she'd been on a course of antibiotics for ten days, along with regular appointments for dressing changes, since it was considered unlikely she'd bother with it herself.

I pulled on some latex gloves and gently removed the old dressing. 'It looks great, Rose. It's healing up nicely now. You'll need to come back tomorrow for another dressing change, and then the stitches will come out, OK?'

'OK.'

'We're in for some scorching weather, apparently,' I said as I put on another dressing.

She mumbled something in reply.

'Knowing my luck, it will rain at the weekend when I'm off work.' I rolled my eyes. 'Doesn't the British weather always do that? Are you doing anything nice at the weekend?'

No response. I didn't really expect one.

I pulled her jumper back down over her protruding ribs and mottled, pale skin. I wanted to ask her if she'd had any word from Katie but Rose always got angry when I tried to find anything out.

She swung her legs over the side of the couch and walked to the door. 'Thank you,' she said gruffly.

'You're welcome. Take care.' I smiled at her retreating hunched shoulders and wondered what Katie was up to. What did she look like now? Was she happy? Had she made something of her life or was she an alcoholic like her parents?

The next patient entering shook me back to the present, and before I knew what had happened Elaine was there to take over and it was time for me to leave.

I grabbed a quick sandwich at home before heading off to see Tom. I was going to take him for a nice walk along the cliffs at Durdle Door. The nursing home encouraged family members taking residents for days out or on trips.

Mary wasn't at the desk when I arrived. A younger nurse called Sue rushed out of a resident's room, looking flushed and harassed, and almost bumped into me.

'Oh, sorry, I didn't see you there!' Sue exclaimed. 'You OK?'

'Yes, I'm just going to take Tom out for a walk up at Durdle Door. I'll bring him back in a few hours.'

'Oh, great. He'll love that.' She grabbed a dressing from a drawer of medical supplies behind the desk and hurried back to the room she'd just come from.

When I entered Tom's room he was wearing thick green cord trousers, a shirt buttoned up wrong and a pair of his walking boots that didn't get much use anymore. He sat in the high-backed chair again, staring out of the window at the grounds. By now, he had trouble dressing himself most days and the nurses helped, although he often tried to redo what they'd already done, hence the odd buttons. Sometimes he forgot to go to the toilet, too, and had to be changed more than once in a day. If he could see himself now he'd be so degraded.

'Hi, Tom.' I kissed his cheek. 'How are you today?'

'Olivia.' His eyes lit up. 'Lovely to see you again. Are we going to Durdle Door? I've been waiting all morning.'

'You remembered?' I grinned. It seemed to be so random now, the things he remembered and the things he didn't. 'Yes. Let's get going, shall we?'

He steadied himself on the edge of his chair with one hand while I took his other and helped him up.

After we walked down the corridor and out of the entrance, I settled him in my Mini. Once it would've been a tight squeeze for him to fit in. Not anymore.

'How's Anna?' he asked, looking out the window.

'She's absolutely fine. She's busy with schoolwork but they break up for summer holidays soon.' I glanced over.

'She's a good girl.' He smiled at me.

'She is indeed. I'm very proud of her. I keep waiting for her to turn into a terrible teen.'

He laughed. 'Like Ethan and Chris, you mean?'

'They weren't terrible.'

'They had their moments.' He sighed with contentment, as if remembering their childhood. 'Nadia was always the good one.'

'What about Chris? He was so into boxing, he didn't have time for much else.' Except Katie, I thought. At one time, he was completely in love with her. The only woman I'd seen him fall head over heels for until his wife Abby. Ex-wife, I should say.

'Chris came to see me. He said his divorce came through.' He shook his head sadly. 'Shame he couldn't give her a child.'

Abby had always wanted kids. Longed for a big brood. After she and Chris got married, they tried madly, the same as me and Ethan, but although I eventually gave birth to Anna, it still didn't happen for them and the strain of IVF and fertility treatment took its toll eventually. I felt for her, I really did. She went a little crazy with the anxiety and stress of it all, and I knew what that was like.

'Where's Eve? She hasn't been to see me.'

I stiffened, not wanting to bring it all back. Every time we had to explain Eve was dead, Tom got hit by a new wave of grief, as fresh as when it had first happened. We all thought it was best not to tell him anymore if he didn't remember it himself.

'That's right. She went to Spain on holiday, didn't she?' he carried on, forehead crinkled up, thinking. 'Oh, it's nice in Spain.' He shrugged and glanced back out of the window. 'They have these strange bits and pieces of dinner. Taps.'

'Tapas. Yes, they're lovely.'

'Something was rubbery.'

'Squid, probably.'

As we pulled up in the car park at the top of the cliffs half an hour later, a little boy and his dad were flying a kite in the shape of something robotic.

Tom sat for a while, watching them. 'I remember Chris had a kite. Ethan hated them. Said they were for . . . for . . .' He looked blank for a moment. 'For turtles.'

'Do you remember when you taught Anna how to fly a kite?' I said, hoping he didn't notice his slip-up. 'You took her up on top of the hills behind the barn.'

'Yes, she wanted one with a cartoon character on it, didn't she?' He smiled fondly.

'SpongeBob SquarePants.' I chuckled.

'I looked everywhere for one, but nowhere had anything like it. I made it in the end, do you remember? I painted SpongeBob on. Copied him off a TV programme. It was almost as big as she was.'

'If I remember rightly, it didn't last long, did it?'

'No. A sudden gust of wind took it away and it ended up smashing on the ground. It took me another two weeks to make a new SpongeBob one, and by that time she said she'd gone off him and wanted one that looked like a ladybird.' He sighed wistfully. 'Those were the days.'

I got out of the car and then went round to open his door and help him out. I linked my arm through his and we walked very slowly along a path over the top of the cliffs, well-worn with years' worth of use. There were signs at regular intervals that read 'Danger! Cliff Edge!' and 'Keep Away from the Edge!'

'I've got a good idea,' I said. 'How about I bring you in some gardening magazines, instead of reading all those horrible stories in the papers that make you worry?'

'What stories?'

'Like the one you mentioned yesterday. The one that you must've seen about Georgia Preston, who was murdered.'

'Georgia?' He shook his head, looking confused. 'Who's Georgia? I never mentioned anyone called Georgia.' He shook his head and narrowed his eyes. 'You're lying.'

I opened my mouth to deny it but thought better of it. It didn't matter, anyway. It wasn't important. 'Yes, I'll bring you some in next time.' I smiled decisively.

After a short walk we sat on our usual bench overlooking the sea. He couldn't manage long distances anymore. As we chatted about the kids and Nadia, Chris and Ethan, he seemed really alert, remembering things we'd all got up to in the past. Even coming out with things I'd completely forgotten, like the time Chris was in a boxing match when he was about sixteen and he knocked out his opponent with the first punch. Chris was always the quiet one of our group, preferring to be on his own a lot of the time, although sometimes his quietness bordered on being broody. Unlike Nadia and Ethan and me, who were outspoken, he was shy and much more introverted than the rest of us, always a bit of a loner. He loved the boxing, and had religiously practised and sparred at a gym in Weymouth when he was growing up. He did it originally to try and lose some of his puppy fat, but I think the main thing he liked about it was he didn't have to talk to anyone else when he was working out or fighting. He could just lose himself in the match.

It wasn't until we were walking back to the car that Tom stopped suddenly and said, 'Did you say something about Georgia? Did you mean Georgia Walker? I killed her, Liv.' He dropped his head in his hands. 'Oh, God, I killed her!'

I froze, my spine erect and stiff.

Chapter Four

'I need to talk to you,' I whispered as soon as Ethan came through the front door.

He raised his eyebrows questioningly before Anna ran out of the kitchen and threw herself into her dad's arms.

I smiled. Or at least tried to.

'Missed you, Shortie Pants,' he said, his nickname for her which was woefully out of date now since she'd be taller than me soon.

'Missed you, too, Dad.' She pulled back and grinned happily. 'I've been helping Mum make focaccia and scones for the picnic tomorrow.'

I pulled a face. 'Yeah, well the focaccia looks more like Poppy's just thrown up on a plate, and the scones are rock hard.'

'They taste OK, though,' Anna said. 'We've still got quiches to do. Are you going to help us, Dad? Go on, please!'

He took his jacket off and hung it on the end of the banister. 'I don't even know what focaccia is, let alone know how to make it, although if it looks like puke I won't be trying it anytime soon. I think you two are better off in there than me, but I'll have a beer and keep you company while you work.'

'Yeah, give your dad a bit of time to relax. He's had a hard week.' I ruffled Anna's long hair, dusty now with flour. 'Can you beat those eggs for me? We'll be there in a minute.'

I waited for Anna to disappear back into the kitchen and slid my arms round Ethan's neck, kissing him hard on the lips. He smelled of mint and coffee and the outdoors. His tongue parted my lips and sought mine.

'I know you're snogging out there! It's gross!' Anna shouted out.

We pulled back and laughed. That was the trouble with having a bright twelve-year-old; it was hard to keep any secrets in the house.

'You'll be doing it one day,' I called back.

'Will not. Boys are gross.' At least I could be thankful she still thought that. It wouldn't be long before she had boyfriends and was getting her heart broken. It didn't bear thinking about. I was buying her a chastity belt for Christmas.

'What's up?' he whispered to me.

'It's about Tom. And this Georgia,' I whispered back.

He rolled his eyes. 'Not again. I thought we went through this yesterday. It's just the ramblings of a senile man.'

'Yes, but he said something else today.'

His shoulders stiffened underneath my touch. 'What did he say?'

'He told me her surname. He said Georgia Walker. I thought he'd just been fixated on a story I found online about a girl called Georgia Preston who'd been murdered by her boyfriend, but it wasn't her. He called her Georgia Walker and said he'd killed her again. Do you know who she is?'

Ethan pulled back. 'I've never heard of any Georgia Walker and there's no way Dad could've killed someone. You've got it wrong. Or rather, *he's* got it wrong. He's confused, like I said. Look, I've had a

41

stressful week, and quite honestly, I don't want to waste my weekend talking about some ridiculous story that can't possibly be true.'

'But I—'

'Just drop it, Liv. It's nuts. I need a drink.' He walked off into the kitchen, loosening his tie.

But I couldn't drop it. Not like that. Not without at least trying to find out anything else about Georgia Walker. It wasn't like Tom had mentioned something casual and inconsequential like a set of keys he'd once lost or a fly he'd killed, and it was niggling away. Even with the Alzheimer's it seemed very out of character for him to say something like that. So, although I was sure it was nothing, and Tom couldn't possibly have killed anyone, I still wanted to find out why he was so obsessed with such a horrible story and where he'd heard it from.

I followed Ethan into the kitchen and went through the motions of drinking beer with him and making the food for the picnic – although I burnt one of the quiches – answering questions when I was asked, nodding in the right places, but my mind was firmly fixed on Georgia Walker. When Ethan headed upstairs for a shower and the final quiche was in the oven I went into the living room and found Anna watching a YouTube documentary on the laptop about prisoners on death row.

'It's terrible, Mum,' she said sadly, eyes watering. 'This man was accused of killing this girl who lived in his town, and he says he's innocent.'

'They all say they're innocent.'

'But what if he really is? And there was this case study I've been reading about where the lethal injection caused such massive pain to the patient when he was—'

'Prisoner, not patient.'

'OK, *prisoner*. And he had loads of heart attacks and it took him about forty-five minutes to actually die in excruciating agony. Don't you remember watching *The Green Mile*, when they were trying to electrocute a prisoner and bits of him caught fire and stuff but it didn't actually kill him for hours?"

'It wasn't hours. That would've taken up the whole film, and I seem to remember it being about a lot more than just that.'

She rolled her eyes. 'Well, a long time, then. Imagine how painful that is. And what if you really did kill an innocent person?' Anna looked horrified at that prospect. 'I mean, what if *I* was wrongly convicted of murdering someone and I got the death penalty?'

'You wouldn't kill someone, sweetheart. You can't even kill those disgusting ticks we find on Poppy, and they serve no purpose in life except to be horrible parasites that spread disease.'

'Actually, everything has a purpose in our ecosystem.'

'Yes, but not ticks. They should be banned. Like scratchy labels in clothes.'

'Yes, but what *if* they were innocent, Mum?'

'Can we talk about this another time? I really need to use the laptop. I can't use the Internet on my phone – it's too slow using the touch screen.'

'But it's just getting to a—'

'*Now*, Anna!' I said, my words coming out harsher than I intended.

She looked up at me sharply. It wasn't often that I lost my temper, and she could sense something was wrong.

She made a big show of pausing the film, and passed the laptop over to me in pouty silence.

I took it into the kitchen and typed in Georgia Walker's name, along with *missing person* and *Dorset*.

I looked down the hits. There was a LinkedIn site for an Emily Walker, a Facebook page for someone called Georgia Williams, a blog about Dorset Walks and, bizarrely, a link to a page about

American slavery. There was also a link to a missing persons website in Georgia, USA, a Walker County Sheriff's Facebook Page (also in the USA – what was that about? I'd thought Google knew everything except, apparently, where Dorset was), and a plastic surgeon in Savannah which was – yes, you guessed it – in the USA!

I deleted *Dorset* and searched again. Maybe she wasn't even local. This time I found a Twitter account for George Wilmington, a website for a dental surgery in London, an article about a man on death row in Georgia (don't tell Anna) and a story about a man called John Hamilton who'd gone missing a week ago from Scotland. Nothing useful at all.

I sat back in the chair with a frustrated sigh. If Tom had heard about this woman, she must've been local, surely. I found British Telecom's online directory. It asked for a surname and location so I typed in *Walker* and *Dorset*.

Too many search results. Please try again, it said.

I tried her surname and narrowed it down to Portesham. There were four Walkers but no G. I tried Dorchester next, where I hit fifteen Walkers but no G.

I gave up after trying Weymouth with the same result. She could be anywhere. Or the phone could be listed in her husband's name. Or she could be ex-directory.

Oh, this is stupid. I was just letting my imagination run away with me. I closed down the search tab and shut the laptop as Ethan wandered in wearing faded jeans and a T-shirt, hair still damp from the shower. I felt a jolt of desire hit me. Despite the fact that his long working hours meant he didn't have much time to exercise, he had a naturally muscular body. At forty-three, his stomach was still flat and toned.

'I'm sorry about snapping earlier. It's been a nightmare week.'

'It's OK. It's forgotten already.' I smiled.

He pulled me to my feet and slid his arms around my waist, nuzzling behind my ear, his lips seeking that place that made me want to melt. Maybe it was an erogenous zone. Whatever it was, I definitely appreciated him doing, oh, yes, that thing right there.

Chapter Five

The doorbell rang at 9 a.m. the next day as I was packing the food into a large cool box. Poppy barked and rushed to the front door, ready to greet the visitor with an excited wagging tail and a wet nose. She'd never make a good guard dog. She'd welcome any intruder into the house with a lick and nuzzle.

'I'll get it!' Anna's feet thundered downstairs.

From where I stood at the island I had a clear view down the hallway to the front door. Anna wore a pink sun top and tiny denim shorts.

'Hi, Anna.' Chris, my brother-in-law, stepped inside and shut the door. 'How's things?'

'Good, thanks. We're almost ready.' She kissed his cheek.

He set down his own large cool box on the floor.

'I'm just going to get my bikini on.' Anna rushed back upstairs.

'Hi.' I waved.

'Bikini?' Chris pulled a face at me.

'What, haven't you got your leopard-skin Speedos?' I arched an eyebrow.

'Yeah. Sexy.'

'It's going to be another scorching day according to the weather forecast.'

'I'm loving this weather, but I doubt very much I'll be going in the sea. It'll be bloody freezing.'

Ethan came in through the back door carrying some fold-up chairs. 'All right, Chris?'

'Yeah. Do you want a hand with anything?' Chris asked.

'No, I'll just put these in the car and then load up with the cool boxes and we're all set.' He nudged me with his elbow, a warm smile plastered on his face. 'Come on. You're always running late.'

Ten minutes later we all piled into Ethan's Range Rover Sport and drove up the road to Nadia and Lucas's house to meet them before driving in convoy through the beautiful Dorset countryside. We headed past Corfe Castle and finally onto the picturesque sand dunes at Swanage.

It was already starting to get busy with families and couples, the promise of a rare spurt of summer weather bringing everyone out of hiding, looking pasty and anaemic. I wondered how many people on the beach would end up with sunburn and heatstroke today. We found an empty spot in between a couple of dunes and set up towels, blankets and chairs.

'Are you coming in the sea?' Charlotte asked Anna as she stripped off her sundress to reveal a black halter-neck bikini.

I lay on a large picnic blanket and watched the two girls walk to the water's edge and test the temperature with their feet, shrieking and giggling as they realised it was colder than they thought.

Nadia lay next to me. 'What a week!' She smiled as if she didn't have a care in the world. As if she hadn't told me the horrible suspicions of Lucas's affair a few days ago. She slathered a high-factor sun tan lotion on with great concentration since she had a tendency to burn. Thanks to my genes, I was dark with olive skin and could get a tan sitting in the shade. I think there was some Mediterranean blood in our family way back.

I turned onto my side, propping my head up with my hand as Lucas, Chris and Ethan stood to one side chatting about football scores or something equally yawn-inducing.

Although Ethan and Chris were brothers, they didn't look alike at all. Ethan was more like his Dad – tall, dark, lean but broad-shouldered, with brown eyes below thick eyebrows. Chris was shorter, stockier and blond like his mum, right down to his pale eyelashes that almost looked transparent. When Chris was younger he was bordering on overweight, which he'd been very self-conscious about. As soon as he hit sixteen he started boxing and doing physical work on the building sites with Tom every day so he'd soon lost the puppy fat. Nadia was a mixture of both parents: blonde like Chris but tall with dark brown eyes like Ethan. Lucas looked as if he could be Chris's brother instead of Ethan's best mate. Nadia always thought Lucas looked like the actor Ewan McGregor, although I couldn't see it myself.

I tuned out their conversation, which was now about some football player who was a right-back, whatever that was. 'So, how are you?' I nodded my head in Lucas's direction. Even though I'd promised her I wouldn't mention it again, technically, I wasn't, even though the meaning was clear.

She glanced over at him and her smile wavered a little, although she tried really hard to hide it. 'We're fine.' Her gaze flicked back to me and she lowered her voice. 'We're meant to be together. You can't argue with that, can you?' She stood up and said cheerfully, 'Now, who wants a drink? I've got a huge bottle of Pimm's in here.' She crouched down next to one of the cool boxes. Knowing her, she probably had enough food in there to feed us all three times over.

After a couple of Pimm's for Nadia and me, and Cokes for the boys, we all played a family game of bat and ball – although the Pimm's had gone to our heads on an empty stomach and Nadia and I spent more time giggling and missing the ball than actually contributing to the game.

Ethan put his hands on his hips in mock annoyance. 'What are you two like? If you can't play then leave it to the boys.'

'Oooh,' I mocked back, grinning as I handed him my bat. 'I've had enough, anyway. I'm going to read my book.'

'Yeah, I'd rather sunbathe.' Nadia swatted Lucas's backside playfully as we walked back to our blanket.

Lucas called Charlotte and Anna out of the sea to take our places and I lay back on my towel next to Nadia, closing my eyes. The comforting sun on my skin permeated my bones, relaxing me, and I was soon drifting off into that pleasant pre-sleep drowsiness.

I was woken a while later with sand being kicked on my leg and the sound of screeching. I sat up abruptly and found Anna being chased round and round by Lucas. In her hand, held high in the air, was his baseball cap.

'Give it back!' Lucas chuckled.

'Nooooooo!' She ran towards the sea as Charlotte grabbed a towel from her beach bag and wrapped it round her wet body. Her hair dripped seawater onto Nadia.

'Ew, that's cold!' Nadia wiped it off, laughing, and tickled Charlotte's stomach.

'Stop it!' Charlotte wriggled away, trying to be serious but erupting into fits when Nadia chased after her.

Ethan kneeled down on the edge of my towel and offered me a bottle of water. 'Here. Don't want you getting dehydrated after that alcohol.'

'It was only two Pimm's.' I raised an eyebrow but took a long swig. He was probably right. Didn't want the sunstroke victim to be me.

Lucas flopped onto one of the fold-up chairs with a can of cider in his hand, putting his cap back on. 'Right, I think the girls should drive back and the men can have a few drinks. What do you think?' he asked Ethan with a grin.

Ethan shrugged. 'I'm not fussed about drinking on the beach. We could all go to the Kings' Arms later when we get back, anyway. Grab some dinner there?'

'Sounds good to me.' Lucas took a swig of cider. 'But I'm having a few of these. It's not very often I actually get a weekend off so I'm going to make the most of it.' He winked at me.

I wondered what he made the most of when he was at work. Patty? I bit back the urge to say something. I couldn't betray my conversation with Nadia since she'd sworn me to secrecy, but still, part of me couldn't quite believe it, part of me didn't want to believe it and part of me was seething with anger, wanting to slap some sense into him. Give him a right mouthful about what an affair would do to his family.

'We should get to the beach more often.' Ethan slung his arm round me. 'I always forget how great it is down here.'

'You're always working.' I rested my head on his shoulder and watched Nadia, who was shrieking now as Charlotte had turned the tables and was tickling her.

'Well, I need to spend less time on work and more on the things that are important.' He kissed my ear.

I smiled, kissing his smooth cheek in return before turning my attention to Chris, who stood at the water's edge staring at something in the sand and kicking it with his foot.

A cry from Nadia pulled my gaze away, and I saw her walking Charlotte back towards us, an arm firmly guiding her. Blood poured from Charlotte's nose, down her face and chin, dripping onto the sand.

I leaped up and got into automatic nurse mode. 'Sit her down.' I went the other side of Charlotte and pinched the bridge of her nose. 'You need to keep pinching here, darling, OK?'

Nadia sat her in Lucas's chair as Lucas grabbed some tissues from their beach bag.

'OK, can you pinch it now?' I asked Charlotte when she was settled.

She nodded and took over on the spot my fingers had vacated.

Lucas put a wad of tissues under Charlotte's nose to stop the blood going all over her.

'She hasn't had a nosebleed for years,' Nadia said. 'Since she was little.'

'It was you. You banged into me with your forehead when you were trying to get away,' Charlotte said with a nasally twang.

'I didn't. I wasn't touching you when it happened.'

'You did!'

'Well, never mind,' I said. 'It'll stop soon.'

Ten minutes later, when Charlotte stopped pinching her nose, it had stopped as predicted.

'There.' I smiled. 'All finished.'

Charlotte glared at Nadia. 'It was your fault.'

Nadia lifted her hands in mock surrender. 'OK, OK, sorry if it was my fault.'

'Why don't we have some lunch now, then, eh? You up to that, darling?' Lucas said to Charlotte, trying to take her mind off it as he handed her a wet wipe for her face. Food usually took her mind off most things.

'Yeah. I'm starved. I want some of those cupcakes Mum's made.' She grinned and put the tissue in the rubbish bag.

There. Crisis averted!

After lunch, Charlotte and Anna were back in the sea again. They'd found a couple of kids with a Frisbee and were playing with them in the shallows.

I sat in one of the chairs, dragging my toe through the velvety-soft sand, not really listening to the conversation going on around me because I was worrying about what to do. I couldn't keep it inside any longer. I didn't want to ruin the family day. And I'd tried, really I had, not to bring it up. I'd tried to forget about it because it was so ridiculous. But, well, as family, I needed their advice on it, not just Ethan's. I knew he wouldn't be happy with me, but I thought it was only fair they knew what Tom had said, as well.

'Something really weird happened when I went to see Tom this week.' I sat forward in the chair and glanced around at Nadia, Lucas and Chris. I avoided Ethan's eyes, but I could feel them burning into me because he knew what I was going to say.

'What, did he catch himself in the mirror again and think his reflection was Gregory Peck?' Chris laughed. 'I had a nightmare trying to convince him otherwise a few weeks ago.'

'No.' I didn't join in with the laughter.

Instead, I told them what Mary had told me about Tom having fitful dreams and then becoming agitated and hard to settle afterwards. About how he'd said Georgia Walker was haunting him. How she was apparently missing. And that he said he'd killed her.

Nadia gasped. Lucas's jaw dropped open. Chris's eyebrows shot up. Ethan glared hard.

'What?' Nadia asked.

'Can you repeat that?' Chris poked a finger in his ear. 'I think I must've heard you wrong.' He let out a slight laugh.

'It's completely crazy. I've already told her.' Ethan shook his head wildly. 'Dad's just confused. Or delusional. There's no way he's talking sense.'

'What, he actually said he'd *killed* her?' Lucas whispered the word, his eyes straying to Charlotte and Anna, safely out of hearing distance as they bobbed up and down in the sea now.

'Yes, that's what he said.' I repeated everything again for them so it would sink in.

'I don't believe it,' Nadia said.

'That's what I said.' Ethan gave me a superior look which made me want to smack him. 'Dad doesn't even know anyone called Georgia Walker.'

'How do you know?' Lucas asked.

'Well, have you ever heard him mention her?' Ethan said.

'No. But that doesn't mean anything.'

'I'm sure it can't possibly be true,' I said. 'But it's bugging me why he keeps repeating it when he's never mentioned anything remotely like it before. Do any of you know anyone called Georgia who Tom might've become confused about?'

One by one they shook their heads.

'I did a search online, but I couldn't find anyone with that name who's mentioned as a missing person. I searched the telephone directories to see if she was in there, but again, I didn't find anything helpful. Do you think we should go to the police and at least ask them if someone called Georgia really is missing?'

'The police?' Ethan snorted. 'Oh, don't be ridiculous!'

'Wait.' Chris plonked himself down heavily on the sand next to my chair and held up a hand. 'How could he have killed someone? Dad's the nicest guy you could ever meet. It's . . . it just doesn't make sense. There's no way.'

'I agree,' Ethan said. 'It's impossible. It's just the Alzheimer's making him believe something he's read or seen on the TV.'

'But what if there really is a missing woman out there?' I said. 'Not that I think Tom's killed anyone, but what if perhaps he knows something about where she is? Something that might help find her?

I've been thinking that maybe he witnessed something that might solve a crime. It could be something that happened a while ago and he's only just remembering it. She could have a family who's looking for her.'

'Of course he doesn't know anything,' Chris said. 'He's just confused.'

'But why is he so obsessed with someone who doesn't seem to have ever been mentioned in the papers? There must be a reason. I've checked for news stories and there's nothing.'

'That's because there's nothing to find out,' Ethan said. 'Honestly, when you get a bee in your bonnet about things, you're a nightmare. Your imagination runs riot! This is all just stupid. I don't even know why we're talking about it.' He glared out to sea.

Lucas stared at the ground, a pensive frown on his face. 'Well, there's a simple way to find out for certain.'

'What do you mean?' Ethan said.

'I mean we go to the police like Olivia said and ask them if there's anyone with her name who's missing.'

Nadia shrugged. 'We'll just be wasting their time. There can't be anything to it. I mean . . . Dad? It's just nonsense. Honestly, Liv, you're always finding something to worry about.'

'I agree he's confused,' Lucas said. 'But there's no harm asking the police. What if Georgia is kid a who's disappeared and Tom does know something about it?' Lucas said.

'I hadn't thought of that. I just assumed she was an adult.' I turned to Ethan. 'We have to go to the police and at least check, don't you see?' I stood up and crossed the sand towards him. 'Tom was very explicit about her, and he mentioned her not only once, but several times. And he was completely lucid when he said it, too. What if there really is a missing child out there and he could help find her?'

'And what are we going to tell them? That our senile dad has confessed to killing someone but, hey, it's probably not true because the other day he thought he was Gregory Peck!' Ethan's nostrils flared with anger.

I reached for his hand. 'Look, I know you don't want to talk about this but—'

'Of course I don't! No one would want to hear that about their father. You're just worrying about nothing again.'

'Look, it seems totally unreliable what Tom's saying, but I think Liv's right,' Lucas said. 'He could be an important witness to something.'

'No, she's not.' Chris said. 'I don't want to go to the police and put Dad through that for nothing. He's ill. He's not thinking straight.'

'So what do you suggest we do, then?' Lucas asked. 'If we're all certain he's never mentioned anyone called Georgia who we can check on, then we have to do something.'

There was a strained silence for a while.

'I'm sure the police will just look into it and confirm that there is no missing person by that name and we'll know for certain. But until then . . .' I shrugged. 'Well, we can't hide something like this.'

'We're not hiding anything because there's nothing to hide. It's not true. Dad didn't kill anyone, and he doesn't know anything about any missing people.' Ethan folded his arms over his chest.

'We'll just be wasting their time,' Chris said. 'I think we should wait until we know more.'

'Weren't you listening, Chris?' I said. 'I've tried to find out who she is but can't. None of us knows who this person could be, and like Lucas said, what if this is something to do with a missing child? What if Anna or Charlotte were abducted and someone knew something, however inconsequential it might sound, but they didn't do anything about it?'

'But this is *Dad* we're talking about,' Chris said.

'I agree with Chris,' Ethan said.

'Well then, the police will just tell us that it can't possibly be true and that will be the end of it,' Lucas said. 'They'll say there's no one of that name on their records and we can just forget about this.'

I nodded. 'Of course they will.'

'Yes,' Nadia agreed.

'I bloody hope so.' Lucas crossed his arms and stared off into the distance.

Chapter Six

Sergeant Downing looked too young to be a sergeant. Or maybe it was just that I was getting old. He sat on one side of the desk in the interview room with Nadia and me on the other. I felt like I was having a job interview and any minute he'd ask me what my strengths and weaknesses were. The walls were painted lilac, or lavender, or something. Maybe it was designed to make suspects feel soothed into dishing the dirt on their criminal activities. It was quite nice, actually. I could see it on our bathroom walls. I couldn't even believe I was even thinking about that as Sergeant Downing frowned for the second time.

'Right. So . . .' he started off. 'Your father-in-law is in a nursing home suffering from Alzheimer's, and he's been mentioning a missing person called Georgia Walker?'

'Well . . . yes.' I nodded firmly and chewed on my lower lip. We hadn't mentioned the fact that Tom said he'd killed her because that was just plain crazy, and they'd probably laugh us out of the station.

'I'm sure it's all nonsense!' Nadia emitted an embarrassed, tinkling laugh, as if she was terribly sorry for wasting their time.

'I agree, but I'm just concerned that maybe he witnessed a crime and he's only just remembering it. We think it's our duty to check, just to make sure.'

Sergeant Downing frowned again. 'Has he ever made any similar statements about missing people?'

'No,' I said.

'What's his full name, date of birth, and last address?' He leaned forward on the desk and wrote as I rattled off the details. 'I don't recall anyone called Georgia being circulated as missing around here, but it can't do any harm to check. Wait here, please.' He stood and left the room.

I glanced at Nadia.

'Ethan's right: this is all just a waste of time. They're not going to find anything,' she said.

'Of course they won't.'

'Did Ethan calm down on the way back?'

'A little bit. With Lucas in agreement, he can't do much else, really. But he's not happy about it.'

'No one's happy about it. This is just stupid,' she barked.

'No, I didn't mean . . . oh, never mind.'

'Sorry. I'm just stressed.'

I squeezed her hand then. Of course she was, what with the worry of Lucas's affair and now this – no wonder she was looking ruffled.

She picked at the hem of her dress. 'I can't believe we're even doing this.'

I jigged my knee up and down as we waited in silence. It seemed like hours before Sergeant Downing came back, but in reality it was probably only forty-five minutes.

I tried to read the expression on his face as he sat down, but I couldn't work it out. I bet there was a lesson on the art of pulling the perfect poker face during their police training. I visualised a whole room of officers pulling different expressions in front of the mirror to see which worked best.

Oh, God, get a grip, Olivia!

I took a deep breath and focused on him. 'What have you found out?'

He took his time looking between Nadia and me. 'There are no missing persons reports for someone of that name.'

I exhaled loudly. 'Thank goodness for that.'

'I checked the voters' registers and there is a Georgia Walker listed in Abbotsbury.'

I leaned forward, heart racing. 'Oh?'

'Unfortunately, there's no telephone number listed for her, like you discovered, so I'm going to take a drive over there and see what I can find out.' He stood up. 'I'll call you when I know something.'

'Thank you.' I stood up.

'You promise you'll call as soon as you hear something?' Nadia asked.

'Yes.' He led us back out to the public area by the front desk and we said goodbye.

I gulped in a lungful of fresh air outside. The interview room had smelled of cheesy feet. Not pleasant.

'Do you want to go home and wait?' Nadia asked.

'No. I don't want to go home with bad news. Ethan's still blaming me for all this. He mostly ignored me on the drive back, and when I dropped them all off at the house before we came here, he stomped off, which is so unlike him. He's not normally a moody sulker.'

She put a hand on my arm. 'I'm still sure there's nothing to it.'

I nodded. 'Shall we get a coffee or something?'

'I fancy a real drink.'

'Yeah. Good idea.'

So we drove back to Portesham and parked up at the Kings' Arms, situated on the village green in front of the road that led to Abbotsbury in one direction and Weymouth in the other.

I bought a red wine and a gin and tonic and carried them outside to the beer garden where Nadia had bagged us the only table left. At six-thirty on a hot Saturday summer's evening, the place was already heaving.

I took a gulp of red wine, savouring the kick as the alcohol hit the back of my throat. Nadia downed a third of hers in one suck of her straw.

I looked at my watch, even though I'd already checked it four times since I sat down. 'What's taking Sergeant Downing so long? He must've got there by now.'

'Maybe she's out shopping or something.'

I pulled my phone out of my bag and checked the signal. Yes, it was fine. And the battery was fully charged. I placed it on the table and knocked back some more wine.

Nadia's phone rang in her mulberry-coloured Michael Kors bag. She delved inside and pulled it out, looking at the display. 'It's Lucas.' She answered it and told him what was going on before hanging up. 'He's coming up to wait with us. I'll get him a pint.' She finished her drink and stood. 'Want another one?'

'Yes, please.'

After she'd disappeared off to the bar, my phone rang, sending my heart pounding again.

'Hello?'

'Hi, is this Olivia Tate?'

I recognised Sergeant Downing's voice straight away. 'Yes. Did you find her? Was she OK?'

He let out a soft chuckle. 'Yes, she's perfectly alive and well. Nothing to worry about.'

A hand flew to my chest. 'Good.'

'I asked her if she knew Tom Tate and she said she did.'

'Really? How?'

'He did some work for her about thirty years ago. An extension.'

'Oh, right. I suppose I should've thought about looking through his building records to see if he had any customers by that name, and then I wouldn't have wasted your time. I'm so sorry.'

'Well, all's well that ends well.' He paused for a moment. 'Alzheimer's is a terrible disease. My mum had it. It was awful watching her losing her mind while her body deteriorated as well. I'm sorry you're going through this.'

'Thank you. For everything. You've been very helpful.'

'You're welcome. Take care now.'

Ethan wasn't there when I got home. Neither was Poppy.

'Has Dad taken the dog out?' I said to Anna, who was watching another documentary about death row on the laptop.

'Yeah.' She pressed 'Pause'. 'Where've you been?'

'Nowhere.'

'You must've been *somewhere*.'

'I was with Nadia.'

'Oh. What's for dinner?'

'You can't possibly be hungry after all the food you ate at the picnic.' I'm sure my daughter has hollow legs. Oh, to have the metabolism of a teenager again.

'I'm starving.' She grinned. 'Did you bring back any of Nadia's muffins?'

'No. There were none left. Chris ate the last one.'

She pulled an unamused face. 'What about the quiche?'

'There's only the burnt one. No one wanted that for some reason. Can't think why. I bet Poppy will love it. Nadia gave me some coffee cake, though, and some chocolate brownies. Dad should've put everything back in the fridge. Go and help yourself.'

She leaped off the sofa. 'Oh, did I mention that the school is having a car boot sale soon to raise money for charity?'

'No. Which charity?'

'It's going to the Dorset Wildlife Protection Trust. I'm going to help out and do a stall. Have we got anything I can sell?'

'We must have loads of stuff we don't need anymore. You can start by clearing out your wardrobes. I bet there are tons of things in there.'

'Yeah, I'll do that later. What about your things? And Dad's?'

'I'll have a look. Check the loft, too. There are probably still boxes of stuff we haven't even unpacked since we moved in. And if we haven't missed it by now, we probably don't need it.'

'Wicked.' She followed me into the kitchen, grabbed a plate, piled it with two brownies and a slice of cake. 'I'll get Emma to come round tomorrow and help me. She's going to do it, too.'

'OK. Why don't you ask her to stay for dinner? You're always going to her house for tea. I'm sure I can rustle up some chicken nuggets and chips.'

'Yeah, that's why I prefer going to my friends' houses for dinner. Because their mums cook real food.'

I pulled a face at her. 'Cheeky.'

She gave me a goofy grin and disappeared into the lounge.

I spotted Ethan through the kitchen window walking on the wooded side of our boundary fence. A few minutes later he and Poppy burst into the utility room. She took one look at me and leaped up, planting her forepaws on my chest.

I ruffled her fur and flapped her ears.

Ethan stared at me from the doorway, thick eyebrows furrowed. 'So go on, then, tell me what happened. Did they think you were mad?'

'There *is* a Georgia Walker who lives in Abbotsbury, but she's very much alive.' I gave him a sheepish smile.

Poppy jumped down and headed for her water bowl.

'There. I told you, didn't I? Told you it was a complete waste of time.' His face instantly relaxed, softening out the tense lines. He walked towards me and hugged me tight.

'You were right. Somehow he'd become confused about her. Tate construction had done an extension for her years ago, so he'd obviously met her before and must've remembered her name for some reason.'

He pulled back. 'Really? Odd that he'd remember a customer after all this time.'

'Who knows? He remembers all sorts of strange things but frequently forgets important things or even how to do everyday tasks.'

'Well, at least this means we can get back to normal now. It's been a stressful week and a stressful weekend so far.'

I ran my hand through the hair at the nape of his neck. 'And how might we fix that?' I raised a seductive eyebrow.

'Early night?' He grinned.

'Absolutely.' I winked.

Chapter Seven

On Sunday morning Ethan and I took Poppy for a walk along Chesil Beach while Anna raided her cupboards for things to sell at the car boot sale with her friend Emma. We leisurely strolled along, hand in hand, laughing at Poppy chasing seagulls. The sex last night had been amazing! Granted, sex was always going to be a little less adventurous now we had Anna, who was old enough to hear and understand everything. There was no doing it on the kitchen table or having a quickie while I was in the middle of washing up anymore, in case Anna came home unexpectedly, but we still hadn't settled into that boring married routine of the missionary position on a Sunday night with the lights off. We were still adventurous, and it was still exciting and sexy and fulfilling. Probably better, even, over the years because we knew each other's likes and dislikes so intimately.

I thought about Nadia and Lucas again. Maybe she'd made a mistake about the texts she'd seen. Lucas had been attentive and loving towards her on the beach, just like he always was. If she hadn't told me, I would never have guessed something might be going on.

They had both acted so happy together. I suppose you can never be sure what really goes on behind closed doors, though, can you? Even if you think you know people really well.

No, of course she hasn't made a mistake, Olivia. Don't be stupid. It's not like you can turn 'I want to fuck you' into 'I want coffee before takeoff, please, not tea'. What if it was serious? What if he left Nadia and Charlotte for this woman? My heart ached for her.

I watched Ethan throwing a stone for Poppy and wondered how women could stay with their partners after they found out they'd cheated on them. I mean, I know there are a magnitude of reasons why you would stay, especially if you have children together. But surely the jealousy and uncertainty that he wasn't out there doing it again would eat you up inside. I couldn't live like that. Lucas was a pig if he was cheating on her. No, I didn't know how Nadia could just pretend everything was normal and act fine.

'Do you want to come with me when I go and see Dad later?' Ethan's voice knocked me out of my thoughts.

'No, I'll go in the week. At least that way he's getting more visiting days, and I need to catch up on some ironing I've neglected.'

'OK.'

'Can you go through your wardrobe when we get back to see if there's anything you want to throw out since you'll be away again all week?'

'For Anna's car boot?'

'Mmm.'

'I think we've got some boxes of old junk in the garage that we've never got round to throwing away. She can go through that, too.'

As we headed home an hour later we drove past the pub and I spotted Chris in the beer garden with a woman who had chin-length wavy red hair.

'Hey, that was Chris.' I twisted in my seat to look back.

'So?'

'He was with a woman.'

'Yeah, he said yesterday he was meeting her for lunch.'

'Really?' I asked as Ethan pulled up at our front gates. I got out of the car, opened the heavy wooden doors and then closed them again after he'd parked up on the block-paved driveway in front of the garage. Even though it had been over two years since Abby had left Chris, and the divorce was now final, it seemed strange to think of Chris dating again. I don't know why. It shouldn't have been odd at all. In fact, I should be happy for him. It was probably that we'd all been such a happy family for so long – me and Ethan, Lucas and Nadia, Chris and Abby, and now we'd have to welcome someone new into the fold. I made a mental note to ask Chris if he'd like to bring his date over for dinner one night. Or better still, go out for a meal. I got too stressed when lots of people came over for a meal and usually ended up making a right mess of it, unlike Nadia, who had four courses planned for weeks in advance and slaved over a hot oven, barely breaking a sweat.

'So, who is she? What does she do? How old is she? What's her name?' I asked.

Ethan laughed. 'I don't know. He didn't really say much about her.'

'Didn't you ask? This is the first woman he's been out with since Abby. Aren't you interested?' I shook my head at him. 'Men. You are so useless at finding things out.'

The rest of the day was a lazy affair. Ethan and I snuggled up on the sofa and watched a DVD. Well, I watched it. He fell asleep, although God knows how he could when Anna and Emma were giggling and banging around in her bedroom so loudly.

Early the next morning Ethan kissed me awake with a mug of tea in his hand before he travelled back up to York.

'I'll miss you.' He put the mug on the bedside table and sat next to me on the bed.

'Me, too. Will you be back Friday or before?'

He shrugged. 'It depends how the job's going. Hopefully before.'

Poppy flew into the room and put her front paws up on the bed, pushing in between us with a wet nose.

I laughed at her. 'Yes, I'll take you out later!'

Ethan kissed my lips softly and stood up. 'I'd better be off, anyway. I'll call you tonight. Love you.'

'Love you, too.' I pushed Poppy off the bed and hastily dressed in cropped trousers and a vest top. The summer was still going strong. Apparently it was the hottest July for twenty-eight years. How long would it last? It would probably be snowing next week.

Forty-five minutes later I was making Anna's packed lunch whilst eating a slice of toast with damson jam that Nadia had made last week. I would've just had butter on it, but I'd miscalculated the amount I'd needed for all the picnic stuff and we'd run out. I needed to do another shopping list. I could swear there was a secret food-eating troll who lived in our house. I tried to remember if Anna needed her PE kit today. Mondays? Did they do PE on Monday? I peered at her timetable stuck on the front of the fridge with a clown magnet Anna had insisted on buying from somewhere or other. It was an evil-looking thing and gave me the creeps but she loved it. Wasn't there an actual phobia about clowns I'd read about once? I wouldn't be at all surprised. I'd seen the film *It* by Stephen King when I was a teenager and it had scared the life out of me.

Anna sat at the table, looking immaculate – hair gleaming and smooth and swept back with a hair band, school shirt buttoned up and neatly tucked into her skirt, cute ankle socks with the frilly edges in perfect ruffles. I thought about what I'd looked like at her age. Wild hair all over the place, one sock up, one down, shirt tucked out of my skirt. Always too late or too distracted to do things properly. She must get her organisational skills from Ethan or Nadia. Still, she had my hair, which was thick and full of body. At least she'd never go bald, thanks to my genes. And she had my snub nose and big blue eyes. Plus my caring nature. That had to count for some Brownie points. Didn't it?

'Where's the butter?' Anna looked forlornly at the peanut butter and jam I'd put on the table.

'We've run out.' I frantically spread strawberry jam on some wholemeal bread that felt like it was on the cusp of staleness again.

Mental note: Add bread to the list!

Anna groaned. 'You know I hate toast without butter.'

I sighed and opened the tin with the last of the brownies in. 'Here, have a brownie instead.' I shoved it on her plate.

She picked off chunks and chewed, watching me. 'It's not healthy to have a brownie for breakfast and jam sandwiches for lunch.'

Who was the parent here?

'And you're not even dressed yet. You're meeting Nadia at the bus stop in ten minutes. I can do my own lunch, you know.'

Honestly, I don't know where the time goes in the morning. I tried, I really did, but there was always something that needed doing to distract me – this morning it had been a gas bill that I'd totally forgotten about which needed paying before they cut us off. Anna didn't share my lack of punctuality. In fact, she hated being late, especially for the school bus. If she missed it, she might end up with a detention. (This had happened before because of me.

I'd felt very guilty about that for weeks. It took a new Horrible History Boxed Set DVD and a Kindle Fire for Anna to speak to me again.) She was such a stickler for following the rules and being the model student and got quite upset if she couldn't because of my tardiness. She hadn't got that conscientiousness at school from me, either.

'It's all done.' I transferred her sandwiches to a plastic container and added the last Satsuma and a packet of crisps still left in the back of the cupboard. 'Here.' I set it down next to her as she finished off her brownie. I dashed out of the room with Poppy close on my heels. She knew it would be walkies time soon.

Ten minutes later, I was dressed but having trouble locating my keys. Where the hell were they? I looked where I usually dumped them, in the pottery bowl next to the fridge that Anna had made at junior school. It was in the shape of a three-legged tiger. Don't ask me why it only had three legs.

No keys.

I looked in the lounge. In my handbag. My coat pockets. When had I last had them?

As I was walking back down the hall I stubbed my toe on a big cardboard box at the foot of the stairs. 'Ouch!' I hopped up and down, thinking a really bad swear word. I rubbed my foot, staring at the offending article. 'Hey, what's this?'

'It's some stuff I sorted out for the car boot sale. I thought I should put everything in one big box so then I know what I've got.' She walked towards me.

'Right. Well, I don't want it left in the hallway. Put it in the garage out of the way when you get a sec.'

'OK. I'm going now. I'll tell Nadia you're on your way.'

'Actually, tell Nadia to walk down and meet me here instead.' I kissed her cheek. 'Have a good day!' I called after her, but she was already rushing up the path.

It took another ten minutes to locate my keys in the fridge. I had a flashback to when Tom was living with us and he'd put the TV remote control in the freezer. It never worked properly after that. The only button that did work was the volume one, for some reason. I shook my head. He was always doing that. Losing things only for them to turn up in obscure places. I didn't have early-onset Alzheimer's, though; I was just distracted, trying to organise a daughter and a house and a husband and job. Who didn't forget things from time to time?

As I shut the front door, Nadia came through the gates.

'Coming! I'm coming,' I called, and Poppy shot down the garden towards Minstrel to say a doggy greeting.

Nadia rolled her eyes at me, tapping her watch.

'Yes, I know. I'm not Super Woman like you.' I gave her a mock glare, shutting the front gate behind us.

We swung an immediate left onto the path that led to the woods and Poppy dashed towards the trees. Nadia let Minstrel off the lead and she chased after her.

'I've just seen Rose Quinn coming out of the village shop.' Nadia scrunched up her face with sympathy. 'She had a few bottles clinking away in the carrier bag. Buying alcohol at this time of the morning is just so sad.'

'She's an alcoholic, so I suppose she doesn't care what time it is.'

'It must be terrible losing a daughter like that and Katie never getting in touch. I couldn't bear it if Charlotte ran away from home and I never saw her again. No wonder she started drinking.'

'Rose never cared about Katie. I think Rose was actually glad when Katie ran away. They never got on.' I tutted. 'And she was an alcoholic long before Katie left.'

'Have you tried to get her into an AA programme through the surgery?'

'Yes, but Rose doesn't want anyone's help.'

'What a shame. If she really wanted to, I bet she could stop drinking. Plenty of alcoholics do, don't they? It's like smoking. Lots of people quit. I did. And they say nicotine is even more addictive than heroin.'

'Smoking was the hardest thing in the world to give up,' I said, remembering the first cigarette I'd had with Katie when I was about fourteen.

She'd brought a packet to school with her and dared me to smoke one at the end of the huge school playing field. It was almost the end of our lunch break and there were a few kids still sitting by the hedgerow, making the most of their last minutes of freedom. If a teacher was looking out of the window at us, they would never be able to see the smoke from that far away, but it still felt scary, rebellious. She lit one up with her back facing the school building, took a practised drag and slowly blew out smoke towards the ground.

'Go on, you have a go.' She handed it to me.

I glanced around. Two second-year girls were dusting themselves off and walking back to class. A couple of fifth-year boys were bundling on top of each other, grass in their hair and on their clothes.

When I took a drag, I'd nearly choked as the disgusting smoke filled my lungs. Coughing and spluttering, I blew it out as quickly as I could, swaying on the ground when the nicotine head rush made me dizzy.

'Whoa!' I put my hand on the grass to steady myself.

'Lightweight!' Katie roared with laughter.

I shrugged and took another drag, trying to look sophisticated. Anything she could do, I could do, too.

'Where did you get them from?'

'Stole them off my Dad. He won't even notice.'

I blew out more smoke, trying not to cough.

'Here, save some for me!' she said when I got halfway through it.

I handed it back and ran my tongue around in my mouth, which now tasted like an ashtray. I was stupid enough to think I'd never get hooked. No one could ever get addicted to something that tasted that bad, right? How naive.

'Anyway,' I waved a hand through the air at Nadia, 'Rose has been an alcoholic for probably thirty-plus years. It's unlikely she's going to change now.'

'Maybe it was a good job Chris didn't stay with Katie, then. Can you imagine if we'd ended up with Katie's dad as an in-law? Jack always gave me the creeps. If I ever saw him out in the village, he always had this leery look on his face.'

I groaned in agreement. 'Oh, he was awful! It was pretty rare for me to go round to Katie's house because she never wanted to be there, – understandably, with Rose and Jack both drinking heavily. But when I did, I'd catch him looking at me in a way that made my skin crawl.'

Nadia did a mock shiver. 'Oh, by the way, I invited Anna over for dinner after school. She asked if I had any stuff for her class's car boot sale, and I've got tons of junk she can go through. It'll take her a while so I suggested she might as well stay. Is that OK?'

'Yes. Fine. How's Charlotte feeling?'

'Um . . . she's still tired. I've made a doctor's appointment at the surgery for her to have a blood test.'

'Good.'

'Are you seeing Dad today? I'm going in tomorrow. I'm organising that charity bash for the Dorchester Children's Charity and I've got heaps to do still.'

'You work too hard.'

'It's the least I can do. I just think of all those kids without families, or who are vulnerable and hurt, and it breaks my heart. I'd feel guilty knowing all that and not doing anything to help.'

'I'll go after work. Let's hope he doesn't come out with any other bizarre statements this week.' I laughed.

'Yeah, I felt quite an idiot going to see the police. I'm sure they've got plenty of real work to be getting on with and don't need people wasting their time with ludicrous wild goose chases like that.'

'You see that purple flower?' Tom pointed to a large bush on the edge of the grounds.

I stopped walking and he stopped, too, since my arm was linked with his.

'It's a tiger's eye iris.'

'Very pretty.'

'I had one of those in . . .' he trailed off, staring at the plant, frown pinched as if he were waiting for a memory to come flooding in. Eventually he shook his head. 'I don't know.'

We sat on a bench at the far end of the garden that looked back onto the home.

'I found out who Georgia Walker is.' I chuckled. 'You gave me the run-around there, for a while, let me tell you.'

'Georgia.' He looked at me and frowned again for a moment, as if rolling the name around in his ravaged brain. Then he smiled and nodded, glancing off in the direction of the flowers again. 'She was kind. Very nice. I built an extension for her, you know.'

'Yes, I know.' I didn't tell him that I'd found that out from Sergeant Downing.

'It had been a long time since Eve died and I was going through a bad patch. Things were getting on top of me. You know how it is?' He glanced at me. 'I was lonely.'

'You were seeing her?' My eyebrows shot up.

'Yes.' He smiled, and for a moment he looked like the old Tom. Loving, strong, kind, happy. The patriarch who had kept the family together after Eve's death.

'I never knew.'

'Neither did the kids. We didn't tell anyone.'

'How long did it go on for?'

'Only about six months. She . . . she didn't want children. She was set in her ways and wasn't maternal or interested in taking on someone else's children.'

'I'm sorry.' I squeezed harder. 'You deserved some happiness and love.'

He shifted in his seat, his eyes rheumy. 'Oh, but I did have that, Olivia. My family gave me that. They were the most important thing in the world. I'd do anything for them.' He squeezed my hand tighter. 'Wouldn't you do anything for your family?'

I thought about Ethan and my precious, miracle daughter. 'Of course I would.'

'That's why I had to do it, you see.'

I nodded. 'Of course. You had to stop seeing her. I understand. Your family came first.'

He stared at me blankly. 'I had to do it. She wasn't supposed to be there. No one was.' He gripped my hand so tight it began to hurt. Tears in his eyes glistened in the sunlight. 'It was an accident, you see. But I buried her.'

I swallowed hard, kicking myself for bringing up her name again. For some reason, whenever he thought about her, he got confused and agitated again. 'No, you're getting mixed up, Tom. There was no accident. Nothing happened to Georgia: she's fine. She's alive and well.' I pulled my hand from his and laid it on top, patting his cold skin. 'You couldn't have buried her.'

He shook his head angrily, a spray of spittle flying from his mouth. 'No, no, no. Not Georgia!'

'What are you talking about? I don't understand,' I said, trying to keep my voice calm and even.

'It wasn't Georgia, it was Katie.'

'Katie?'

'Yes. Katie. You know her. Your friend.'

I dropped my hand from his and sat upright. 'You're talking about Katie Quinn? Are you . . . You killed Katie? Is that what you're saying, Tom?' A bitter taste washed through my mouth.

'Why did you think it was Georgia?' He gasped and tears fell from his eyes. 'It was Katie. I had to do it, though, don't you see? I buried her.'

Despite the hot sun beating down, my core temperature dropped. Goosebumps broke out on my skin.

He wiped his eyes with the cuff of his shirt and nodded, looking shrunken and shrivelled and broken, like a seventy-five-year-old child.

His words snatched my breath away for a moment before I forced myself to breathe. 'Where did you bury her, Tom?' My voice came out a gravelly whisper.

'I'm sorry, I'm sorry. I had to do it. It was an accident. It was—' He clutched his chest and fell sideways on the bench.

'Tom?' I crouched over him.

His eyelids fluttered as he rasped for breath. 'It . . . hurts . . . chest.'

'Tom!' I patted his pale cheeks gently. 'Stay with me, Tom. You're OK, do you hear?' I put my arms around him and sat him up. 'There. You're going to be more comfortable sitting. Now, breathe.' I stared him in the eyes, taking exaggerated breaths for him to copy. 'That's it. Just keep breathing. You're doing great.'

He moaned.

I felt his pulse for rhythm and strength. His skin was grey and sweaty. There was a blue tinge to his lips. I was pretty sure he was having a heart attack. 'I'm going for help now. Keep breathing. Just keep breathing.'

He moaned again, clutching his chest.

'I'll be back soon. Don't worry. You're doing all right. We'll get you sorted in no time.' I ran across the garden and burst through the front doors to reception. I knew that we couldn't resuscitate him if his heart stopped. Tom had a DNR attached to his medical records – a 'Do not attempt resuscitation' order to tell his medical team not to perform CPR should the need arise, although it didn't affect other treatment. It was Tom's choice, one he'd made when he was first diagnosed, and it supported his autonomy past the stages when he could no longer clearly express his own wishes. But at least we could get him into bed and make him more comfortable and hopefully pain-free.

'I think Tom's having a heart attack. We need to get him into bed and start him on oxygen and Aspirin NOW,' I shouted at Kelly and rushed back outside. At least if he did go, I'd be by his side at the end.

Kneeling on the grass beside him, I monitored his breathing which was slow and laboured. 'Tom? Can you hear me? Tom?'

His eyes opened. 'I'm . . . s . . . sorry.'

'Shhh. Don't talk. Just breathe, all right?' I brushed his hair off his sweating, chilled forehead. 'You'll be OK. You'll be fine.'

Chapter Eight

I'm so sorry, Ethan, but Tom's had a heart attack,' I said down the phone.

'What?' He gasped over the noisy office sounds in the background. 'Hang on; I was just about to go into a planning meeting. Give me a sec.' The noise grew quieter until I could no longer hear it. 'Dad's had a heart attack? Is he OK? Is he still alive?'

'Yes, he's OK. It was only a mild one. I was with him at the time. He's on some anticoagulants to thin his blood, Aspirin, and medication to reduce his blood pressure. They're monitoring him closely at Mountain View, which is the best thing in the circumstances. With the DNR order, the staff felt it was better to keep him in familiar surroundings, and I agreed. There wouldn't be much to gain by taking him to hospital.'

'Shit.'

I pictured him running his hand through his hair, pacing up and down.

'I should come back. It'll take me hours, though, before I get there.'

'Chris and Nadia are with him now, but he'd love to see you, I'm sure.'

'Christ. How did . . . ? Oh, never mind. I'm leaving now, OK? I'll go straight to Mountain View.'

'OK. Text me when you're on your way back to the house and I'll sort something out for you to eat.'

'Will do. Love you.'

'Love you, too.'

With everything that had happened I'd forgotten to go food shopping again so I grabbed my keys, which surprisingly were where they should be in the pottery bowl.

I put my head round the door to the lounge. Since Nadia was with Tom, her dinner plans for the girls had backfired and I had them here instead. Anna was painting Charlotte's toenails a glittery purple colour while she asked her history revision questions for an exam Charlotte had tomorrow. They both looked up with glum faces when they saw me.

'Is there any more news about Granddad?' Anna asked, mouth turned down.

'Is he going to be OK?' Charlotte gave me a sheepish look, as if somehow this was all her fault.

I kissed Charlotte on the head before sitting down next to Anna on the sofa and drawing her close. Anna was a sensitive girl, taking on other people's pain and anguish as her own.

'Is he, Mum?' Anna's eyes welled up.

'Come on, now.' I stroked her hair. 'He's fine at the moment. He's resting and they don't think he needs to go to hospital.'

She sniffed and nodded. 'I want to go and see him, but . . . he kind of scares me now. He's not the same as he used to be.'

'I know, darling.' I sighed sadly. 'But inside he's still the same man who loves you both very much. He's probably had a bit too much excitement for one day, anyway. Your Dad's driving back now so he'll see him tonight. We'll go soon, OK?'

Another sniff. 'OK.'

'I want to go, too.' Charlotte glanced up. 'But I feel a bit like Anna. And I never know what to say to him anymore. He doesn't even know who we are now,' she said.

'I know. It's very difficult to see someone you love change like that.' I gave them both a solemn smile. 'Let's just see how he's feeling in the next day or so and then we can talk about you girls visiting him again, OK? I'm going food shopping now. Is there anything you fancy for tea?'

'Pizza?' Charlotte asked.

'We had pizza the other day when you forgot to go shopping,' Anna said, an edge of accusation to her voice.

'Sorry, sweetheart, I'll hand in my notice as your mum on the grounds that there was no butter in the fridge and I made you eat pizza for tea. OK?' I forced a smile. 'You can get a new mum from MumsRUs who'll do a better job, although most kids would love eating pizza twice in one week.'

That got her smiling again. 'How about spaghetti Bolognese?' She was a pasta addict.

'Sure.' I glanced at Charlotte, who looked so pale she could probably do with a hefty dose of red meat. Maybe she was anaemic. I made a mental note to get Nadia to test for that, too, when they went into the surgery. 'That OK with you?'

'Yep.'

I drove to the supermarket with thoughts jumping around in my head.

Would Tom be OK? One heart attack didn't necessarily mean he'd have another anytime soon. He could go on for years, but was it fairer on Tom if he did slip away quickly before the Alzheimer's interfered with the part of his brain that made his lungs and heart stop functioning? Wasn't it better not to suffer like that?

What did he mean about Katie, though? How could he possibly be telling the truth?

He couldn't be. It was a simple as that. Yes, Katie had run away from home when she was eighteen, and no one had heard from her since, but she'd left a letter. A goodbye letter. So Tom couldn't have killed her, could he?

What was it he'd said? *It was an accident but he'd had to do it.* Those two statements completely contradicted each other. He was confused. Delusional. Maybe even hallucinating. He obviously remembered that Katie had run away but had distorted things in his mind. He was getting mixed up again. His memories were lying to him, that was all.

I walked round the supermarket, flinging the usual things into the trolley. Wholemeal bread – I kept trying to like it since it was supposed to be healthy – orange juice with no 'bits' in as Anna hated that one – milk, ham for sandwiches, butter, plus another butter since I obviously couldn't have enough in my house and needed a spare, potatoes.

A picture of Katie swam before my eyes. It was during a netball lesson one day when we were about thirteen. She'd just dived to her side to catch the ball but misjudged it and went crashing to the floor, landing awkwardly on her arm and breaking it. She sat on the ground, staring at the bone which was actually poking through the skin. The teacher almost threw up when she saw it, as did several other girls, but Katie just stood up calmly, supporting her injured arm with the other and asking the teacher if she could have a lift to A&E. She never cried. I would've been screaming in agony, tears streaming down my face, but she never did. Not then. Not ever.

Katie usually hid her feelings well, whereas I wore mine on my sleeve. If she was upset about something that had happened with Rose or Jack, she never really talked about it; she kept it all inside. The only way I could tell things were really bad would be if she turned up at my house late at night after a row with her parents or something. She'd throw gravel up at my bedroom window to wake me up, not wanting to go back home, and I used to make up a bed for her on the floor with a couple of huge beanbags I had. The next morning she was always gone before I woke up. Even though I had repeatedly asked her over the years about her home life, she always refused to tell me.

She didn't seem able to hide her grief about splitting up with Chris, though. They'd been together for nine months, and although she never told me she was in love with him, I guessed she was. It seemed obvious to me by how she acted around him. Whenever she looked at Chris she softened around the edges. Her face lit up. She was happier, freer, lighter somehow. He had loved her, too, but it just wasn't meant to be. When he'd finished with her, she was devastated. She'd refused to come out anywhere with me, preferring to cry and mope around at home, which I'd never seen her do before. Katie was usually strong, resilient and independent – she had to be. She always had a strength that I envied – although I'm sure some people would call her hard, bitchy and selfish. The thing is, you can never understand someone until you've walked in their shoes, and even then it's probably impossible. No one's perfect, are they? So maybe she had a reputation, for a lot of things, but maybe it wasn't her fault. Anyway, she was my friend, and I was nothing if not loyal. I tried to get her out of the house when she split up with Chris. Tried to get her to do things with me again, take her mind off the break-up, but she wasn't interested. The last time I saw her, after weeks of being heartbroken, she'd looked like her old self again, like there was a kind of determination about her. A new resolve. I'd thought it was just that she'd made a decision to herself to go out and get on with her life again, but it wasn't that at all. She'd decided she was leaving the village. Running away from Rose and Jack and her broken heart.

I studied the freshly made pizzas under their shiny cellophane wrapper. Ham and cheese or roasted veg?

Who cared? Who cared what pizza I bought if what Tom had told me was true?

But, of course, it wasn't true. Couldn't be.

So why hasn't anyone ever heard from Katie again? In twenty-five years, why hasn't she contacted you?

Because you were a bad friend. A friend who obviously ignored her when she was in need and she felt the only thing to do was run away. A friend who was too busy with her nursing diploma and her fabulous boyfriend to notice how much she was hurting. Yes, a selfish friend who never stopped to think what was really going on in Katie's life.

I chewed on my lip and put both pizzas in the trolley.

But plenty of people ran away and were never heard from again. I googled it once, a long time ago. Of course, there was no Internet when Katie went missing, but one day, oh, probably about six years ago now, I thought about her out of the blue and actually looked up how many people go missing a year. I was shocked. It was thousands. About 300,000, if I remember rightly.

And Katie had been eighteen. An adult. The police said at the time that they couldn't do anything. It was her choice. And, of course, there'd been the letter she'd left, addressed to her mum and dad. The village policeman had been satisfied that Katie had just run away and she'd probably turn up again.

I picked up a packet of minced beef and flung that in the trolley.

So, really, it was Katie's choice not to get in touch with anyone and tell them where she was. She'd left for reasons that none of us ever really knew for certain. But Tom couldn't possibly have killed her because of the letter.

There. That letter was complete proof that Tom's memories were just distorted with Alzheimer's.

I shook my head to clear the thoughts and grabbed a bottle of dried oregano and basil. Did we need salt? I got some, just in case.

I couldn't tell Ethan what Tom had said. Not after the last time when he'd got so angry. Not after the whole thing about Georgia had been proved to just be the ramblings of a mixed-up mind and we'd wasted the police's time. Not after Tom's heart attack when everyone was so upset and worried. It would sound like my imagination was going into overdrive, neurotically piecing together events that couldn't possibly be true. I couldn't tell Nadia, either. She was devastated about Tom's heart attack, too, as well as worrying about Lucas's affair. She didn't need any extra stress now. Plus, it was all completely crazy because of the goodbye letter.

And yet . . .

I'd always wondered what had happened to Katie. When she first left, I'd felt so guilty. I hadn't been there for her enough. Hadn't been sympathetic enough. If she'd only just talked to me about things, we could've come up with something to make her feel happier. I didn't have any clue she was intending to up and leave. I mean, I knew her home life wasn't happy. Living with Rose and Jack drinking all the time couldn't have been much fun. Katie had had to grow up quickly if she wanted to survive. She was the adult in that household, not her parents. She'd been carrying a tremendous load since she was a kid and I hadn't understood just how bad things were until she left. Until I got older and became a proper adult myself. She hid things so well, you see.

I chucked some ketchup, tinned tomatoes and baked beans in the trolley.

Losing Chris must've been the last straw for her, though. She'd talked about them getting engaged, getting a house together. Chris was working for Tom as a builder and earning decent money, and she'd left school at sixteen and was working in a shop in Weymouth, so they could've afforded to rent somewhere as a starter home. And Tom would've helped Chris out, I was sure, since Tate Construction was doing really well. Better than well, actually. Tom was loaded, but he worked really hard for what he had. It was Katie's dream for her and Chris to be a family. Sometimes when I saw her at Tom's house for a Sunday BBQ or something, she'd be taking everything in, studying the whole family – Nadia, Chris, Ethan, Tom – with a look of . . . God, what was it? It was like a mixture of envy, satisfaction and happiness. She wanted a happy family, wanted to be a part of theirs, and she finally was. And who could blame her? I knew what it felt like, too, to be included in this big, close-knit family. Even though my childhood was great and my parents doted on me, I'd always longed for brothers and sisters. Being an only child was tough sometimes, and Katie's life was a lot tougher than mine. She wanted the son of a rich developer, the security, the protection that she'd never had from her own family. But somehow her dream shattered. They were only eighteen but she wanted to get her own home and get married. Have kids. It was too much, too soon for Chris, and even though I believe he really did love her, he panicked.

I chose a big bag of crisps and some honey-roasted peanuts Ethan liked, then scoured the bottles of wine. I needed a drink.

I think Chris felt too pressured to settle down, and rightly so, I supposed. Eighteen was so young. He wasn't ready. And instead of sticking around and waiting for him to *be* ready, enjoying just being together and being in love and having fun like I'd been doing with Ethan and Nadia had been doing with Lucas, Katie had pushed and pushed and gone on and on about settling down until Chris couldn't take it anymore and had ended things.

So, yes, I felt guilty that I hadn't been there for my friend. Guilty that I'd thought about her less and less over the years as I got on with my life. Guilty that I hadn't known what had happened to her or where she'd ended up. But I didn't think Tom had buried her. Of course I didn't. It was mad. Did I mention the letter?

No, it wasn't because I believed Tom at all that I went in search of Katie Quinn. It was so I could absolve myself. I had to find out that she was having a good life. A better life than the one she would've had if she'd stayed in the village and married Chris. I had to make sure she was happy.

At least, that's what I told myself.

Chapter Nine

How do you find someone who wants to stay hidden? I didn't have a clue. I was a nurse and a mother – what did I know about finding a missing person?

Google was becoming my new best friend. Or BFF, as Anna's annoying TV programmes would say. When she went to bed that night I typed in Katie Quinn's name and was met with an author website for a Katie Quinn who'd written a cookbook. There was a Twitter page for someone who looked about a hundred years old and definitely wasn't her, along with a Facebook page, a photographer, a journalist, an actress and a doctor, all with the same name. I checked through them but none was my Katie Quinn.

Poppy barked, making me jump, a few seconds before Ethan slid his key in the door. I closed the laptop, uncurled myself from the sofa in the lounge and went out into the hall to meet him. He looked exhausted, with his hair sticking up where he'd been running his hands through it, an unconscious habit of his when he was worried. He'd done it so much when Anna had scarlet fever I thought it would stay permanently spiky at the front.

'How is he?'

Poppy, sensing the mood, refrained from a full-on greeting and just sat there staring at Ethan, her tail thumping loudly on the stone floor.

Ethan met my inquisitive look with a watery gaze. 'He's pretty weak, but surprisingly he was quite lucid. Told us all to stop fussing over him and get back home to our families.' He set his briefcase down on the floor. 'They're just making him comfortable. It's all they can do, really.'

'Are you going to stay down here for a while or are you going back up to York tomorrow?'

'If I stay here, Dad will only moan at me. And as sad as it's going to be to lose him, he could still go on for months or even years yet.'

I opened my mouth to tell him what Tom had told me earlier, but the words died on my tongue. With everything going on I had to make some more enquiries before I mentioned anything. *If* I even told him at all. I'd find Katie alive and well and there would be no need to say anything, anyway.

'. . . back to York in the morning.' Ethan's voice pulled me from my drifting thoughts.

I squeezed his arm. 'OK. There's leftover spaghetti if you want some.'

'I actually had a bite with Chris and Nadia. We went to a pub on the way back.' He followed me into the kitchen.

'Tea, then?' I filled the kettle.

'No, thanks. I'm going to have a shower and go to bed.' He sat at the island, shoulders slumped, tie askew. 'Is there something going on with Lucas and Nadia?'

I snapped my head around. 'Why?'

'It's just Lucas was a bit odd.'

'Odd how?'

'Well, he was really quiet. You know how he's usually so energetic – the life and soul of everything – but tonight he didn't hardly say two words. Even Chris said more than Lucas for once.'

'He's probably just upset about Tom. It's not like he's going to be all lively after his father-in-law's just had a heart attack, is he?'

'No, I know. He was just . . . miles away, really, like he wasn't even in the room. He kept fiddling with his phone.'

I wondered if there had been a development with the woman he was having an affair with. Was Lucas preoccupied with deciding whether to leave Nadia or whether to end the affair? I hoped it was the latter, for Nadia's sake.

Ethan shrugged. 'I don't know. Maybe you're right. He's just upset about Dad.' He walked up the stairs.

I made a chamomile tea, hoping it would help me sleep but it didn't. As I spooned myself against Ethan's warm body, Tom's words echoed in my head.

I had to do it. She wasn't supposed to be there. No one was. It was an accident, you see. But I buried her.

It didn't make sense.

I tried to think about what happened when Katie ran away, but the memories were twenty-five years old, lying deep under layers of others that made up my history. She'd left the letter, I remembered that bit, but what had it said? I don't think I ever actually saw it. I remember . . . what? I turned on to my back and stared at the ceiling, willing my brain to trawl through my mind. A policeman had turned up on my doorstep one morning. It must've been a Sunday as I was having a lie-in because there was no college. I think I'd had a late night . . . I'd been to . . . Where had I been the night before? No, I can't remember. Anyway, the policeman. Yes. He was the village bobby, back in the days when we still had a community policeman who actually lived in the village and knew pretty much everyone and everything that went on. PC Cook – that was his name. He always had the reputation of being firm but very fair, although I'd never had anything to do with him until then. So, there PC Cook was on my doorstep on a Sunday morning saying Rose had called him and told him Katie had run away from home and left this letter. He asked if I knew where she'd gone, but she hadn't said anything to me at all. I had no clue. No warning sign she was about to do that.

No, that's not strictly true. Looking at it with hindsight and the benefit of years of wisdom, maybe there were clues. I just didn't recognise them at the time. I suppose after the event, we're all experts, aren't we? Shame it's too late by then.

It hit me then where I'd been the Saturday night before Katie left. There was a band playing at the Kings' Arms, one we'd seen before and really liked. They were called something like the Jazz Iguanas, or Jazz Lizards, or something else peculiar. Anyway, I was going to go with Ethan, Chris, Nadia, Lucas and Tom. By then I hadn't seen much of Katie for months since her break-up with Chris. Every time I'd asked her to go out, she made excuses. I finished college in Weymouth on that Friday afternoon and walked into town to the shop where Katie was working to ask if she wanted to come with us the following night. I thought it was probably too soon for her to want to see Chris again – even though it had been about seven months by then – but at least I would've tried to include her. I didn't want her to feel left out just because she wasn't part of the 'Tate' crowd anymore. She looked different that afternoon. She'd had her long blonde hair cut into a choppy jaw-length bob, and instead of her usual skimpy, figure-hugging, cleavage-enhancing clothes and stilettos, she was wearing leggings and a long baggy jumper and flat shoes. It was like she was trying to reinvent herself into something frumpy or old before her time.

Even her makeup wasn't the usual hard black lines around her eyes and vampire-red lipstick. It was toned down to a clear lip gloss and just a swiping of mascara.

What had she said when I asked her to come out with us all? Something strange. Damn, what was it? Something like 'Well, if he thinks I'm going to fuck him again, he can fuck off.' She had an odd smile on her face, equal parts secretive, sly and spiteful. I vaguely remember laughing it off. If she'd met Chris since the break-up to have sex I didn't really want to know about it. It wasn't my business, and I wasn't going to judge her for it. I knew how hard it was for her to let go of him. Maybe enticing Chris with sex was her last-ditch attempt to get him back, but it hadn't worked.

That was the last time I ever saw her. After PC Cook left me, I went to see Rose to try to find out what had happened, but Rose was drunk and angry. Jack was strangely quiet, sitting in his favourite armchair, already with a glass of amber liquid in his hand, staring into space while his wife ranted and raved about how ungrateful Katie had been and what a sad excuse for a daughter she was. I'd left then. They were a pair of hypocrites. They'd never given her a happy home life, and what with Chris breaking up with her, it had obviously been the last straw so she'd gone in search of something better. Something happier. What I do remember distinctly is silently wishing she found it.

Over the next few days, there were whispers in the village. The rumour mill had started, of course, as it's bound to in any village. The gossip was that she'd stolen something from Rose and Jack who had then chucked her out. Then it changed to she'd run away to London to work at King's Cross as a prostitute. Then something about her aunt had collected her one day and taken her on holiday. She didn't even have a bloody aunt!

After that, I frequently went to see PC Cook to ask if he'd found anything else out but he always said no. Since Katie was eighteen and an adult, and had obviously left of her own free will, there was nothing really they could do. After finding out from Mr Google just how many people go missing each year, I'm not surprised it had gone no further.

But now there was a big question mark in my head. Had she really left of her own free will?

Chapter Ten

It was 9.30 a.m. when I knocked on Rose's door. She lived in one of the few remaining local authority-owned houses in the village. The same one they'd lived in all those years ago. Recently, the council had sold most of them off to private buyers in an attempt to boost their sagging budgets. You could spot the difference between the private ones and Rose's a mile off. Her concrete path had suffered years of wear and neglect, broken in places with thick weeds protruding through and covered with moss. It was an obstacle course just to get up to the front door, whose navy blue paint was peeling in thick flakes onto the step. Ivy clung in a death grip on to the front of the house, trailing over the windows, even, and the guttering bowed in the middle. I didn't fancy being around when that fell down. I bet there were tons of leaves and mud inside. Probably a few dead birds, too.

A memory flooded in then. Just after we'd bought the barn from Tom and he was living with us, we had a dove nesting in our guttering outside Anna's window. Anna had called it Mrs Lovey Dovey and was so excited to watch her tending an egg, spending hours with Tom in her room just staring at it. When the chick finally did arrive she'd called it Baby Davey Lovey Dovey, and Tom had gone out in the garden and dug fresh worms for Mrs Lovey Dovey every day, leaving them in the guttering for her, saying to Anna how hard it was to be a bird parent. Those aren't the actions of a killer, are they? Someone who could murder and bury a young woman couldn't possibly gather worms to feed a baby bird. They'd more likely kill animals, wouldn't they? Isn't that how serial killers start?

A smell hit me as I knocked on Rose's door. Urine. I hoped it was cat's and not human's. Rose wasn't the first drunk I'd ever dealt with as a nurse, and I was sure she wouldn't be the last. I knew whatever would greet me inside wouldn't be pretty.

I knocked again when I got no response.

An elderly woman with grey curls walked past with a Jack Russell on a lead. 'She'll still be in bed, that one. Never gets up 'til the afternoon,' she scoffed and walked off.

As I waited I thought about the last time I'd stood here, calling for Katie. It was months after Chris had split up with her and she hadn't been round to see me, which was weird. I mean, I knew she was devastated, but she practically lived at my house whenever she could. She never wanted to be at home. And yet, after Chris, she avoided me. I'd stood in the doorway asking Jack if she was in. It took a few seconds for his drunken eyes to turn into something lecherous and predatory, as if he was about to lunge forward and attack me. It had creeped me out. I fought the urge to run back down the path, screaming, or to throw up. Or both. I couldn't wait to get away from there when he said she wasn't in. After he closed the door and I was walking back up the path I felt that horrible sensation of someone watching me. I glanced back, expecting to see Jack leering out of the lounge window, but instead, the corner of the curtain in Katie's room dropped suddenly.

I shivered then, just thinking about Jack again, and was about to turn and go when a dark figure loomed behind the glass panel in the door and Rose appeared.

'Hi.' I smiled when she opened the door. 'How are you?'

She didn't smile back. 'There must've been a mix-up. I had the stitches out yesterday at the surgery,' she said gruffly. 'I don't need a nurse's visit.'

'Oh, right. Good. I'm not here about that. I actually wanted to ask you something about Katie.' I braced myself for an outburst of anger but she just stared at me impassively. 'Can I come in for a minute?'

She turned around and walked up a tight corridor with the original threadbare carpet that had been in fashion in the seventies but was now stained, garish. I left the door ajar slightly, just in case I needed to make a quick getaway, and followed her into the kitchen, which was also stuck in a seventies time warp, all avocado green Formica and mustard lino on the floor. Dirty cups and plates were piled up in an equally dirty sink stained with a thick layer of grime and limescale. The surfaces were covered with crumbs and food-encrusted utensils. A packet of butter was open, oozing its yellow creaminess down the front of a cupboard and onto the floor. Empty bottles of gin and vodka and whisky spilled out of a black rubbish bag in the corner of the room. The overpowering odour of urine and alcohol made the back of my throat close. I pictured Katie living in amongst all this and felt a stab of sadness.

She unscrewed the top from a bottle of cheap supermarket brand whisky and poured out half a pint glass. She took a big gulp and narrowed her eyes at me over the rim. 'Want a drink?' As she set it back on the Formica worktop, some whisky sloshed onto the floor.

'No, thanks. I wanted to ask if you'd ever heard from Katie.'

'Don't be stupid.' She took another gulp. Swished it round her mouth. Swallowed. Her gaze locked on mine. 'Why?'

'I was just . . . I was just thinking about her. You know, wondering what happened to her. Where she was. What she was up to. Don't you ever think about it? The last time I asked you if you'd heard from her you got really angry with me for bringing it up, and I'm sorry, but I—'

'That's because Katie's an ungrateful bitch.' She slammed the glass down.

I tried to suppress a gasp but I'm sure a little slipped out. No matter what Anna did, I would never call my daughter a bitch. And seeing things now, really seeing things for the first time, it was actually a miracle that Katie hadn't left home before she was eighteen.

'Fucking ungrateful from the minute she could talk. She was a nasty piece of work. A liar! She left me here to look after myself in my old age. I gave birth to her and she never gave a toss about us!' Her voice rose with contempt.

I wanted to mention that the state she was in was entirely her own doing, but I pushed the thought away. No one would ever persuade Rose she was in the wrong. That she was the selfish one. The despicable parent who didn't even deserve to have a child. Not when there were so many people out there who desperately wanted them and couldn't.

'Right. So, you've never heard from her at all, then, in the last twenty-five years?' I asked, wanting to make quite sure so I could leave.

'No. And I'm bloody glad. Useless cow.' Her eyes glinted with steel and something else. Hatred, it almost looked like.

I took a step backwards towards the corridor. 'Do you remember the letter she wrote you when she left?'

'What about it?'

'Do you remember what it said?'

She shrugged. 'No. I ripped it up.'

'But it was definitely Katie's handwriting, though?'

She snorted. 'Of course it was. Whose handwriting did you think it would be? The Queen's?'

I was halfway through my morning patients when a thought struck me. Maybe I'd been surrounded by a clue to Katie's whereabouts all this time and I'd never even realised.

What do you do when you leave a doctor's surgery and move to another location? Katie would've had to register with a new practice at some point in the last twenty-five years. Even if she was perfectly healthy and never had a reason to see a doctor, she would surely have been having regular smear tests.

I typed in Katie's name and date of birth. Before I started at the surgery all the old paper records had been transferred onto computer so it only took a few seconds for her name to ping up in front of my eyes.

It took another few seconds to realise that the last entry in the records was from when she was seventeen for a repeat prescription of the contraceptive pill, and no doctor or hospital had ever requested a copy of her records.

I sat back in the chair. No. That couldn't be right, although there could be a good explanation. Maybe they'd been requested but someone had forgotten to add an entry. Or maybe the request had been written in the paper records but accidentally omitted when the information was added to the computer all those years ago.

My eyes scanned the screen, wondering if maybe a request had been filed at the beginning of her notes, rather than the end. I scrolled back through the most recent entries and turned the pages, going back in time. And that's when I saw something disturbing.

From the age of eight, Katie had been treated for repeated bouts of cystitis and vaginal thrush and inflammation. Eight?

Sexual abuse was the first thought that popped into my head. I remembered Jack's predatory looks. Katie's promiscuity. She'd started having sex with boys at fourteen. I thought it was her way of trying to find love and attention when she couldn't get any at home, but could it have been more than that? Was it learned behaviour? Had Jack been abusing her from an early age?

Then again it might mean nothing. Although vulvovaginitis, thrush and chronic urinary tract infections can be signs of sexual abuse, they can also be caused by other circumstances, such as lack of hygiene; using soap, shower gel, or bubble bath; diet; and taking antibiotics.

I bit my lip and stared at the screen. She'd been prescribed antibiotics for a couple of bouts of tonsillitis, and I knew her diet was pretty poor at home.

Was I looking for something that wasn't there because I didn't want to believe that Tom had killed and buried her like he'd told me?

Katie had never mentioned anything about Jack abusing her. But now I realised that she'd never said anything about a lot of horrible things that would've been going on in her life, and I was too stupid to understand back then. If I'd been her, I would've been complaining to my best friend about the state of them – that I had to fend for myself, get myself to school, wash my own clothes, make myself dinner, survive on pennies because both parents were living off their unemployment benefits and using most of it to buy alcohol – but Katie had never complained. She just got on with things. And that was how she survived, until she turned eighteen and left it all behind.

After my last patient I had a half-hour gap before Elaine came in and took over from me. There was no way I could call every single doctor's surgery in the country trying to find any trace of

Katie, but every patient was registered in the NHS database, and they would definitely have a record if anyone had ever requested her medical notes. For the first time in my career I found myself wishing a patient had had an operation or an illness over the years, just so I could try and find her.

I called the NHS records line and got through to a woman called Linda who I'd spoken to in the past. She checked once, and I made her recheck, but she still gave me the same answer.

Katie Quinn's records hadn't been updated or requested in the last twenty-five years.

My head was still spinning when I took Poppy out for a walk along Chesil Beach later. The pebbles crunched under my trainers as I stared out to sea, thoughts crashing into each other like the waves onto the shore.

Had Jack sexually abused Katie? Had she really written that goodbye letter or was it all a convenient cover-up? I had only Jack and Rose's word that it even said she was running away. Maybe Jack had killed her and faked the letter. But if that was the case, why was Tom saying he'd killed her? Tom couldn't stand Jack and Rose. I was sure he wouldn't have had anything to do with Jack. So, what, then?

Tom's words drilled into my head again. I was sure now that this wasn't just a confused old man mixing up fragments of memories. Somewhere in those words was the truth about what had happened to Katie. A truth I had to find out.

Move over, Pandora. Katie's box was about to be prised wide open.

Chapter Eleven

Nadia returned the favour the next night and had Anna over for tea. Nadia was making sweet and sour chicken balls and jasmine rice. From scratch, not out of a jar. I don't know how she found the time. Lucas was on his way to New York on a two-day stop-over and Nadia said she wanted the company, although I'd forbidden Anna to talk about death row prisoners whilst she was there. Not only was it depressing, but I thought her latest obsession was a bit unhealthy. She'd been signing online petitions the last few days, trying to get the death penalty abolished in America! Luckily, she was distracted enough by the excitement of being able to go through Charlotte's and Nadia's stuff to search for anything they could give her for the car boot sale and hadn't mentioned it once all day. Anna had always been a bit of a magpie. As a kid, she'd always loved anything shiny and sparkly, but she also had this urge to examine other people's things. If we went to a new house she'd pick up people's photos and ornaments and knick-knacks and study them, asking how they got them and if there was a story behind them.

So at 7.15 p.m. I was child free and standing on Chris's doorstep with a lasagne still warm from the oven. The ragout and béchamel sauce was out of a jar, unlike Nadia's, and the cheese came pre-grated, but, hey, it's the thought that counts. And the jar stuff tasted much better than I could make on my own. Sometimes I wished I had Nadia's talent for, well, for everything, really, but that wasn't going to happen any time soon unless I was body-snatched and replaced by a totally different entity. At any rate, I admit that I wasn't delivering food on a purely altruistic basis: I had an ulterior motive for wanting to talk to Chris because he was the last person to see Katie after she left home, and I wanted him to jog my memory.

'Olivia?' Chris came to the door wiping his hands on a towel. 'You OK?' He gave me a concerned frown.

I smiled, holding up the dish. 'Meals on wheels.'

He took a sniff. 'Mmm, that smells gorgeous. Come in. I wasn't expecting you.'

'I know, but I was making dinner and made an extra one for you. Then I thought that since both Ethan and Anna weren't at home we could eat it together, too. It's not a bad time, is it?' I suddenly remembered the woman I'd seen him with at the pub. 'I mean, if you've got company, I can just leave it with you.'

'No, course not.' He stepped back and waved me in. 'I was just about to stick a jacket potato in the microwave so this is an unexpected pleasure.'

We sat in the kitchen at the sleek black ash table in the white kitchen that Abby had chosen when they'd first moved in together twenty years ago. In fact, the whole house had a black and white theme going on, with just splashes of colour here and there. I wondered how they'd decided who got what in the divorce. How did you divide things up into neat little bundles? *You have the microwave and I'll have the ornamental frog, you bastard! No, I want the frog, you bitch – you never loved it like I did!* In that moment, part of me could understand Nadia's reluctance to confront Lucas about his affair. It would mean the change of everything. Life as you knew it would collapse. And, yes, although you would get over it eventually, in the meantime you were looking at a whole heap of pain, heartache and stress. At least Chris and Abby hadn't had any kids, although ironically that was the main reason for the breakdown in their relationship. Love could be a vicious and destructive thing sometimes. I didn't realise then just how vicious and destructive.

Chris piled a huge serving onto a square white plate and set it down in front of me.

'Whoa, that's massive!' I stared at it.

He shrugged. 'Just eat what you can.'

I tucked my fork into the corner and broke off a piece.

'That's apparently what Mum always used to say to us, although I was too young to remember that.' Chris sat down. 'She'd give us gigantic portions of food all the time. Thought that we were growing kids so we should eat a lot. That's probably where my being overweight stemmed from.' He blushed, embarrassed. 'I was pretty chubby as a kid.'

You'd never know it to look at him now, though. The years of building work and boxing had turned his body into a chiselled physique that any male fitness model would've been jealous of.

'I went to see Dad again today.' Chris took a bite of food and set his fork down, chewing.

'I'm going to go tomorrow. How was he?'

'Better than yesterday. He had more colour in his cheeks and he was sitting in the chair. He said he wanted to go for a walk and the staff were keeping him prisoner.'

'A bit of exercise is good for him, actually.'

'He may not have much time left. He should be able to do whatever he wants.' Chris leaned his elbows on the table and clasped his hands together. 'I hope he does have another heart attack.' He caught my eyes warily, as if expecting me to get angry at that.

I reached out and laid my hand over his. 'I think it would be kinder for him to go suddenly.'

'But then I feel guilty for thinking like that. I shouldn't want my dad to die.' He pulled his hand away and picked up his fork again.

'Don't feel guilty, Chris. You don't want him to suffer any more than he has to. That's natural.'

'I need a drink.' He stood up and grabbed a couple of bottles of beer from the fridge. 'Want one?'

'Yes, please.'

He flipped off the caps and brought them back to the table. 'I don't know how Dad did it, you know. Looking after three young kids and running a company at the same time. I never once felt neglected or unloved. If I had a problem he was always there for me. The same with Nadia and Ethan. He was always running us around to various clubs. Me to boxing, Nadia to dance, Ethan to football. We always came first, you know.' He tipped his head back and took a long sip of beer. 'I mean, Nadia was great, too. More like a mum sometimes than a big sister.'

I took a drink and pushed my food away, my appetite vanishing suddenly. It was hard to equate the Tom that we all knew and loved with the Tom who could kill an eighteen-year-old girl. Almost impossible. And if I was finding it hard, how would Nadia, Ethan and Chris feel if I told them what I'd discovered so far?

'You remember Katie?' I picked at the label on the beer bottle.

'Yeah.' He sighed. 'I feel guilty about her, too.'

My head snapped up and I locked my gaze on his face. 'Why? Why would you feel guilty?'

'She left the village because of me, didn't she? Because I finished with her. I broke her heart.' He stared down at the bottle in his hands. 'She wanted us to move in together and get married and have kids and all that stuff, and I just wasn't ready for it. I . . .' He sighed. 'We were too young.'

'But you did you love her, didn't you?' I thought how different Katie and he were. She was the brash, mouthy, hard girl and he was the quiet loner. Still, didn't they say opposites attracted?

'Yes. I was gutted when she left. Even though I was the one who broke it off, it didn't stop me loving her still. You can't just turn your feelings for someone off. I thought maybe if she'd stayed we might've got back together later when she wasn't trying to pressure me so much – when we were both a bit older and more ready for such a commitment.'

I thought about what Katie had said that last time I saw her, about fucking him again. 'But you did meet up with each other after you split up, didn't you? I mean, you were sort of seeing each other.'

'No.'

'You didn't . . . you know?' I raised an eyebrow.

'What, meet up for sex?'

I shrugged. 'Well, sometimes it's hard to let go, isn't it? You go back and forth a bit, confused, until you make your final decision.'

'No. We never did. In the seven months after the split, I only saw her round the village a few times.'

'But you were the last person to see her that day she ran away, weren't you? Tell me what happened again.'

'I told that policeman at the time. What was his name?' He shrugged. 'I don't know. It's not important.'

Except maybe it was. 'PC Cook?'

'Yeah. It was really early and I was waiting for the bus to take me to the boxing gym. We'd been to the pub the night before to see some band. What were they called?'

'The Jazz Iguanas or something.'

He laughed. 'Yeah, that was it. Crap name. But I left early because I didn't want to be too tired to spar the next day. Anyway, the Sunday morning Dad was supposed to be giving me a lift to the gym but he said he had something urgent to do so he couldn't take me, and I remember seeing her walking past, coming from the direction of her house. It was awkward. Like I said, I'd only seen her a few times since the split, and even then not to say hello to because she was too far away. I didn't know whether to stop her and talk to her, or whether it was better to just pretend I hadn't seen her. In the end, I decided to say hi.'

'Did she speak to you?'

'She just stopped and stared at me for a moment. She looked really different. Her hair was short and she didn't have all that heavy makeup on and her clothes were a bit . . . I don't know, grannyfied. It was weird. I thought she was going to say something. Swear at me at the very least. Tell me to fuck off or something. But she didn't say a thing. Then she just carried on walking.'

'I vaguely remember you telling me all this at the time, but I can't remember what happened next. Did you see where she went after you saw her?'

'Yeah, she was walking towards your house.'

'In Back Street?' I asked, thinking about my parents' three-bed cottage I grew up in, long sold now after they'd retired to sunny Spain twelve years ago.

'No, Tate Barn. Well, it was our house then. Dad was renovating it at the time for us to live in.'

'Yes, I remember when he was working on it.'

Since our house is the last in the village, she could only have been heading towards Abbotsbury, the next village along the main road, or cutting through the woods alongside the barn and hiking up over the hills. 'So she was going to Abbotsbury?'

'She must've been. That's what that policeman thought, too. She was carrying a big rucksack. I didn't think anything about it at the time, but then later, after I heard she'd left a letter and run away, it all made sense.'

'You're absolutely sure?'

'Positive. When I found out she'd left home I kept replaying the scene in my head over and over, wishing I'd done something differently. Said something to make her stay. I can even remember what she was wearing because she still looked beautiful to me, and, like I said, I kept thinking about it afterwards. Don't you remember I used to bend your ear about it all the time?'

'Yes, that's right. You did.'

He stared off into the distance, lost in an old memory. 'She had on some shiny black leggings and a big yellow button-down shirt. It looked strange, to tell you the truth. Nothing like she usually used to wear. And she was wearing these massive yellow hooped earrings and a silver necklace with a sun and a star on it.' He rubbed his hands over his face. 'Then the bus pulled up and I got on. If I'd known it was the last time I'd ever see her, I never would've let her go.'

Chapter Twelve

I stood outside the old police house in the village the following day, mentally rehearsing what to say to PC Cook, or Mr Cook as he was now. He'd retired years ago and bought the house he'd lived in as a serving officer.

If Chris had seen Katie walking towards Abbotsbury with a large rucksack, then the letter she wrote couldn't have been a fake and she must've really been running away. Which meant Tom couldn't have killed her and he was just completely muddled.

But would Mr Cook remember what was in that letter?

I knocked on his door and looked around at the immaculate front garden. There were no prizes for guessing what Mr Cook had been doing in his retirement.

He opened the door and it was as if I was transported back in time to the day he asked me if I knew where Katie was, only this time our roles were reversed. I was on his doorstep and would be asking the same questions.

'Hi.' He frowned in surprise. 'It's Olivia, isn't it?'

'Yes.' I smiled. 'Olivia Tate.'

He smiled back in recognition. 'Yes. You're a nurse at the doctor's surgery.'

'That's right. Um . . . I wanted to ask you something.'

'Something?' He tilted his head in a question.

'Something about a runaway you dealt with a long time ago.'

'You mean Katie Quinn? I remember talking to you at the time.'

'Do you?' A spark of hope ignited. 'Do you remember the goodbye letter she wrote, by any chance?'

His gaze drifted into the distance somewhere above my head, thinking. He was silent for a while before finally saying, 'Why don't you come in?'

His house was small and neat and tidy. Definitely male-oriented, with dark grey and brown and navy accent colours.

I perched on the edge of the grey velour sofa as he sank into an armchair opposite that had a nice view of a back garden equally as beautiful as the front.

Tom would love it.

But Tom was the reason I was there.

'So, you want to know about the letter Katie left?'

I nodded.

'Do you know how many people run away each year?'

'No.' I played it vague, not wanting to give away that I'd been Googling like mad.

'Hundreds of thousands. People go missing all the time. Especially youngsters.'

'Right. But you saw the letter, didn't you? And you were satisfied that Katie had written it and it wasn't a fake.'

'A fake?' He eyed me calmly.

'Yes. I mean, did you compare the handwriting with something else of hers?'

'Yes, I did. I even took it to our handwriting analysis officer, who told me it was a match.'

'Oh. Did you ever manage to find out where she'd gone when she left?'

'No, I didn't.' He hesitated for a moment, his eyes searching mine with something that looked like expectation. 'I remember you kept asking me at the time if I'd heard anything – every few months or so for a long time.'

I was suddenly an eighteen-year-old again, sitting in this very room, which was then his police office, asking if he'd had any updates about Katie's whereabouts. I'd been hoping one day to get a letter from her, telling me all about her new life, but it never came. One half of me had felt like I should try to find her, although I didn't have a clue how to go about it. If PC Cook couldn't find her, then how could I? As the time wore on, I felt angry and hurt that she'd just upped and left without even a goodbye. We had been close. Like sisters for a long time. But not as close as I'd thought. I'd felt betrayed in the end, and so I'd stopped asking him. Stopped thinking about her.

'Why are you asking now, after all this time?' His voice jerked me back to the present.

I couldn't explain the real reason – that my father-in-law had admitted to killing and burying her somewhere. Not yet. Not until I was certain she was really missing. So far it could all be some great big coincidence that I couldn't find any trace of her.

He cocked his head slightly, waiting for me to say something.

'Well, I've just been thinking about her a lot lately. Wondering why she didn't get in touch when she was settled wherever she went.' It wasn't strictly a lie. I *had* wondered a lot, especially in the beginning. 'At first I thought she'd come back. That she'd just had a row with her parents or was trying to run away from a broken heart.'

'Yes, I remember you saying that at the time.' He leaned forward, elbows on his knees.

'But don't you think it's weird she never got in touch with anyone in all this time?'

'Are you suggesting something happened to her?' He stared at me intently.

My cheeks flushed with warmth. Could he tell I was hiding something? Surely, as a policeman he was used to spotting lies. 'I don't know.'

'Well, you don't just disappear without a reason, do you? And from what I found out at the time, Katie didn't get along with her parents, and she was running away from a troubled home life and a recent traumatic break-up with your brother-in-law, so it may not be that strange that she didn't get in touch with anyone again. Although plenty of runaways do turn up later, some just don't want to be found. Katie was an adult when she left. It was her choice to leave home, and I'm certain she left of her own volition. I made enquiries with the local hospitals, just in case she'd been in an accident. I searched the house and didn't find anything that made me suspicious. I questioned Jack and Rose, and you and other people who knew her, and was satisfied there was no foul play. But I was pulled off the inquiry as soon as I established that, and there was nothing more I could do at the time.'

'Did you keep a copy of the letter she left?'

His eyebrows pinched in an intrigued frown for a moment before he stood up. 'Wait here.' He disappeared out of the room.

I glanced around while I waited. There were several trophies for lawn bowling on top of the grey slate mantelpiece, along with a photo of him in his police uniform at an award ceremony, looking much younger. On the desk in the corner of the room was a laptop with a stack of hand-written notes at the side.

When he came back he handed me a clear plastic folder with a few sheets of paper inside.

'What's this?'

'It's the notes I wrote up when Katie went missing. And a copy of her letter.' He tilted his head towards his laptop. 'I always intended to write a book when I left the force. I've got a big interest in the history of the village, and I thought it might make good reading, all the things that happened here. So I always kept personal notes on everything.'

Tears pricked at my eyes as the possibilities of what might have happened to her bombarded my thoughts. I gripped the letter and started reading.

I'm leaving this place and you can't stop me. You know what you both did. I hope you rot in hell!
Good riddance!

That was it. No *To Mum and Dad*. No *from Katie*. It was definitely her writing, though.

I paused to gather my thoughts. Her medical notes flashed into my head. 'What do you think she meant by "what you both did"?'

'I asked Rose and Jack that at the time but they said it was just referring to a row they'd had the night before she left and Katie was just being melodramatic. It wasn't an unusual occurrence for them to argue, as I remember. Rose told me the argument started because they wanted Katie out of the house now that she had a full-time job. Jack said she was lazy and they'd had enough of her attitude and it was time for her to get her own place and fend for herself.'

'They were throwing her out?' I asked. Why had I not heard that at the time? I put the letter on the arm of the sofa.

'Yes.'

'So you don't think she was referring to . . .' I trailed off, unable to ask if he thought Jack had been abusing her. Maybe because I didn't want to say it out loud. Saying the words made the possibility stronger, and if it was true, the thought of what Katie could've endured over the years went way beyond neglect.

He picked up the letter and read it again. 'Referring to what?'

'Um . . .'

'I think I know what you're asking, but I never found any signs of abuse going on – just neglect. I suspected Rose and Jack liked a drink, I suppose, but they hid it well behind closed doors. After Katie left, they didn't really bother to hide it any longer. God knows how long they'd been alcoholics. So, you see, that's what I think Katie meant in her letter. Her parents had neglected her. She didn't get on with them and they were threatening to throw her out anyway, so she left. Her running away wasn't unusual under the circumstances.'

I looked down at the carpet, feeling the weight of guilt crushing down on my shoulders again. I should've done more. Done something. I'd called myself her best friend, but I was the worst friend in the world. I'd let her down.

But you were only young, too. You can't know everything when you're that age, even if you think you do.

I shook off the inner turmoil and tuned back in to what Mr Cook was saying.

'I found myself being glad that she'd run away in the end. I'm sure she would've had a better life on her own, without her parents.'

'I hope so,' I said. Maybe Katie really had run away. Maybe she'd just disappeared like the thousands of people who are never heard from again. But an uneasy thought hovered in my head and refused to go away. Something bad had happened to my friend: I was sure of it. 'It's . . .' The room swam before my eyes and I suddenly felt stiflingly hot. I needed air. 'I have to go.' I shot up and made my way to the front door.

'If you ever find out anything . . . if you ever hear from her, will you let me know?' he asked as I turned the handle.

But I had a horrible feeling no one would ever hear from her again.

Chapter Thirteen

I had a hard time keeping everything straight in my head as I drove to Mountain View Nursing Home, hands gripping the steering wheel. I got blasted with a horn from the driver behind when I failed to notice some traffic lights had changed from red to green. Then I had to swerve to avoid a mum with a pushchair at the zebra crossing that I swear I didn't see in the middle of the road until the very last minute. What the hell was I doing? I was a liability.

I sat in the car park in my Mini, staring at Tom's window on the ground floor, chewing on my thumbnail. I didn't want to be here. I wanted to be reassuring a patient, or walking Poppy. Mucking around with Anna, having sex with my husband, or at home making dinner. OK, not making dinner, but I wanted to be doing something normal. Something a world away from asking my father-in-law exactly where he'd buried my best friend's body.

It was mad. Crazy. Insane. It couldn't be happening. It wasn't real.

And yet it was.

Kelly made conversation about something as I signed the visitors' book, but I couldn't tell you what she said. I just smiled and nodded automatically and headed down the corridor in a daze, fighting to keep the anxiety and dread inside.

I waved a hello to Mary, who was thankfully on the phone and couldn't engage me in any conversation, and I stood in Tom's doorway, staring at the sleeping, shrivelled form of a man who was possibly a murderer. A man I'd known for over twenty-five years. A man I'd looked up to and loved deeply. The father of my husband. The doting grandfather of my beautiful child. Whenever Charlotte or Anna were ill when they were little, he'd be the first one round, reading stories to them, making up all these funny accents for characters in the books. He spent hours with them, trying to keep them entertained so it took their mind off how they were feeling. When Anna had chickenpox one year, he read her stories by Roald Dahl all night, doing all these amazing voices and making her laugh. Ethan and Nadia and Chris said he'd always done the same thing for them when they were growing up. Even though he was rushed off his feet, he still always had an infinite amount of time for everyone else.

If it was true, the world as I knew it was about to slip from underneath my feet and send me crashing to the ground. And what about Ethan and Nadia and Chris? How would they feel? Charlotte and Anna and Lucas? This wasn't just about Tom; it would involve the whole family. We lived in a small village. People would gossip and stare and point fingers. How could we face Rose if we knew Tom had killed her daughter? How could we face anyone? We'd have to move. That was all there was to it. Leave the village and move to a town miles away where no one knew us. But what about Charlotte's A-levels and Anna's school? Anna loved it here. She loved her teachers and was doing really well.

I rubbed at the throbbing ache behind my temples and sat down in a chair next to his bed, suddenly feeling light-headed. I gripped the armrests, staring out of the window as the severity of the situation increased in magnitude. I worried about what would happen, desperately hoping there was still room for error and Tom was just confused about Katie.

I don't know how much time passed as the afternoon drifted by and my stomach churned. I wanted to wake him and get it over with but I was afraid to, as well. Eventually, Tom's voice made me look over sharply at him as he woke.

'Who are you?' He blinked sleepily at me.

'Olivia,' I said with none of the gentleness I usually reserved for my visits. 'How are you feeling?'

'Are you a nurse?'

'Yes, but I'm not your nurse. I'm your daughter-in-law.'

He looked sceptical. 'No, you're not. She's blonde. Who are you?'

'That's Nadia who's blonde. She's your daughter.'

'I don't have a daughter.' He sat up in bed and began fiddling with the blue waffled blanket.

'I need to ask you something, Tom.'

'I don't need to go to the toilet.'

'That's good, but I need to ask you something else.'

'It wasn't my fault. It was an accident.'

I gripped the arm of the plastic chair harder, steadying myself for what he would say. 'I'm sure it was, but I need to know exactly what happened.'

He shook his head, tears springing into his eyes. 'It wasn't my mess. I didn't do it on the floor. Someone else . . . someone came in and did it when I was asleep.'

'What?'

He pointed slowly to the bathroom with a shaky hand. 'Accident. I forgot.'

'You're talking about having a bathroom accident? You didn't get to the toilet in time, is that it?' I tried to keep my voice calm while my heart pounded so hard I could hear it in my ears.

He was getting agitated, flapping his hands in the air, his breathing coming fast, so I grabbed his hands and placed them in mine, even though I didn't want to touch him.

'It's OK, don't worry. The nurses see it happen all the time. Just breathe slowly.'

Tears dribbled down his cheeks. 'It's not me.'

'Everything's all right. No need to get upset, OK?' I grabbed a wad of tissues from a box on top of his bedside cabinet and wiped his eyes.

He stared at the blanket and wouldn't look at me. 'You're not like her, are you?'

'Who?'

'Eve. She doesn't come anymore.'

I decided against telling him again Eve was dead. I didn't think he could handle a fresh tide of grief in his fragile state. 'She's a bit busy today, but she'll come soon.' I patted his hand. 'I'm Olivia. Do you remember me?'

He looked at me then, his eyes watchful, flitting back and forth in their sockets. 'You made me a chocolate cake.'

I was hit with a memory of his seventy-first birthday, just after we'd bought Tate Barn and moved in with him. Nostalgia rose up inside. I'd wanted his first birthday with all of us living in the house to be a special occasion for him, not knowing how much time we'd have left before the Alzheimer's took its toll. I bought him one of those old newspapers you get online, dated the year he was born, which he loved. Anna made him an impression of her hands encased in pottery at school and painted it red. I don't know what happened to that. Ethan bought him some fifty-year-old single malt whisky that he shared with the guys. I can't remember what the rest of the family bought. It was a great day, though, and Tom was on top form. He had a blast. Didn't even get confused once.

My eyes stung behind my eyelids, but I blinked back the tears threatening to flood out. 'Yes, I made you a chocolate cake.' It was awful. It tasted rubbish but Tom had pretended it was the best thing he'd ever eaten, and I'd loved him for it.

His face softened, the lines smoothing out as he smiled, his eyes lighting up in recognition. 'You like pink nail varnish.'

'No, that's Nadia.'

'No, you had it on your toes when you got married. You looked beautiful. I was so proud when I gave you away.'

It was definitely Nadia but I wasn't going to argue.

'Tom, do you remember what you told me the other day about Katie? About how you buried her?' I said gently, trying to ignore the cramping in my stomach.

He stared blankly at me.

'Katie? Katie Quinn? Do you remember her? She was my friend. She left the village when she was eighteen.' At least I very much hoped she had.

'Katie,' he whispered and fiddled with the edges of the blanket again, twisting it one way and then the other.

'Yes, she was going out with Chris. She was at your house a lot that summer. Do you remember her, Tom?'

He nodded and screwed up the edge of the blanket in his fist.

'What happened to her? Did you do something to her? If you did, it's all right.' Even though it wasn't all right at all. What was I talking about? 'If you did something, we can sort it out. I just need to know what happened.'

He took a shallow breath. The tears fell down his cheeks, splashing onto the blanket, which he gripped tightly. 'I didn't mean to do it.'

'Yes, you said it was an accident, wasn't it? Just a bad accident?'

He closed his eyes for a long time and I thought he may have fallen asleep. Eventually his eyelids flew open and he said, 'I got rid of her. It's OK; no one will find her body.'

My stomach lurched. Acidic bile rose up my oesophagus into the back of my throat. 'Where, Tom? Where did you get rid of her? Where did you bury her?'

He wiped his wet cheeks with the back of his hands and looked at me, shaking his head. 'You won't tell them, will you? I was just protecting my family. I was just doing what a parent should.'

'I won't tell them, but I need to know what happened to her. Where is she? Did you really bury her?'

He muttered something so quietly that I had to lean forward, unsure I'd heard him correctly. Hoping with all my might I hadn't heard him correctly at all.

'What was that?' I asked as a wave of dizziness hit me. 'Can you tell me again?'

'My house.'

'Which house? Not Tate Barn?' I squeezed my eyelids shut tight and took a deep breath in and out, willing my stomach to stop spinning. When I opened them again he was staring at me, his bloodshot eyes etched with sadness.

'Yes.'

'Where at Tate Barn?' I managed to say, even though it felt like I had cotton wool stuffed in my mouth.

'I'm sorry, Olivia. I'm sorry.'

'I know. Where at Tate Barn? I need you to tell me. Where's her body?'

His voice, when it came, was raspy and cracked. 'Underneath the garage.'

Chapter Fourteen

I don't know how I made it home without spilling the contents of my stomach at the side of the road. Even then part of me was still trying desperately to cling on to the idea that this was all one huge innocent mistake, but I couldn't ignore the facts that were piling up.

Katie went missing and was never heard from again. She'd vanished without a trace. Tom had confessed to killing her and burying her under the garage of the barn he'd been renovating at that time. The barn that we now lived in.

Had Katie really been under our feet this whole time? For twenty-five years? Had I parked my car overtop of her body without knowing? Walked over her skeleton? Ethan had worked on his bike there. Anna had helped him, when she was going through a tomboy stage and wanted to do everything her dad did, following him around, copying his every move. Had we all been just inches away from a corpse?

I'd seen and heard some horrific things in my time as a nurse, and I wasn't squeamish, far from it, but this . . . this went above and beyond anything I could comprehend.

Terrible thoughts chased around in my head. And the real question, the one ballooning in my brain, was what to do about it. I was convinced Tom was completely lucid when he was talking about Katie. But should I tell someone or should I keep quiet?

It's going to destroy the whole family. You can't tell anyone!
You can't NOT tell. This is a murder!
You don't know that. It could've been an accident.
Why would he have tried to hide it so long if it was just an accident?
Can you really stay silent about it? This was your friend. Don't you want to know what happened to her?
You'll wreck everything. Think of Anna and Ethan, and everyone else if you're wrong!

Back and forth I went. I didn't want to go home yet. I needed to think. I drove to Chesil Beach and walked along the shore, agonising over what to do. But after three hours of soul searching, the only thing I was certain of was that I needed to talk to someone. I needed to talk to my husband.

———

When I finally drove in through my gates, I saw Ethan's Range Rover parked on the driveway, outside the garage that just maybe happened to have my friend's body buried under it.

Bile rose again and my mouth flooded with saliva. Beads of sweat broke out on my forehead.

Do not be sick.

I took a deep breath, got back in the Mini and drove it forward, parking behind Ethan. Then I closed the gates and headed for the house.

'Hey, Mum.' Anna swung the door open before I could even unlock it. 'Guess what? Dad's back early.'

I forced a smile and kissed her on the cheek before stepping inside and dropping my handbag on the quarry-tiled floor in the hallway next to the stairs. The place was now thankfully boxless, returned to our usual semi-tidy chaos of a few pairs of shoes randomly kicked off by Anna and Ethan, and Ethan's briefcase.

'Yes, I saw his car,' I said brightly. Or tried to, anyway. I think it came out sounding more wobbly and off-key. 'Where is he?'

'He's in the shower. He said he was going to take us to the pub for dinner before he goes to see Granddad.'

'Right. I think we're going to have to do that another night.' I marched into the kitchen and picked up the hands-free phone.

'But Mum, I already know what I'm going to have!'

I dialled Nadia's number and listened to the ring tone on the other end.

'Mum! Are you listening?'

'Huh?'

'I'm going to have their carbonara. It's yum.'

'Hello?' Nadia picked up, breathless, on the other end.

'Hi, it's me.'

'Can I ring you back in a minute? I'm just in the middle of working out some costings for the charity bash and—'

'No,' I butted in.

'What?' she asked incredulously

I turned to Anna. 'This is a private conversation. Can you wait in the lounge for me?'

'What's going on?' Nadia said down the phone

'Why are you acting all weird?' Anna frowned. 'I want to go out for dinner. Dad said—'

'I'm not acting weird!' I snapped again, unable to control myself any longer. I didn't do this. I wasn't a snappy person, but under these circumstances I thought it was justified, plus I think I was a little hysterical by that point. 'And we're not going for dinner! Go in the lounge and shut the door.'

A flash of hurt sparked in Anna's eyes before she turned away. 'Suit yourself.' Then she muttered something that sounded like 'weirdo'. She slammed the lounge door and turned on the TV to ear-splitting volume. Even for a good girl, she still had her moments. She wasn't an angel.

'Can Anna come over to yours tonight?'

'What's going on?'

I debated whether to tell her yet. She had a right to know, but I still wanted to cling on to that little sliver of doubt that I couldn't trust what Tom was saying. Even though he'd been pretty clear in what he'd done and where he'd put her body, I couldn't reconcile the Tom I knew with someone who would murder Katie, and I didn't want to tell anyone else until I had concrete evidence. There was no point upsetting the rest of the family until I was one hundred per cent certain.

'Just a family emergency,' I said. 'So, can she?'

'Have you had a row with Ethan?'

Not yet, but I can guarantee one will be happening in the next few minutes. 'No. But we need to sort something out in private.'

'Oh, God.' She dropped her voice. 'You don't think *he's* messing around, too, do you?'

'No! It's nothing like that. Look, can I drop Anna round or not?' I said impatiently.

'Yeah, of course.'

'She hasn't had any dinner yet, though. Can you feed her?'

'We haven't eaten yet, either. We were waiting for Lucas, who should be here any minute. I've made miles too much, as usual, anyway. Yeah, she can come over whenever.' She paused. 'Are you OK? You sound really weird.'

How did I answer that? No, I wasn't OK. I wanted to vomit and yell and cry. Probably all three at the same time.

'I'll be there in a minute.' I hung up, grabbed the car keys I'd only just put on the island and opened the door to the lounge. 'Anna, you're going to Charlotte's for a few hours,' I shouted over the noise of the TV.

'What? Why? I want to go out with you and Dad.' She pouted.

'Sorry, but we're not going out. There's been a change of plan. I need to talk to him about something important. Come on, you love going to Charlotte's.'

'But I'm hungry,' she whined.

I didn't have time for this now so I rolled my eyes and jerked my head to the door. 'Come on. Now. I'll explain later.' Which was probably the worst thing to say because Anna questioned me over and over on the short car ride there.

'If you're going to tell me later, you might as well tell me now. Come on, Mum, why can't you tell me? I wanted to go out with you and Dad. Go on, tell me. What's the big secret?'

I'd never been so glad in my life to get rid of my daughter for a few hours, but as soon as she was out of the car I felt guilty. Then I was angry at Tom for putting me in that position in the first place.

By the time I got home, hot and harassed, Ethan was on the phone in the kitchen. He put it down as I came through the hallway.

'I was just calling your mobile. Where's Anna? I thought we could all go to the pub for dinner.'

'What are you doing home?'

He raised his eyebrows and laughed in mock annoyance. 'Well, that's nice, isn't it? I've rearranged some things so I can stay for a bit and spend some time with Dad.'

I rubbed my forehead. 'I didn't mean it like that. I thought I was going to have to tell you over the phone. But . . . shit.' I dropped onto the stool at the island before my legs gave way.

'Tell me what?' The grin slid off his face. 'What's wrong? Is Anna OK? Where is she?'

'No, Anna's fine.' I ran a shaky hand through my hair.

'Oh, no. It's Dad, isn't it? They didn't ring you to say he's had another heart attack, did they?'

'No, he's . . . um . . . he's not ill.' I stared at the exterior kitchen wall that was nearest to the detached double garage, as if I could see through the layers of brick and concrete with X-ray eyes.

'Then what's up? You look a bit ill, actually. Have you been overdoing it?' He sat next to me and pushed a tendril of hair behind my ear.

Was Katie really buried under our garage? 'Bloody hell. I don't know how to say this.'

'You're scaring me now. What's wrong?' His voice turned hard and deep. He cupped my chin between his thumb and forefinger and turned my face away from the wall back to him.

'It's Tom.'

'You said he was OK.'

'No, not like that.' I stared into his worried face. 'It started with Georgia, but it wasn't really about her. He was just getting two different stories mixed up together.'

'What do you mean?'

'It wasn't Georgia he killed. I think it was Katie.'

'What?' His eyebrows shot up to his forehead.

I swallowed hard and talked slowly, telling him about how Tom had confessed to me that he'd killed Katie. That I checked her medical records to see which doctor's surgery she'd used in the years since she went missing but there was no trace of her. It was like she'd vanished. That I'd spoken to Chris, who'd reminded me he was the last one to see her, and that she was walking towards our house. And that Tom had told me exactly where he'd buried her body.

'Not this again! You've got to be joking!' He shot off the stool so quickly the movement sent it clattering to the floor. He ran a hand through his hair, his mouth gaping open.

'I wish I was.' Despite the summer warmth in the air I felt chilly and wrapped my arms around myself, rubbing up and down.

'You can't seriously think he knows what he's saying.' He paced the floor. 'He said he'd killed Georgia and that was just a waste of everyone's time. This is the same. He's just fixated on some strange, messed-up story. Katie is alive and well somewhere.'

'I don't think so. He was getting the story about Georgia mixed up with what he'd done to Katie.'

'No.' He shook his head vehemently. 'No.'

'Then where is Katie?'

'She ran away! The whole point of running away is so no one can find you!' He threw his hands in the air.

'I don't think that's what happened. If she did, why didn't anyone ever request her medical records?'

He blinked for a moment, taking that in. 'I don't know. Maybe she's never been ill.'

'What, in twenty-five years?'

'When was the last time *I* went to the doctor?'

I shrugged. 'At the very least she'd need a smear test every five years from the age of about twenty. And she was on the pill, she'd need a prescription to carry on with that, but there was nothing, Ethan. No record in all these years.'

'That doesn't prove anything.' He paced the floor.

'Tom told me! He told me she was buried under the garage. The garage we've been walking over all this time. Right next to where we've been living. Where Anna's been living!' I shouted and pointed in the direction of the garage. 'We have to find out if she's under there. I couldn't live with myself if I didn't.'

He stopped pacing, leaned against the oven, his face red with anger. 'No bloody way.'

'This is my house, too. We have to tell the police. We *have* to. How can we not?' I shrieked. 'Katie's buried under the concrete floor and Tom killed her. I know it.'

'You don't know anything. Why would he kill her? Answer me that. What reason could Dad possibly have for killing her?'

My neck shook in a nervous twitch. 'I don't know. I've been thinking that they might've been having an affair.'

'What? Are you mad? She was eighteen and he would've been . . .'

'Fifty.' I'd had time to work out the age difference. 'So what? Plenty of men have affairs with younger women.'

'Dad wouldn't have had an affair with his own son's girlfriend! He loved us. He would have never done something to hurt us.'

'But I remembered something she said to me at the time and I thought she was talking about Chris, except now I think she was actually talking about Tom.'

'What did she say?'

'She implied they'd had sex, but Chris says he never slept with her after they split up. She was talking about someone who was with us at the pub that jazz night before she left. Now I think she meant Tom.'

'That's ridiculous!'

'Is it? He could've been secretly sleeping with her. After all, he'd been involved in a relationship with Georgia before without anyone knowing.'

'Katie always was a troublemaker. I never knew why you liked her so much. She was sly and lied and she even stole stuff from Nadia's room when she was here seeing Chris. Did you know that?'

'What?'

'Look, I know she was your best friend and everything, but it's true. When Katie first started going out with Chris, Nadia didn't think anything of it. Little things would disappear from her room and she just thought she'd misplaced them, or Dad had moved them when he was tidying up. But then it was bigger things. Sometimes Dad would give her her weekly pocket money and she'd leave it on her dressing table, but then later she'd discover a couple of pounds missing. Or she'd look for some clothes that she hadn't worn for ages and they'd be gone. And jewellery, too. Then she worked it out that it always happened after Katie had been in the house visiting Chris.'

A vivid memory flashed into my head of Katie and me when we were about sixteen. My mum had given us a lift into Dorchester to spend my Christmas money and we were in a new trendy shop that had just opened, trying on piles of outfits in the changing rooms. It was a Saturday and madly busy. The staff were harassed at the tills with a long queue and hadn't had time to take out the discarded clothes left in the changing rooms by shoppers who didn't want their selected items. Katie went into her cubicle with a couple of dresses and a pair of jeans while I took the one next to her with a few skirts and a new bra in hand. We took our time, slipping in and out of the cubicles as we got changed into our new items and parading them up and down the centre of the room for each other in front of the mirrors, doing a bizarre walk that was supposed to make us look like a couple of catwalk models but really made us look like we both had one leg shorter than the other.

My stuff looked awful on me but the two dresses looked great on Katie. I asked if she was going to get them but she said she couldn't afford to. I even offered to buy her one. I was sick of seeing her in the same old clothes all the time. Probably not as sick as she was, though, thinking about it now. She waved me off and said she didn't like them that much, anyway, so it was no biggie. It wasn't until we were on the bus on the way home that she opened her big handbag and showed me the dresses folded up into tiny bundles inside.

I was shocked, of course, but I just thought it was daring and brave of her. It was my rebellious streak coming out again. Yes, Katie could be a troublemaker and a live wire, but she was fun and wild and reckless and exciting, too. No one would stop her doing what she wanted. And anyway, didn't most youngsters dabble in a bit of shoplifting? She justified it by saying that if the staff weren't interested enough to try and stop people stealing, then why should she feel bad?

I shook the memory away and tried to question what Ethan had said, but I knew deep down it was the truth. 'Was Nadia sure it was Katie? She never stole anything from me.'

'She said she was positive.' He shook his head at me. 'You always see the good in people instead of the bad.'

'Maybe.' I shrugged. 'Did Nadia confront her about it?'

'Yeah, but Katie denied it. Then Chris finished with her a few days later, which I was glad about.'

'Well, people change, don't they? We all do things when we're younger that we regret. Are you saying you were the model child?' I snorted.

'No, of course not, but she was a thief and a liar and a troublemaker.'

'Well, whether she was a thief or liar is not the point.'

'What is the point, then? That you'd rather believe Dad is a murderer than that Katie didn't just run away? She could've changed her name.' He gave me a knowing smirk. 'That's why there are no medical records. Did you think about that?'

I hadn't thought of that. It was possible, I supposed, but in my heart I knew that wasn't right.

'Or she could've moved abroad.'

'No, I remember asking Mr Cook that almost a year after she'd gone and he said she'd never applied for a passport. And anyway, why would Tom tell me he'd buried her under the garage?'

'He told you he'd killed Georgia, for God's sake, and she's perfectly fine!'

'Like I said, he's mixing up the stories. I could understand him getting confused about Georgia, but Katie's different. She really did go missing and hasn't been heard from again.'

'We are not digging up the garage because Dad's mixing up *stories*.' He opened the fridge door, pulled out a beer without offering me one and unscrewed the cap. He took a big swig, his eyes angry narrow slits.

'Look, I know how this sounds, but—'

'I don't think you do. Are you actually listening to what you're saying?'

I stood up, poured a glass of chilled white wine from the fridge and slumped back down on the stool. Sod the headache. I needed to feel the warmth of alcohol as it broke through the cold, hard horror and softened everything around the edges, making it all fuzzy and less real, less horrific.

'We're not going to the police. If we do, we'll have forensics and officers swarming around. We live in a village! Everyone will find out about this. Imagine how they'll react! This is going to affect all the family, and the ones who will suffer the most of all will be Anna and Charlotte, so you need to think very carefully before you carry on with your crusade.'

'I've thought about that. Of course I have. I've been plagued with thoughts about what this could mean for all of us. The damage it will do to the whole family. But how can we ignore it? Just because he's got Alzheimer's doesn't mean he's not telling the truth. We have to tell the police! How can we suspect she's under there and not do anything?'

'*We* don't suspect anything. You do.'

'So, you're perfectly happy with walking over a skeleton, if she's down there, are you?' I challenged him with a tilt of my head. 'You're perfectly happy with Anna and us living in this house with the possibility there's a *fucking body out there?*' I knocked back a third of my wine.

He blew out an angry sigh, hand on hip.

'You should've heard him. He was scared and upset and he kept saying it was an accident.'

Ethan clamped his jaw shut tight, the muscles working under the skin.

'I think that she was seeing him secretly. I think she wanted him to get her away from Jack and Rose because—'

'Why would she want that? It's insane!'

'Because Tom had money. She'd set her sights on Chris – don't you remember? How she kept pressuring him to get a place together and settle down?'

'Exactly. So she wouldn't get involved with Dad, would she?'

'But when Chris finished with her I think she got more desperate. She couldn't afford to get her own place with the wages she earned in the shop so she was probably trying it on with Tom because he would be able to support her. Give her the family security she must've longed for. She just wanted to get away from Rose and Jack but couldn't afford to do it on her own. And when it looked like she couldn't get Chris to help her, maybe she turned to Tom. And maybe she was threatening to expose their affair and Tom got angry with her.'

'Oh, God.' The colour suddenly drained from his face.

'What?'

He scrubbed a hand over his smooth cheeks. 'She tried it on with me once.'

'What? When? Why didn't you say anything?' My eyes widened.

'Because I wasn't interested and it didn't seem important at the time. Chris had finished with her but he was obviously still in love with her, and I wasn't about to upset him or you over it by mentioning what had happened. It was best left untold. Like I said, she was a troublemaker. She probably did it to try and split us up because she was jealous.'

'My best friend trying it on with my boyfriend's not important? Of course it is.' I slammed my glass down on the island. 'What happened?'

'It was nothing. I was at the Kings' Arms one night with Lucas and Chris. We were having a game of darts or snooker, or something. An old school mate came in just before last orders. Do you remember Colin Montgomery?'

I thought back. Colin always used to smell of lemons for some reason.

I nodded.

'Anyway, I got chatting to him, and Lucas and Chris left before me. At chucking out time, I said goodbye to Colin, who was heading in the other direction, and walked home. As I was going past the bus stop, I saw Katie there, sitting down. The last thing I wanted was to get into a conversation with her, but I knew the last bus had already gone at that time, and I didn't want to see her waiting there on her own. Didn't even really understand why she was waiting there, anyway. I mean, where was she going at just after 11 p.m.?

'Anyway, I stopped and we had a bit of small talk, then before I knew it she stood up and made a play for me.'

I tilted my head. 'What do you mean, "a play"?'

'She actually walked up to me and put her arms round my neck and tried to kiss me. I took a step back and unwound them, holding her at arm's length. I just laughed and made a joke of it at first. She stunk of alcohol, too. But she tried again. Tried to pull me towards her, and she said something about us going in the woods for a fuck, and that you'd never find out.'

A stabbing pain squeezed at my throat like something sharp stuck inside. 'Go on.'

'Well.' He shrugged casually. 'I just laughed. I told her she was pissed and she should go home. Then she got angry, called me fucking queer or something, and I just walked off and left her there.' He drained the dregs of beer. 'And that was that. I turned her down and forgot about it.' He threw his bottle in the bin underneath the sink with a loud crash and opened another. 'Do you want a top-up?' He glanced at my now-empty glass.

'Yes. I think I need it.' I forced the igniting anger back down.

He sloshed more pale golden liquid into my glass and put the bottle back in the fridge before sitting down next to me.

'When was that?'

He shrugged. 'I can't remember exactly. I don't know how long it was after Chris had dumped her.' Before I could think any more about what a betrayal Katie's actions were, he said, 'Do you seriously think she then tried it on with Dad and they had an affair?'

'It seems the most likely thing.'

'That bitch.'

'She wasn't a bitch,' I said automatically, used to defending her like I always had. But now I didn't know what she was. In return for my loyalty and friendship she'd tried to sleep with my boyfriend. A boyfriend she knew I was in love with. Still, it was years ago. Too late to worry about it now. We had more important things to worry about. 'She was . . . she was living a shitty life with no one to love her. That's what she was after. All the sleeping around was about searching for someone to love and take care of her. I just didn't get it at the time. She kept everything locked deep inside. I never saw her cry, you know. Never once in all the years I'd known her. And now I think about what it must've been like in that house with Rose and Jack pissed out of their heads, having to look after herself and grow up before her time.'

The words in her letter swam into my head again.

I'm leaving this place and you can't stop me. You know what you both did. I hope you rot in hell!

Good riddance!

'And if Jack abused her, then . . .' I trailed off. 'Well, wouldn't you want to get away?'

'Abused her?'

I told him about my suspicions.

He slumped further down on the stool. 'I can't bloody take this in. Wouldn't she have said something if Jack had been . . . well, I can't even say it. I mean, Katie wasn't some quiet wallflower. She had a mouth on her. Why wouldn't she tell anyone?'

'A lot of child abuse victims blame themselves. Maybe she was scared to tell the truth in case no one believed her. Maybe Katie did tell Rose but Rose ignored it and let it carry on. Maybe Katie didn't want to admit it was even going on.'

'Then isn't it more likely that if something happened to her, it was Jack?'

I shook my head. 'I don't know. If Jack was involved in her disappearance, why did Tom say he'd buried her?'

'It doesn't make sense. None of this does. He's just confused.' But his voice sounded doubtful now.

'I don't want to believe it, either, but too many things aren't adding up.' I reached out and threaded my fingers through his. 'But we have to see if she's under there, Ethan. You know that, don't you?'

Chapter Fifteen

They came with their vehicles and white suits and equipment. From the kitchen window I could see the double garage at a diagonal angle. The wooden doors were open, but I couldn't see what they were doing inside. Didn't want to see that.

I stood, cradling a cup of cold coffee, wondering if I should go out there and offer them all one. What was the proper hospitality etiquette when police were looking for a dead body on your property?

There was only room for one van on the drive with both Ethan's and my car already there, and it belonged to the scene of crime officers. The plainclothes police officers who'd introduced themselves as Detective Inspector Spencer and Detective Sergeant Khan parked their black Ford Mondeo on the road outside, along with another woman's BMW. The gates to the drive were open and anyone walking past could see the van emblazoned with 'Crime Scene Investigation Unit' in plain view. That would get the gossip-mongers' tongues firing on all cylinders.

'What are we going to say when people notice that van on the drive?' Ethan sat at the island, laptop open in front of him on the counter, eyes bloodshot and hair spiked up where he'd been running his hands through it. He was supposed to be sending some work emails that couldn't wait, but really he'd been staring out of the window since they arrived with some kind of imaging equipment, like I had. 'Maybe we should just say the garage was broken into.'

I glanced at him with exasperation. 'And say what, that someone broke into the garage and deposited a body under the concrete floor, then left? Oh, wow, how did that happen?'

'Well, they're not going to find anything. This is all a ridiculous waste of everyone's time. Just like it was with Georgia. Not to mention the expense of digging up the bloody floor and relaying it. And, more importantly, what are we going to tell Anna when she sees a hole in the floor?' He shot me a filthy look.

I chewed on my lip. I'd dropped off her school uniform over to Nadia's late last night and asked if she could stay there. Anna was pretty chuffed about it in the end since she got to spend a school night having a sleepover with her cousin. We hadn't told Nadia what it was all about yet. Ethan insisted there was no point. He thought the police would discover that Katie really wasn't down there and we could all forget about it. No point upsetting everyone for absolutely no reason, he'd said. He thought it was all some kind of macabre mistake. I thought he was in denial.

A loud noise from what sounded like a hammer drill reverberated through the windows.

Poppy shot out of the kitchen and ran up the stairs to get away from it. She probably thought it was thunder, which she hated. I could picture her now, cowering in the shower cubicle, shaking. Usually, I'd sit with her, stroking and reassuring her, but I couldn't then. I had to see what was going on. Like a rubbernecker at an accident scene, I was glued in place by an invisible tape.

My stomach cramped and the orange juice I'd drunk for breakfast burned inside. I hadn't been able to eat any real food for fear of bringing it back up again.

'Oh, my God.' I dropped my head into my hand, tugging at my roots. 'If they're digging, they must've found something with that imaging stuff.'

'I can't concentrate with all that racket going on. I'm going to take the dog out. I need some air.' Ethan slammed the laptop shut so hard I'm surprised he didn't crack it. He managed to coax a shaking Poppy out the door and when he left, I suddenly felt calmer, as if his anger had been permeating into me by osmosis. He was like that, you see. If things went wrong and he felt powerless or unable to protect his family in some way, he let it out by shouting or being defensive. Maybe he felt like I was criticising him, or that I thought he was a failure or something. I don't know. Men really are from Mars sometimes.

I'm not sure how long I stood in that position while the drilling pounded inside my head and out. When it stopped some time later, my ears were hypersensitive and I could still hear ringing, like a bad case of tinnitus you get after going to a nightclub. I took the ironing board out of the utility room, plugged in the iron and got to work tackling a big pile of clothes I'd been putting off, hoping the mundane task would take my mind off things.

It didn't. Every few moments my gaze strayed back to the garage again.

DS Khan emerged in her all-in-one white jumpsuit and stood outside the garage doors, talking on her mobile phone. She was Indian with smooth dark skin and almond-shaped eyes. Tall, slim and, before she'd donned the suit, immaculately turned out in black skinny trousers tucked into calf-high leather boots and a navy blue silk mac. She could easily have been a model. I wished the window was open so I could hear her, but I'd shut it to drown out the noise. I watched her, craning my neck, straining to hear, but the double glazing Tom had put in all those years ago was so efficient I couldn't make out anything. She nodded a few times, frowning deeply. I wanted to tell her not to do that too often or she'd end up with a wrinkled forehead later in life. Nadia always frowned from between her eyebrows, so she had two tiny vertical lines above the bridge of her nose that were barely noticeable. I, on the other hand, had a more expressive face. My forehead was always creasing up in surprise, or with a question, or when I made a humorous remark, and the result was a very lined forehead.

I heard a sizzling sound and glanced down, noticing I'd burned a brownish stain onto one of Ethan's favourite salmon-pink work shirts.

'Shit!' I yelled, as a raging anger exploded to the surface, which wasn't like me. I was usually pretty calm in a crisis, but I was angry with Tom for putting us in this position. Angry with Ethan for walking out and leaving me to deal with it when it was his own dad who was involved in all this. Angry with myself for not doing more to help Katie when I had the chance. And angry just because I could be.

I practically threw the iron back in its holder on the ironing board as tears sprang into my eyes.

When I glanced up DS Khan was off the phone and watching me through the window. I gave her a half smile but it twitched on my face and probably made me look as if I was having a stroke. She didn't smile back. Not a good sign. Instead, she disappeared back inside the garage.

I switched the iron off, unable to concentrate on even that, and left it sitting in the ironing board to cool, scowling at it. My stomach gurgled with a mixture of hunger and acidic reflux.

The phone rang, then, making me jump.

'What's going on?' Nadia said when I picked it up. 'I just drove past your house and there's some crime scene van there. Don't tell me you've been burgled.' She carried on before I could say anything. 'Is that why you wanted Anna to stay? You should've just said!'

I stared at the garage again. 'Not quite.' Although I did feel the same as if we'd been burgled – violated, angry, stressed, upset, vulnerable.

'What's going on? You sound weird.' Her voice became suspicious. 'I'm coming round when I've dropped off some paperwork to the office, OK?'

Before I could protest, she'd hung up.

Great. Now Ethan would blame me for shooting my mouth off to Nadia, too. I worked my neck from side to side, trying to get rid of the painful knots of tension forming, gaze firmly back on the garage.

DI Spencer emerged first, followed by DS Khan. Spencer was older than Khan, who appeared to be in her mid-thirties. If I had to hazard a guess, based on the grey at the temples of his fair hair, the paunch around his stomach and the bags underneath his eyes, I'd say he was in his early fifties. I watched them strip off their white suits, walk up the part of the driveway I could still see at this angle and then disappear. A few seconds later there was a knock at the front door. I'd been expecting it, but it still made my stomach jump into my throat and my heart beat in an irregular pattern for a fraction of a second before settling back into rhythm again.

I wiped my clammy palms on my denim cut-off shorts and walked towards the door.

'Can we come in?' DI Spencer said with an expressionless face. Close up, the bags were more pronounced and his eyes were red. I wondered briefly if he suffered from hay fever. The rape seed had been terrible this year.

It sounded like a question but it really wasn't. I didn't have a choice in the matter, so I held the door open and waved them through into the hallway, and they followed me into the kitchen.

'Um . . . do you want a coffee or . . . something?' I leaned my hip on the island to keep me upright.

'No, thanks.' DS Khan smiled but it was practised and sympathetic. A smile I often used at work when I had to give a patient some bad news.

There was banging at the front door then.

'Sorry, hang on.' I walked down the corridor and felt them watching my back, their eyes assessing me.

As soon as I saw Nadia there I burst into tears. I couldn't contain it any longer. I knew from their sombre expressions and their air of quiet seriousness exactly what they were going to tell me.

Katie Quinn really was buried under my garage.

Nadia took one look at my face and, without saying anything, she enveloped me in her arms, my head resting on her shoulder.

'What's going on? Did they take much? Did they do a lot of damage?' She asked.

'It wasn't a burglary.' I took a big sniff and wiped my eyes with the heel of my hands. 'Come into the kitchen.' I gripped her hand and pulled her behind me, introducing the new addition to the dig-up-my-best-friend party. 'This is my sister-in-law, Nadia, Tom's daughter. This is DI Spencer and DS Khan.'

Nadia looked at me, eyes wide with worry. 'Has something happened to Ethan? Or Dad?'

'Maybe you'd both like to sit down?' DI Spencer indicated the oak dining room table in front of the French doors that led to the courtyard garden.

Nadia sat. I stood.

'You found something, didn't you?' I asked.

DI Spencer and DS Khan exchanged a stern look.

'Found what?' Nadia frowned – just from between the eyebrows, mind you. 'I don't understand.'

'It's OK,' I said. 'Whatever you're going to tell me you can say in front of Nadia.'

'I'm afraid we discovered bones consistent with a young woman buried underneath the concrete floor of your garage, Mrs Tate, just like you suspected,' DI Spencer said, and the room swam in front of my eyes.

Chapter Sixteen

I put my hands over my face, as if to shield myself from the reality of it. The floor seemed to wobble underneath my feet.

'What?' Nadia shrieked. 'What do you mean?'

I dropped my hands limply to my sides. 'It's Katie,' I told her. 'Katie Quinn.'

'Katie?' She looked between Spencer, Khan and I, head going back and forth. 'What the . . . How can she be under there? She ran away.'

'We can't say who the remains belong to at this stage,' DS Khan said. 'Although, given Mr Tate's confession to you, it seems most likely.'

'Confession?' Nadia said.

'Who else could it be?' I kept my eyes on DS Khan as I sat down before my legs gave out completely. Tears burned in my eyes.

'The scene of crime officers and a forensic anthropologist are recovering the remains at the moment, along with any evidence they find,' DI Spencer said.

The front door opened and Poppy bounded down the hallway, first coming up to me and wiggling with excitement, then turning her attention to Nadia and finally DI Spencer and DS Khan, who gave a tight smile but ignored her. I called her to me absentmind-edly and stroked her head as she lay on the floor, panting.

My gaze met Ethan's as he stood in the kitchen doorway. He could tell from my expression what was going on.

He uttered one single word loudly. 'No!'

I nodded, allowing the tears to fall now, not caring. 'Yes. She's really there.'

'How did you know?' Nadia's jaw dropped open.

'Tom told me.' I squeezed her hand as Ethan shook his head, his features dissolving into blankness.

'He told you?' Nadia asked again, her own eyes welling up. 'Are you saying . . . that stuff with Georgia was just where he was getting mixed up?'

'Georgia? Who's Georgia?' DI Spencer asked.

DS Khan retrieved a notebook and pen from the pocket of her mac and started taking notes. Why did she even have a mac on when it was about twenty-six degrees? Surely that alone would make her unable to judge things properly. How could she be a proper policewoman if she couldn't even dress herself according to the weather?

'Do you want to sit down?' I said to Ethan, who glared at me in response.

'So, who's Georgia?' DS Khan repeated.

Through the sniffs and tears, I started at the beginning, telling them how Tom had become agitated lately, having bad dreams, fix-ating on someone called Georgia Walker who he said was missing and that he'd killed. I said how Sergeant Downing had actually traced her to the next village of Abbotsbury and she was very much alive and well, and how we'd thought that was the end of it.

'But then I went to see Tom again and he told me he wasn't talking about killing Georgia: he was talking about Katie.'

'And he actually mentioned Katie Quinn?' DS Khan asked. 'The young woman who apparently ran away from home twenty-five years ago?'

I nodded.

Ethan ran his hands through his hair again. It would all fall out at this rate.

Nadia wiped her eyes with a tissue from her pocket; her cheeks were devoid of their usual rosiness.

'Shouldn't we get Chris here?' I said. 'This is going to involve him, too.'

'Who's Chris?' DI Spencer asked.

'Our brother,' Ethan spoke his first words since his 'No!' outburst and sat down, too. 'He's at a building site in Weymouth.'

'We can speak to him later,' DS Khan said. 'For now, we need to get some more background information from all of you since you're here.' She locked her gaze on me. 'Go on, please. What exactly did Mr Tate tell you?'

'That he wasn't talking about Georgia. And that he'd killed Katie. Um . . . he was rambling a lot, like he does these days, but he said it was an accident, that she wasn't supposed to be there. And then he said something about how he had to do it. I tried to get more out of him but he became very distressed and suffered a minor heart attack.'

'You mentioned on the phone when you reported this that he was alive but very frail.'

'Yes, the Alzheimer's is taking its toll on his heart and lungs,' I said. 'He signed a DNR order when he was diagnosed and still in control of his mind, so they just gave him medication and made him comfortable after the heart attack.'

'He's not up to being questioned by you lot,' Ethan said brusquely.

DI Spencer studied him for a moment. 'I know this is very difficult and upsetting for you all.'

Ethan snorted. 'That's an understatement.'

I reached out and squeezed his hand but he snatched it away.

'And then what happened after the heart attack?' DI Spencer asked.

'I went to see him a few days later and that's when he told me that he'd . . . Oh, God!' I shook my head. 'That he'd . . . that he'd buried her under the floor in the garage.'

'It's been two days since then. Why didn't you call us immediately?' DS Khan asked.

I glanced at Ethan. The agitation, disbelief and stress coming off him were almost tangible.

'Don't look at me. I didn't even know until last night,' he said.

'I didn't know until just now,' Nadia said, gulping back a sob. 'It's . . . I just can't . . .' She replaced the balled-up, soggy tissue with a fresh one from a pocket-sized packet in her bag.

'I didn't want to believe it,' I said. 'And after the last time, when we'd just wasted everyone's time with the Georgia business, I wanted to make sure.'

'And what made you suddenly sure?' DI Spencer asked.

'Well, it was the medical records that made me suspect it was really true.'

'Medical records?' DI Spencer frowned.

'I'd thought about her over the years, and always wondered what happened to her. You know, I thought it was weird when she didn't get in touch again. But plenty of people run away and never contact the people they know, plus she'd left that letter to Rose and Jack, so I never thought to look at her medical records before. Not until Tom said what he did. And, it wasn't strictly ethical for me to check them. Data protection and all that.'

'Right. But you checked after Tom told you this, and what did you find?' DS Khan wrote something down.

'That no one had ever requested a copy of her medical records in the last twenty-five years since she'd disappeared. She would've had to have regular smear tests, plus she was on the pill, so some doctor's surgery or clinic would've got in touch with the surgery.'

DS Khan exchanged another look with DI Spencer.

'She could've changed her name,' Ethan said weakly.

'Of course she didn't change her name!' It was my turn to snap as I pointed towards the garage. 'She didn't change her name because she was buried under the garage!'

'We don't know it's her!' He gave me a brittle stare.

'OK, OK, let's all try to calm down.' DI Spencer waved his hands in what he thought was a calming gesture but only seemed to inflame Ethan even more.

'Calm down?' Ethan said. '*Calm down?* You're accusing my dad of murdering someone and you want me to be calm?'

'Ethan! They're just doing their job.' Nadia laid a hand on his arm.

His shoulders heaved up and down as he breathed hard.

'We're just trying to establish the facts, Mr Tate,' DS Khan said gently.

'How do we know the facts? Who's going to remember anything after twenty-five years?' Ethan shook his head but at least he sat back down.

For some reason, I wanted to slap him. Pretending it wasn't happening wasn't going to solve anything. Yes, he was upset by this, but we all were. We had to deal with it whether we liked it or not. It wasn't like we could brush it under the carpet – or concrete – and forget all about it. Not now.

'It's true that most people won't remember what they were doing twenty-five years ago, but we still have to ask,' DI Spencer said. 'This is a murder enquiry now, and if you remember anything, no matter how small, it could help us piece together what happened.' He turned to me. 'What did you do after you checked her medical records?'

'I went to see Chris next, because I remembered we'd talked a lot about Katie running away when it happened. I thought maybe he might remember something I'd forgotten.'

'Chris, your brother-in-law?'

'Yes.'

'Can we have his contact details?' DS Khan asked.

I gave them his full name, address, landline and mobile phone number.

'And did he remember anything?' DI Spencer asked.

'Well, mostly. He was going out with Katie for about nine months, you see, and he'd broken things off with her about seven months before she . . . um . . . went.'

'Why did they break up?' DS Khan again.

'Well, he was still in love with her, but she was pressuring him to settle down and move in together and get married and he wasn't ready for it.' I glanced down the table, trying to recall what he'd said the other night. 'Apparently, he was the last person to see her. He said he was waiting at the bus stop just up the road here and she walked past. He said hi to her but she didn't say anything back, and then he watched her walking towards our house. We thought at the time she was going to Abbotsbury. That was the last time he saw her.'

DI Spencer leaned an elbow on the table and rested his chin in his hand with a pensive look. 'Did Chris say anything else?'

I shrugged. 'Not much. I also went to see Mr Cook. He was the village policeman at the time Katie went missing and he made a few enquiries after Rose and Jack found the letter Katie had left. Um . . .' I paused.

Everyone waited, watching me.

'Well, it's about her dad, Jack. I always thought he was . . . I don't know. Odd,' I said.

'He gave all the girls the creeps.' Nadia grimaced.

'Odd, how? You thought something inappropriate was going on between Katie and Jack?' DS Khan narrowed her eyes slightly.

'Not at the time, I didn't, but looking back on things, I think it would explain a lot. Her behaviour, for one,' I said.

'What do you mean?'

'She was the village slag is what my wife means,' Ethan said. 'From the age of about fourteen she'd sleep with anyone.'

'She was looking for attention and love,' I insisted, still defending her even though the discovery of her propositioning Ethan was still raw in my mind. 'Also, I found something else in her medical notes that could raise a red flag for possible sexual abuse.' I told them what I'd discovered about the vaginal infections.

Nadia let out a horrified gasp.

'Anyway, then I went to see Mr Cook, to see if he remembered what her goodbye letter said, to make sure she really wrote it. Katie put in the letter that she was leaving the village and they couldn't stop her. She said, "You know what you both did".'

DS Khan wrote that down. 'Did the letter say anything else?'

'Just that she hoped they rotted in hell.'

DS Khan wrote frantically in her notepad. 'Did she ever mention her father was abusing her?'

'No. Never. And, of course, there could be reasonable explanations for her symptoms.'

DI Spencer stared over my shoulder, looking deep in thought. 'What was her relationship like with her parents?'

'Not good. She hated them and they argued a lot.'

'She was a thief, too,' Ethan butted in. 'When she was seeing Chris, she was here at the house all the time and things kept going missing. She stole stuff from Nadia.'

'Is that right?' DS Khan asked Nadia.

'Yes, I'm afraid. She took things from my room. I confronted her and she denied it but it must've been her.'

'I was glad when Chris finished with her,' Ethan said. 'She was a troublemaker. She would've messed his head up if he'd married her.'

'Rose and Jack were alcoholics, although I don't think anyone realised how bad they were until after Katie left,' I added, still feeling as if I had to stick up for Katie. 'Looking back, they must've neglected her from an early age. I think she had to fend for herself most of the time, although she never admitted that to me. As she got older, she didn't spend much time at home if she could help it.'

'Did Katie drink, too? Or was she into drugs?' DS Khan asked.

'She liked to drink, I suppose. We both looked older than our age so we used to sneak into pubs when we were seventeen,' I said. 'But it was just usual teenage experimenting. She wasn't like Jack and Rose or anything. And she never did drugs that I knew of.'

DI Spencer looked pensive. 'Did she ever steal anything from Tom?'

Nadia and Ethan looked at each other and shrugged.

'Not that I know of,' Nadia said.

'He never said anything if she did,' Ethan said. 'But it wouldn't surprise me.'

A memory flashed into my head then. The last time I'd seen her. Something else she'd said to me that had seemed insignificant at the time but now it put a new slant on things. 'Um . . . I think she might have taken something.'

'What do you mean?' Nadia turned her hands palms up in a question. 'What did she take?'

'I don't know. But I just remembered something weird that she said to me the day before she supposedly ran away. We were all going to the Kings' Arms on the Saturday night to see a band. There was Nadia, Lucas, Ethan, Tom, Chris and I going. I'd been spending a lot of time with Ethan then, and Katie hadn't wanted to go out much because she was still upset about breaking up with Chris. I went to the shop where she worked and asked if she wanted to come with us all.' A picture of Katie in the shop swam clearly into my head, then. How she'd looked frumpy and dowdy and plain, but how her head was cocked as she spoke, her hand on her hip, her defiant body language in complete contrast to her new meek look. 'First of all she said, "If he thinks I'm going to fuck him again, he can fuck off." Which I thought meant at the time she was talking about Chris. And then she said, "I've got something he wants and I'm going to make him pay".'

'You just happened to remember that, word for word, all this time later?' DS Khan looked up from her note-taking and raised her eyebrows.

'Well, I thought about it a lot at the time because I felt so guilty afterwards that I wasn't there for her more. I think it was etched into my brain and must've just needed a nudge to resurface again.'

'So, it's possible she meant she'd stolen something from Tom?' DI Spencer tapped the table lightly.

'Yes, I suppose.'

'Who's Lucas?' DS Khan asked, pen poised.

'My husband.

'So if Katie was here at the house a lot when she was going out with Chris, did Tom have much to do with her?' DI Spencer looked round the table.

'Well, we weren't living here when Katie . . . um . . . left,' Nadia said. 'We lived in another house on the other side of the village. This barn came up for sale and Dad was renovating it around that time.'

'So the garage was built at the same time he was renovating the barn?' DS Khan asked.

'Yes,' Ethan said.

'Who would have had access to the garage when it was being built?'

Ethan shrugged. 'Dad and Chris. Other builders and contractors working for Tate Construction. But the site wasn't secured while they were working on it. At the weekends or evenings when no one was around, anyone could've just walked in.'

'But in order to hide a body under the floor of the garage, it would have to have been someone who was involved in the renovation?' DI Spencer asked, although it was more of a statement than a question.

Ethan stared at a spot above DI Spencer's head. 'I suppose so, yes. I'm the company architect, but I wasn't working there then. I was at university, getting my architecture degree.'

'So you don't remember which employees would've been here?'

'No.'

'I was working for Tate Construction at that time, in their offices,' Nadia said. 'But I just dealt with the accounts then. I didn't have anything to do with which employee was working on which site.'

DI Spencer crossed one leg over the other and sat back. 'Did Katie and Tom get on with each other?'

Nadia shook her head. 'I never noticed anything strange between them, although I don't think he approved of her. He thought Chris could do better, but he never said anything bad about her to me.'

'Dad didn't like her,' Ethan muttered quietly.

DI Spencer tilted his head. 'Pardon?'

'Dad didn't like Katie,' he repeated. 'He thought she was trashy. He was glad when Chris saw sense and dumped her.'

'He said that?'

'No. Not in so many words. But I thought it was obvious.'

'Did Tom and Jack have much to do with each other?' DS Khan asked.

'What? No way.' Ethan frowned. 'He thought Jack and Rose were even trashier.'

'How was Katie's state of mind before she disappeared?' DI Spencer asked me. 'Was she angry, happy, depressed?'

'I'm not sure.'

'You were her best friend, weren't you?'

I thought about how she'd changed her appearance following her break-up with Chris. How she'd avoided me and confined herself to her house. A house she usually hated with vehemence. Analysing it now, it was entirely possible she was suffering from depression. 'Yes, but I hadn't really seen her much for the six months before she left so I don't know for certain. But now I think maybe she was depressed. The only thing I really know for certain is that she hated her parents and they didn't get on, and apparently they wanted her to leave home, anyway.'

DS Khan made more notes.

'When was the last time you saw her?' DI Spencer asked Nadia.

'I don't know. I wasn't friends with her. Probably when Chris was still going out with her.'

'How about you?' he asked Ethan.

He shrugged. 'I haven't got a clue.'

'Has Tom Tate ever made any other confessions to you about crimes in the past?' DI Spencer asked.

'No, of course not!' Ethan said.

'Are you sure you don't want something to drink?' I asked them.

'No, thanks.' DI Spencer stood. 'I think we've got enough for now.'

DS Khan clicked the top of her pen closed and followed suit.

'The scene of crime team will be here for a while longer, but we really need to go and speak to Mr Tate.'

'I don't think that's a good idea,' Ethan said. 'He gets agitated and confused easily. I don't want him getting upset and having another heart attack.'

'Well, I was going to suggest that one of you accompany us to try and keep things as calm and familiar for him as possible,' DI Spencer said.

'I agree.' Nadia nodded. 'I'll come with you.'

'You're not questioning him without me.' Ethan stood, towering over DI Spencer.

DI Spencer looked at me, silently asking my opinion.

'I'd like to go, too,' I said.

'Right. Well, shall we all jump in our car together?' DS Khan asked.

'I'll take my car,' Nadia said. 'I have to stop at the supermarket on the way home.'

I wondered how she could even think about eating at a time like this but stress and anxiety affected people in different ways. Who was I to judge? Nadia's drug of choice was comfort food. I'd be numbing the anxiety later with wine.

'I'll drive, too.' Ethan grabbed his car keys from the island and clenched them in his fist before anyone could challenge him.

As we drove in convoy to the nursing home, I had the feeling that my normal life would never be normal again.

Chapter Seventeen

Tom's room was crowded with all of us in there. I stood in front of the window while DI Spencer and DS Khan stood at the end of Tom's bed. Nadia sat on the edge of the bed next to her father, stroking his hand. Ethan stood protectively on the other side, fists clenching and unclenching, looking as if he was about to explode, or hit someone or . . . do something volatile. My heart squeezed in sympathy for him. He still wanted to believe the impossible, to hang onto the insane idea that Tom hadn't committed this terrible crime. That there was some other explanation. I got it, of course. I understood why no one would want to believe their parent could be capable of something like his. I didn't want to believe it, either. Not of Tom. His words from a few days ago floated in my head. *I was just protecting my family. I was just doing what a parent should.* It was exactly what Ethan was doing then, trying to protect his father. I was torn between wanting to protect Tom and wanting him to rot in hell, just like Katie had told Jack to. Even if she'd stolen something or blackmailed Tom, or slept around and lied, or dared to dream of a better, more secure life, or tried to have sex with Ethan, she didn't deserve to be murdered and buried under a pile of earth and concrete like a piece of rubbish.

'I don't want an enema.' Tom looked at DI Spencer and DS Khan.

Nadia squeezed his hand. 'They're not doctors, Dad.'

'Why are they in my room, then?' Tom turned his head to her for guidance.

'They want to ask you some questions.' Ethan's voice was laced with contempt for the officers that he didn't bother to hide.

'I'm tired.' Tom rested his head back on the pillow and closed his eyes. 'I'm going on holiday later and I want a nap. I'm going to Spain. It's nice there – have you been?'

I pictured us all about five years ago, before the Alzheimer's was really rearing its ugly head, when we had all taken a family holiday out to stay with my parents at their converted *finca* in Andalucía. I didn't get to see them that much after they moved abroad so it was a great time, with both the Tates and Maxwells spending lazy days around the pool, reading books or playing water volleyball or bat and ball. We'd taken Charlotte with us, too, and both girls were hardly out of the pool for two whole weeks. On days out we soaked up the history of the area, then went for early evening walks to the local restaurants and ordered tapas that, surprisingly, Anna loved. Even the squid! Who'd have thought things would end up here?

'We won't take long, Tom,' DI Spencer softened his voice slightly, making it sound soothing and relaxed, and it struck me that he was probably a bit like a chameleon, changing his persona when relating to different types of people as he tried to eke out more information. 'Do you remember telling Olivia about Katie Quinn?'

Tom's eyelids flew open and his gaze sought mine. The skin around his eyes wrinkled at the edges as his face crumpled in on itself.

I blinked back the tears. 'I'm sorry, Tom. I had to tell them what you told me.'

Ethan glared at me again, and I looked away, out of the window at a magpie on the lawn, squawking as it chased away a blackbird. What was that saying about them? *One for sorrow.* Was it a premonitory warning? I swallowed and turned back.

'Do you remember telling Olivia that you'd buried Katie under the garage?' DI Spencer tried again.

'She's lying. Olivia's always lying.' Tom clamped his mouth into a thin trembling line.

'Was it an accident? Is that what happened?' DI Spencer asked and waited patiently in the silence that followed. When Tom didn't speak, he said, 'We found a skeleton buried where you said it was. Is that Katie?'

Tom started coughing, a hacking, dry sound. He leaned forward and Nadia patted his back.

I poured him water from a jug on his bedside cabinet and tilted the glass in front of him. 'Have a drink.'

His eyes streamed as he took some small sips, but I couldn't tell if it was from the coughing fit or because he was crying.

'We need to find out what happened to her, Mr Tate,' DS Khan said gently.

Tom wiped his mouth with the back of his hand and let the tears wind down his cheeks. 'I . . . it's . . . was a long time ago.'

'We know. That's why we need to piece things together,' DI Spencer said. 'Can you tell us?'

'She shouldn't have done it.' Tom looked up and stared at me but he wasn't looking *at* me, he was looking through me, as if drowning in some distant memory.

'Done what?' DI Spencer asked.

Tom opened his mouth to speak and then shook his head.

'*Please,* Dad,' Nadia pleaded with him in a tiny voice.

Suddenly Tom snatched his hand back from Nadia's and fumbled with the bed covers, trying to pull them down but really just flinging them around. 'You're not taking me away. I know your type!' he snarled, managing to free his pyjama-clad legs and swing them over the edge of the bed. 'No, no, no.' He shook his head manically. 'Not taking me. Not.' He tried to lift himself off the bed with his forearms but he was breathing hard, face red with effort and anger. 'I'm not going with you! You'll put me in one of those . . . one of those . . .' He pointed a shaky finger at DI Spencer.

Ethan, who had managed to contain himself so far and stay quiet, erupted then. 'Right. That's it. You'll have to leave. Can't you see you're upsetting him? He's had one heart attack already. Do you want another one on your conscience?' He took a step closer to the end of the bed, as if to shield Tom from them.

Alerted by the commotion, Mary entered the room. 'Is everything all right in here?' Her eyes sought out Tom, who was shaking now and fiddling with the buttons of his pyjama top, trying to get it undone.

'Tom, let's get you back into bed now, eh?' She lifted his legs to try and swing them back under the covers but he protested.

'No!' He flung his arm out, pushing her away. For someone who had seemed so feeble a minute ago, he had surprising strength. 'Get away from me. You're all trying to kill me! You're trying to KILL ME!' He shrank away from her, curling sideways into his pillows. 'Go on! Get away!' He opened his mouth, took out his denture plate with false teeth attached and threw them in the direction of DS Khan and DI Spencer, who darted sideways to avoid a direct hit.

'Come on, now, Tom, it's OK.' I stepped forward into his direct sightline and sat down in front of him on my haunches. 'No one's taking you away. You're safe.'

Nadia started crying. 'Dad, oh, Dad, don't worry. Just calm down.'

'Look what you're doing!' Ethan barked out.

'I think it would be better if you came back another time,' Mary said to DI Spencer and DS Khan. 'When he gets like this it'll take a long time to get him settled again.'

DI Spencer nodded and looked at us all. 'We'll be in touch. In the meantime, if you remember anything, please give us a call.' And then they left the room.

'I can give him something to calm him down,' Mary said.

'You're all right, Tom. Nothing's going to happen.' I looked up into his eyes and saw a flicker of recognition there.

'Olivia?' he said, his voice distorted without his dentures. 'Are you taking me to Durdle Door? I want to see Durdle Door.' He grabbed hold of my arm, his fingernails digging into the skin. 'Want to go to Durdle Door. Take me. You take me, don't you?'

I looked over at Ethan, whose dark eyes reflected back anger and pain. 'Shall we take him?'

'Is he OK to go out, though?' Nadia asked Mary. 'He only had the heart attack the other day.'

'He's got a DNR order and he's going to . . .' Ethan's voice cracked and his eyes watered. 'We should make this time as nice as possible for him.'

'I agree,' Mary said. 'Plus, he still needs to have some exercise, and a visit out there always relaxes him. You can take one of the wheelchairs out in the corridor for him in case he's not strong enough to do his usual walk. It'll fold up to go in the car.'

'I'll take him,' Ethan said.

'Why don't we all go?' I suggested.

'No,' Ethan said forcefully. 'I want to spend some time with him.' He looked at me and I knew what he was saying without words: *before he dies.* 'Dad? I'm going to take you out to Durdle Door, OK?'

Tom visibly relaxed then, his shoulders dropping from their rigid hunch up around his neck. 'Will you, Tom?'

'I'm Ethan, Dad.' He blinked rapidly and sniffed. 'Now, shall we get you dressed, eh?' He found Tom's clothes in the small cupboard in the corner of the room and pulled out some trousers and a shirt.

'All right, now, Tom?' Mary stood back. 'Shall I bring you a nice cup of tea first and a few biscuits before you go?'

Tom nodded slowly.

Mary patted his hand, gave us a sympathetic smile and picked up Tom's dentures. 'I'll just clean these and I'll be back with some tea.'

Nadia kissed Tom on the cheek. 'I'll see you soon, Dad. Love you.'

'Bye, Tom. See you soon.' I squeezed Ethan's shoulder as I walked past. 'I'll see you at home later. We need to talk about what we're going to tell Anna.'

Nadia and I didn't speak until we were sitting in her car.

'That was awful. The whole day's been awful,' she said.

'More than awful.' I couldn't think of a word to describe what it was.

'You're right, though: what are we going to tell the kids?'

'I don't know.' I leaned my head back on the headrest and let out a sigh. 'How do you tell your daughter that the granddad who's always doted on her is a murderer? That he killed a young woman and buried her in the garage of the house she's been living in for the last four years?'

But as it turned out, something worse delayed me telling Anna about Katie.

Chapter Eighteen

Nadia and I sat in the corner of a coffee shop in Dorchester high street, trying to process what had happened. We were still both in shock.

'I just can't believe it.' Nadia took a sip of her espresso, her pale blue eyes looking grey against the pallor of her skin. 'It's . . . bloody hell.' She balled her hands into fists.

'Anna won't want to live in the house anymore, will she? I don't want to live there anymore! We'll have to sell it.'

'You can come and stay with us. We've got room.' She blinked back tears.

My stomach rumbled, and I remembered I hadn't eaten anything all day. 'Maybe that would be best. For a while, at least. Anna's going to have nightmares. Do you remember when she saw that story on the news about those Japanese fishermen in Taiji who hunt dolphins to either capture them for aquariums or slaughter them for food? She had nightmares after that for months. She kept waking up saying she was drowning in their blood. It was horrendous. Actually, I couldn't stop thinking about that afterwards, either. It's horrific what humans do, isn't it?'

'She's a lot stronger than you think.'

'She's sensitive.'

'What are we going to tell them, then?' Her foot tapped an erratic beat against the table leg.

I stirred my spoon around in my cappuccino, staring down as if it hid all the answers. I held my breath. Finally, I exhaled and put the spoon on a napkin on the table. This was a parent's worst nightmare. Your family was supposed to be a safe haven. Not capable of great cruelty and viciousness. Not capable of this. My thoughts wandered to Jack again. Was he Katie's worst nightmare? Her home should've been a safe haven, too, but had he abused her? Had Rose turned a blind eye to it or was she too drunk to notice? Could I have prevented this somehow? Everything we do, every event in our lives has a domino effect. If Jack and Rose were sober, model parents, would Katie have grown up to have a normal life? If Jack was abusing her, was that the real reason she'd been running away? If Chris hadn't split up with her, would she still be alive? If I'd paid more attention, would it have come to this? We all had a part to play in how things had ended up.

'Maybe we should just say there's been an accident for now, not go into specifics.' Nadia's voice dragged me back to the table. She patted her now wet cheeks with a napkin and took a long, hard breath. 'Just that the police found some old bones but they don't know who they belong to or what happened.'

'You know as well as I do that as soon as the police start asking questions, people in the village are going to know what's happened. Everyone's going to be talking and speculating. Do you remember when Jody Spencer was having an affair with Dave Potts? The ridiculous stories people came out with then about how they were both into dogging and went out to a local playing field in the middle of the night to have sex with people? I mean, where the hell did they get that from? They must have some amazing imaginations to think up rubbish like that.'

She sat upright, looking more like the in-control, calm, organised Nadia I knew so well. 'Yes, but we can deal with the gossip when it happens.'

I nodded, not really believing her, but anything to delay the inevitable sounded like the better option to me.

'I just don't understand,' I said, my stomach lurching again. 'Why would Tom do it? Why would he kill her? What makes a lovely, kind man kill a teenage girl? There must be more to the story.'

'I just don't believe Dad killed her. It's impossible.'

'Well, someone did. Someone with access to the garage who wouldn't be discovered. Oh, God.' I sat back in the chair, the enormity of everything sinking in like a kick to the solar plexus. I had a physical pain behind my breastbone and rubbed at it, shaking my head.

Nadia swirled the bitter dregs of coffee round in her tiny cup, blinking back more tears. 'I need another one of these.' She nodded to my untouched drink. 'Want one?'

'No, thanks.'

She came back with another espresso and two huge chocolate muffins. She slid one of the plates towards me. 'You look like you're about to pass out. You need some sugar.'

'I can't face food.' My stomach contracted at the sight of it.

'I need to eat. Comfort food.' She pulled apart the muffin and picked off a chunk but her hands shook so much, she dropped it and it fell back onto the plate, scattering crumbs across the table.

I leaned forward, watching her scooping up the crumbs with trembling, mechanical actions, trying to stop my own tears from falling. 'Why would he do it?' I asked again. 'I need to understand this. I need to know what happened.'

She shook her head. 'He didn't do it. Someone else must've put her body there.'

'But you have to admit he obviously knew about it, otherwise he never would've known where she was buried. Maybe she did steal something and wouldn't give it back.' I swallowed a mouthful of coffee to lubricate my dry throat. 'You know that last day I saw her in the shop and asked her to come out with us? I told her who was going and she said about having something he wanted and she'd make him pay, and she said about fucking him again. I thought she was talking about Chris, but Chris says he never slept with her after they split up. What if she was really talking about Tom? What if they really were having a secret relationship?'

'He wouldn't have.' She shook her head adamantly. 'Dad didn't like her that much. He was glad when Chris finished with her. And he was old enough to be her father! There's no way he would've been involved like that with her.'

'Yes, but she was young and attractive and wasn't shy about having sex. What if he was tempted? What older man isn't going to find that tempting?'

'No way. Not Dad.'

'He kept Georgia a secret from everyone. What if he kept Katie a secret, too? I know none of us wants to imagine our parents having sex, but it's not that unlikely when you think about it.'

'Even supposing they were in a relationship, why kill her?' Nadia shook her head solemnly, wringing her shaking hands together.

'Don't they say most people are murdered by people they know?' I paused, trying to ignore the pulse thumping in my forehead. 'When Katie said that she had something he wanted, she *must've* been talking about something she stole from him that he wanted back. Maybe Tom arranged to meet her at the house to get it from her before she left the village and they argued about it. Maybe she'd already sold whatever it was she stole to get money to run away with. That's the most likely explanation, isn't it? I don't think she was walking towards Abbotsbury at all. She was walking towards the barn.'

Nadia stared at me blankly. 'How do we even know it's her body?'

'Who else would it be? How many other people do you think he's *murdered?*' I hissed the word, glancing around me to make sure none of the other customers could hear us. 'It's got to be her.' I chewed on my lip. 'But I think I can count on one hand the number of times I've ever seen Tom lose his temper in all the time I've known him. I know sometimes Tom and Lucas don't see eye to eye about things, but Tom never gets *angry* with him, does he? Whatever happened, it must've been pretty bad for him to have killed her.'

'He only ever used to get angry with things, not people. Frustrated, more like – if the vacuum didn't work, or some tool or other went wrong, or he was fixing the car and it wasn't going right. But he was never angry with us or anyone else.'

'Yes, but he did hit that man once in that car park in Weymouth, didn't he?'

'That was different! The man had already punched his wife in the middle of the street and was going to do it again if Dad hadn't intervened. He was just protecting her.'

I looked at my watch. 'We need to get back home. I want to be back in time to meet Anna off the school bus in case the crime scene people are still there. I'll have to explain something to her at least.'

Nadia stood, squaring her shoulders. 'We'll have to be strong for the girls. I think it will be best if I bring Charlotte back to yours and we can tell them together. That will be easier. At least it's the last day of term and they won't have to go back to school while this is all still fresh in people's minds.'

As we headed out the door, my mobile phone rang.

'It's Chris,' I said to her, looking at the name on the display.

'What the hell is going on?' he said when I answered. 'I've just had the police up at work to talk to me, saying Dad killed someone and buried them under your garage!'

'It's true. It's unbelievable, but it's true.'

'And he just confessed this to you?' he asked dubiously.

'Yes. I don't know why, but, yes. I wish he hadn't.'

'I just don't believe it.' He sounded exactly like Ethan and Nadia.

'Look, Nadia and I are going back to the house. I'm hoping the police have finished there by now. But we need to say something to Charlotte and Anna. Why don't you meet us there?'

'OK. I'm on my way back. Where's Ethan? I've been trying to get hold of him but his phone's turned off.'

'Maybe it's run out of battery, or sometimes the signal at Durdle Door is not that strong.'

'Has he taken Dad up there?'

'Yes.'

'What, in the middle of all this shit?'

'Look, just come to ours, OK? We can talk more then.'

'All right. I'll see you soon.'

I held my breath as Nadia's car approached my house. The gates were shut now, which was hopefully a good sign that the police had finished collecting whatever evidence they needed. I didn't exhale until I got out of the car to swing them open.

The garage doors were closed, too, and there was no sign that anything untoward had even happened inside them earlier that day. No white suits. No crime scene tape. No officer stationed at the entrance. Thank goodness for that. I didn't want Anna to see it.

Nadia pulled in behind my Mini as I walked to the front door. I was opening it just as Chris swung in behind her.

He jerked his pick-up truck to a stop and shot out of the car, his face pale, eyes wild. 'What is this? It's got to be some kind of joke. The Georgia thing wasn't true. This can't be, either.'

I tried to hug him but he stepped away.

'Come inside.' Nadia tugged his arm.

In the kitchen, the only telltale sign of what had been discovered earlier was DI Spencer's business card on the oak table. I picked it up and shoved it in a drawer, wanting it out of my sight.

'Do you want a drink?' Nadia took charge, filling the kettle with water and turning it on to boil.

'When's Ethan coming back?' Chris ignored her.

'Probably soon.' I explained what had happened when the police questioned Tom earlier and how upset he'd become. 'I don't know how long it would've taken to get Tom dressed after we left. Mary was going to make him a cup of tea. Maybe Tom and Ethan are still on their way to Durdle Door.'

'Christ. He's going to die soon, anyway. Why do the police have to harass him?'

I sat at the table, feet up on the edge of the chair, arms wrapped around my knees. 'They have to find out what happened. They have to ask questions.'

Nadia pulled her mobile out her bag. 'I'm going to call Lucas and get him to come over, too.' She dialled his number and walked out into the hallway with it pressed to her ear. I heard her mumbled voice as Chris sat down so hard on the chair I thought it would collapse beneath him.

'I bet they think I had something to do with it.' His knee jigged up and down.

'What? Why?'

'Because I was the last one to see her.'

'Is that what they said?'

'No, not in so many words. But they didn't sound like they believed me.'

'Why shouldn't they believe you? Tom's confessed to it.'

He shook his head. 'Have you got any whisky?'

I pointed to one of the cupboards. 'Help yourself.'

He grabbed a cut glass tumbler and poured himself a hefty couple of inches. Staring out of the kitchen window at the garage, he swallowed half of it in one go. 'This is bloody mental. She was really under the garage this whole time?'

Nadia came back in and grabbed some mugs, filled them with coffee granules. 'Apparently, yes.'

'I thought she was leaving. She was supposed to be leaving.' He threw his head back and drained the remains of the glass, then winced and coughed.

'Do you want tea or coffee?' Nadia asked him.

He wiggled the glass in the air. 'No, I'll stick to this.' He poured himself some more whisky. 'Dad couldn't even kill a spider. Don't you remember, when you were a kid and you were scared of them all the time?' His gaze darted in Nadia's direction. 'He never killed them. He always captured them between a glass and a bit of cardboard. Said that everything deserved a chance to live.' He threw a hand in the air wildly. 'So how could he kill her?'

'People can snap,' I said. 'Lose their temper and do things they regret. It must've been an accident. That's what Tom told me, that it was an accident.' It's what I kept trying to tell myself, although exactly what kind of accident, I couldn't even imagine. And if it was, why hadn't he told the police at the time? Why cover it up?

'What did the police ask you?' Nadia poured boiling water into the mugs and stirred them with a spoon.

'Just . . .' He sniffed. 'Just what had happened between me and Katie. I told them about me finishing with her about seven months before she left, and that I hadn't really seen her until that day when I was waiting at the bus stop and she was leaving home.'

'Are you sure you never slept with her after you'd split up?' I asked.

'Of course I'm sure! I think I'd know that. Why?'

'It's just that she said something weird the last time I saw her. At the time I thought she meant you but maybe she really meant Tom. She said, "If he thinks I'm going to fuck him again, he can fuck off".'

Chris looked at me as if I'd punched him. 'She wasn't sleeping with Dad. That's just . . . sick.'

Nadia handed me a mug of steaming coffee and sat opposite. My hands shook as I took it. I'd probably had far too much caffeine for one day.

I told them what Ethan had said about Katie trying it on with him. 'Maybe she was sleeping with Tom to get you back for dumping her. She could've been doing it out of spite, planning to tell you so she could rub your face in it, or she'd set her sights on Tom when you broke up with her so he could support her.'

'Oh, come on, she wouldn't have done that,' Chris said. 'She wasn't spiteful.'

But trying to sleep with Ethan was pretty spiteful, wasn't it? What was she planning on doing if he'd slept with her that night? Rub my face in it? Try to split us up because she wasn't with Chris anymore so she thought I didn't deserve to be happy, either? And it got me thinking about something that happened one day at school when we were coming out of science block after a lesson. There were these heavy metal and reinforced glass doors with wire mesh inside, and I'd opened the door first with Katie behind me. The next thing I knew, one of the annoying, mouthy girls in our class was scream- ing and crying behind us, her nose pouring with blood. She'd told everyone Katie had slammed the door in her face on purpose, but Katie had denied it, saying it was an accident and the wind had banged it shut after her, but she had this amused glint in her eyes when she said it. Months later she told me the girl had called her a slag and no one got away with calling her names. I knew then for certain it hadn't been an accident.

'If she was going to say something to hurt me she could've done it on that last day I saw her, but she never said a word.' Chris shook his head and stared out of the window again. 'And what about the letter she wrote, then?'

'She must've written the letter intending to run away but then Tom killed her before she actually left the village,' I said. 'Maybe she saw him when she was walking past the barn, or she could've already arranged to meet him here to get money or something. Maybe she was blackmailing him about something she'd found out or had stolen something from him. Or maybe it started off as something innocent where he saw her walking along the road and picked her up, offering her a lift somewhere. Whatever happened, she paid an awful price for it.'

'It's my fault, isn't it?' he muttered. 'If I'd stopped her that day . . . if—'

'You can't play "what ifs",' Nadia said. 'It's too late for that now. There's no point looking back and trying to think of things you should've done differently. It's happened and we can't change it. Now we have to concentrate on getting through this.'

There was a knock at the door and Nadia got up to open it. 'That's probably Lucas.'

Lucas took one look round the room at our faces and said, 'So, it's really true, then? What Nadia's just told me about Tom and Katie?'

'Apparently so.' Nadia hovered beside him, her hand touching his arm. 'Do you want a drink, darling?'

'Have one of these.' Chris tilted the bottle of whisky in Lucas's direction. 'Or are you flying later?'

'No, I've got a couple of rest days. I definitely feel a Scotch coming on.' He poured himself a large one and sat down opposite me. 'I can't get my head round this.'

'You and me both,' Chris muttered, clutching the worktop so hard his hand shook with the force.

'He really killed Katie?' Lucas asked.

'It looks like it,' I said as Nadia sat next to him, sliding her hand through his.

'And it was my fault!' Chris cried.

'It wasn't your fault. Don't be ridiculous!' Nadia sighed impatiently, her shock being replaced with anger. 'Stop being so full of self-pity all the time. No wonder Abby left you.'

'Hey, that's not fair,' I said to her. 'Come on, we're all upset. It doesn't mean we have to go round attacking each other. That's not going to get us anywhere.'

'Sorry. I'm sorry, I didn't mean it.' Nadia scrunched her face up. 'This is really difficult.' She looked at Lucas. 'We've got to tell the girls something and I'm dreading it.'

'Me, too,' I said.

'What shall we do?' Lucas stroked his glass absentmindedly. 'I'm all for delaying telling them but they'll have to know some time. The police will be asking questions, looking for witnesses. It won't take long to get round the village.'

'That's what I said,' I agreed.

'Do you want to come and stay at ours?' Lucas asked. 'I can't imagine what Anna will think of living next door to where Katie was found.' He jerked his head in the general direction of the garage.

'Thanks. Nadia already offered. I think it's probably a good idea for the moment, but I need to talk to Ethan.' My gaze strayed to my watch again.

'The police want to talk to you, too,' Chris said to Lucas, picking up the whisky bottle and bringing it to the table before he slumped down on a chair.

'Well, I won't be able to tell them much. I can't remember anything about the last time I saw Katie. It was years ago.'

Nadia's hand strayed to Lucas's arm again. He grabbed it and held on tight, giving her a loving and supportive smile. There was still no outward sign he was having an affair. He was obviously as good at hiding things as Nadia was. As Katie had been.

'No, I didn't remember much, either,' Nadia said. 'I'd forgotten all about us going to the pub that night until you mentioned it. How can we be expected to remember what happened twenty-five years ago?'

'I remember some things because I thought about it a lot after she left.' I cradled the mug. 'I felt guilty that I hadn't stopped her or done more for her. I feel even more guilty now, knowing what's happened.'

'Me, too,' Chris said.

'You had nothing to feel guilty about, mate.' Lucas gave Chris one of those men slaps on the back.

'I still loved her and I let her walk off.'

'You were too young,' Nadia said. 'It wouldn't have worked out even if you'd got back together. There was a reason you split up with her.'

Chris looked up through hooded eyes at her. 'You can be so cold sometimes.'

'It's not being cold. It's being practical. I'm trying to help.'

'Well, it's not helping.' Chris swallowed some more whisky.

'OK, OK. Olivia's right – there's no point arguing amongst ourselves,' Lucas said gently. 'We should all be supporting each other instead. We've got to stick together and somehow get through this with as little damage to the family as possible.'

'So what do you suggest we do, then?' Chris said bitterly, his words beginning to slur. He muttered something else unintelligible.

I didn't hear the rest of the conversation, though, because my mobile phone rang from somewhere in my handbag on the island. It was Ethan.

'Hi, how is he? Has he calmed down now?' I said before he could even say hello.

His next words came out of nowhere and blew me away.

Chapter Nineteen

D ad's killed himself.' Ethan's voice sounded wrong. Far
away and disjointed, as if he was in a long tunnel.

'What?' I gasped, hoping I'd heard him wrong.

'He . . . he stepped off the cliff. He just . . . went over.'

'What do you mean, "went over"?'

'I don't know if he meant to do it or if it was just an accident.
I . . . I'm waiting here for the police.'

'No.' I shook my head, staring at the others with wide-eyed
shock.

'He was so agitated when you left, it took ages to get him dressed.
When we finally got to the car park at Durdle Door he refused to
go in the wheelchair – he wanted to walk. We were walking along
the usual path and we got to near the bench we always sit on. And
then . . . Christ, Olivia. It was just so . . . it was like everything
happened in fast motion. We were talking, and then he got angry
with me. He was confused. I didn't really know what he was going
on about and he wasn't making any sense. We were standing near
the edge of the cliff and he told me to leave him alone!' Ethan's voice
rose to a shriek. 'He pushed me away from him. He . . . he . . .'

'It's OK, darling, take your time.'

'I tried to calm him down, but he wouldn't listen, so I thought I should give him a bit of space. I turned back and walked towards the bench, hoping it would give him time to calm down. But when I got there and looked back at him, he was staring at me. And then . . . then there was this moment, where he had this expression of clarity on his face, and then he turned around and stepped off the cliff. By the time I got to where he'd been standing he was . . . he was gone. Shit!' He yelled so loud it made me pull the phone away from my ear for a second. 'I can't . . . I can't believe it happened.'

I tried to avoid looking at the others, who were all wearing expressions of worried expectation.

'Liv, it's . . . oh, God.'

'I'm so sorry. So sorry.' I closed my eyes, the tears smarting behind my eyelids. Part of me felt a rush of emotion. Part of me felt numb, disbelieving.

'Oh, the police are here now. I have to go. I'll see you soon.' He hung up.

I stood there, phone still pressed to my ear, blinking away the tears, not really seeing anything in front of me.

'What's happened?' Nadia rose and walked towards me. 'Has Dad had another heart attack?'

I couldn't speak, just let the tears snake down my cheeks.

She grabbed my shoulders and shook me. 'What's happened?'

I stepped out of her grip, took a tumbler from the cupboard and sat down at the kitchen table. 'Tom's just taken his own life.' I poured myself a large whisky and didn't stop drinking until I'd swallowed the whole lot. It burned on the way down, igniting fire inside the pit of my stomach, which was already delicate from not eating all day, from the constant jangling nerves. I wanted it to anaesthetise me. Make everything go away.

'Suicide?' Nadia sat next to me, her expression dazed, shaking her head. 'No. How on earth could he do that?'

'He . . . um . . . he stepped off the cliffs at Durdle Door.' I poured myself another drink. The bottle was almost empty.

Nadia leaned her elbows on the table and flopped her head in her hands, her hair falling over the table and shielding her face as her shoulders shook with sobs.

Lucas's face drained of colour. He slid his arm around Nadia and drew her closer, rubbing her head in soft strokes. 'I'm really sorry, darling. This is . . . wow. I can't believe it. Any of it.'

'He can't have killed himself.' Chris shook his head vacantly.

I retrieved another bottle of whisky from the cupboard – an old, expensive single malt thing that Ethan had been saving for a special occasion. Murder and suicide trumped special occasion, any day.

I topped up all our glasses. We were silent for a while, lost in our own stunned thoughts, grief filtering in slowly.

'Who knows what was running through his mind,' I said. 'Ethan said he wasn't sure if he meant to do it or he was just confused because he was angry and upset. Maybe it's a good thing. What was the alternative?'

'But surely the police wouldn't have prosecuted a seventy-five-year-old Alzheimer's patient for murder?' Lucas said. 'It wouldn't be in their interests, would it?'

'I very much doubt it,' I said, rocking back and forth in my chair, wrapping my arms around my stomach.

Nadia let out a shuddering sob. Lucas kissed the top of her head.

I wiped away my tears with the back of my hand. 'But he was dying, anyway. Either another heart attack would've got him or the Alzheimer's would've given him a slow death. As painful as this is, I think it was better for him.' *But what about for us?* I wanted to say. What was best for us now? How could Tom do this to us all and then just jump off the cliff?

'This is your fault!' Nadia suddenly sat up straight, pointing an accusing finger at me, her eyes wide, eyelashes clumped together with damp, salty tears. 'If you hadn't said anything, none of this would've happened and Dad would still be here.'

A ball of guilt exploded in my chest at the force of her words. 'I'm sorry. I'm so sorry. I never meant for this to happen. Any of it. Maybe I should've kept quiet. I just—'

'Yes, maybe you should have,' Nadia hissed.

'How could she have kept quiet about it, love?' Lucas stroked Nadia's shoulder. 'Olivia couldn't have kept it a secret. It's not fair to give her the responsibility of all this.'

Once again we were lost in our own silent thoughts. The only sounds permeating the room were sniffs and sobs and the ticking of the kitchen clock that seemed to reverberate right through me.

'We've got to tell Charlotte,' Nadia suddenly muttered, smoothing away the hair from her damp cheeks. She gripped Lucas's hand. 'I don't want to tell her. I don't want to get her upset.'

'Darling, we have to say something. This isn't something we can hide.' Lucas's eyebrows furrowed together.

'But that means it'll be the end of it now, won't it?' Nadia tried to give a brave smile but it wavered on her face. 'Dad confessed and now he's . . . he's gone, so maybe we can keep a lid on this. There won't be a police investigation and . . .' She looked around the room wildly. '. . . and maybe we won't have to even tell the girls. We can just say there was an accident and Dad fell off the cliffs.'

'People are going to talk, though,' I said. 'We can't avoid this forever. The police have to tell Rose about what happened to Katie, and it will get out like that. It will be in the papers. Maybe even on the TV.'

'Oh, no,' Nadia groaned.

Chris downed more whisky, seemingly oblivious to the discussion going on around him.

'Poor Ethan, witnessing that,' I said. 'He told me Tom was angry and that he walked off to give him a bit of space to calm down, but then he looked at Ethan and just stepped over the cliff. The police arrived when we were on the phone so he couldn't tell me any more.'

'Shall I go up there?' Lucas suggested. 'He might need a bit of moral support.'

'By the time you get there, they'll probably be sending him home,' I said.

'Do you think Tom knew what he was doing?' Lucas asked.

Chris pressed the heels of his hands to his eyes. When he released them again, his eyes glistened with sadness and something else. Anger. He reached for the bottle and poured another couple of inches into his empty glass. He missed the edge and some of it spilled onto the table. 'Yes.' He sneered. 'I think he knew exactly what he was doing. Why would take his own life otherwise? He killed Katie and he couldn't stand the guilt anymore. I didn't want to believe Dad could do something like that, but now I do. He killed her all right. Why else would he jump off a cliff?'

'How can you say that?' Nadia shrieked at him.

I put a hand on Chris's shoulder but he shook it away.

Lucas gripped Nadia's hand. 'I know you want to protect him, darling, but—'

'Don't, OK?' She jerked her hand out of his grasp. 'Just don't.'

'Look, I've got to go and meet the school bus now – I can't leave it any longer.' I stood up.

Nadia wiped her eyes. She blew her nose forcefully with a tissue from her bag and thrust it in her trouser pocket. Then she squared her shoulders and stood up. 'I'll come with you. We'll bring them back here and then we can all tell them together,' she said firmly, back in control.

'Shall I come with you?' Lucas said.

Nadia waved him off. 'No, I can manage.'

Nadia and I walked up the road in silence and waited at the bus stop. The same bus stop where Chris was sitting when he saw Katie walk past, heading towards her death. What if she'd stopped and spoken to him that day? What if they'd chatted and Chris hadn't gotten on the bus, and she hadn't walked towards the barn? Would she still be alive now? If she was five or ten minutes later going down the road, would that have made a difference? Would Tom still have killed her and buried her body?

An uncontrollable shudder shook me. I rubbed my arms and shifted from foot to foot in the silence. There were no words to say. Nothing seemed good enough for the events that had unfolded and shattered our family like an atomic bomb mushrooming through our lives. No words would make sense of it. I could feel Nadia's anger towards me coming off her in waves. She blamed me for all of this, just like Ethan did.

When the school bus arrived Anna and Charlotte were the last off, chatting excitedly about some boy at school called Howie whom Charlotte fancied.

'Mum!' Anna grinned, full of energy. 'What are you doing here?'

Charlotte said goodbye to one of her friends before turning to Nadia and frowning in annoyance. 'We don't need a chaperone.' Then she turned to me and grinned brightly. 'Hi, Aunty Olivia.'

Teenagers. They can blow hot and cold in the blink of an eye.

Charlotte started walking off in the direction of her house.

'Wait! We all need to go to the barn,' I called out after her.

'What? But it's the last day of term. I said I'd meet some friends later since we don't have any school now. We've arranged to go bowling.'

'No. We're going to Olivia and Ethan's,' Nadia said, her voice croaky.

'Are you all right?' Anna said to me. 'Have you been crying?'

'But *Mum!*' Charlotte whined. 'I promised them.'

'We've got some news we need to talk about, I'm afraid.' I took Anna's hand in mine and held the other out to Charlotte. 'Come on. You've got the whole summer holiday to see your friends. This is important.'

Charlotte sighed and walked back towards us. Or rather, stalked.

'It's Granddad, isn't it?' Anna gave me a worried sideways glance as we made our way up the road. 'He's had another heart attack, hasn't he?' Her eyes welled up with tears.

I slid my arm around her shoulder. 'Let's wait till we get home.'

'But it is, isn't it?' she wailed.

'Is it, Mum?' Charlotte asked Nadia behind us.

As I opened the gates Anna started crying.

'He's dead, isn't he? Just tell me, Mum.'

I gripped her hand as I opened the front door. 'Come on, let's go in the kitchen.'

Charlotte immediately went to Lucas, standing next to him and putting her arm round his shoulder. He slid an arm round her waist. 'Hi, sweetie.'

Anna gripped my hand hard. 'Tell us.'

I looked at Nadia's face, etched with pain.

She looked at me. Took a deep breath. 'I'm sorry, girls, but Granddad had an accident earlier today. He was . . .' She trailed off and looked back at me for help.

'Ethan took him out for a trip to Durdle Door and there was an accident,' I stepped in. 'Granddad fell off the cliff.'

Anna's forehead scrunched up in a frown that looked like a scowl. I knew that look well. It was a prerequisite to a full-blown hysterical crying fit.

'No!' Anna cried, tears streaming down her cheeks, which were rapidly turning red, her shoulders shaking up and down with the weight of her sobs as she gulped for air.

'Mum, he's still alive, right?' Charlotte said disbelievingly to Nadia. 'Right?'

I pulled Anna to me so her head rested on my shoulder and smoothed a hand over her forehead repeatedly, a gesture that had always relaxed her when she was younger and couldn't sleep. 'I'm sorry, darling. I know how much you loved him. But no one could survive that fall. He's gone, sweetheart. And he's not suffering anymore.'

Nadia reached for Charlotte but she buried her head in Lucas's chest.

'Well,' Chris slurred, his eyes glassy. 'At least things can't get any worse.'

But he was wrong about that. Things were about to get a whole lot worse.

Chapter Twenty

It felt like a lifetime later when I slipped under the cotton sheet in bed. Ethan lay on his back, hands laced together behind his head, staring at the ceiling. He hadn't cried yet but it looked like the tears weren't far off. The room felt oppressive, and not just because the heat from the summer day was trapped inside. The weight of Ethan's grief, of mine, too, lay heavy and stifling in the air.

'Is Anna asleep now?' he said as I turned and nestled into his chest. He brought one arm around me. His heart beat in a steady rhythm against my cheek.

'Finally. She kept asking me all sorts of questions about what happened. I was trying to explain that maybe this was kinder to Tom in the long run. And that he's not in pain anymore and will always be in our hearts and memories, even though he's no longer physically here anymore.'

'And how did that go?' He blinked rapidly.

'Not too well.'

'This is the first time someone close to her has died. It's bound to be confusing for her.'

'I know. But now she's angry and upset with me because she didn't get to say goodbye to him. She wanted to see him after the heart attack but I didn't think it was a good idea just yet. And – oh, God, we haven't even told her the whole story still. Imagine how she's going to react then.' He didn't reply, so I said, 'Chris is still asleep on the sofa.'

'Passed out, more like. He was so drunk.'

'I took his shoes off and left him there.' I stroked my fingers lightly along Ethan's flat stomach muscles, tracing a line over his hip bone.

He twisted a lock of my long hair round and round his finger.

'I can't stop thinking about everything. I'm so confused. If Katie dying *was* an accident, like Tom said, then why didn't he just call the police when it happened? Why not confess to it at the time instead of covering it up? And then the next minute he said he *had* to do it, which makes it seem like it wasn't an accident at all. I mean, there must've been other people working on site when he was renovating the barn. Chris was working here as one of the builders at the time, wasn't he? And there would've been electricians, plumbers. Maybe Tom knew something about the murder but he didn't actually do it. Well, he must've known *something*, otherwise he wouldn't know where she was buried, would he? But I keep hoping that he wasn't directly involved. Although, I suppose—'

He pressed a fingertip to my lips and rolled sideways so he was angled over me, forearms taking his weight. 'Don't. Just stop. For just a few moments I don't want to think about it. I don't want to hear about it.' His brown eyes looked almost black in the darkness of the room. They glistened as they roved my face.

Before I could agree to stop talking, he'd crashed his lips against mine, his tongue desperately delving inside my mouth with a fiery need usually reserved for make-up sex. We were lost in a tangle of legs and arms and lips and groans, and then I was pressing myself against him and he was inside me. It was short. Fierce. Electric. Something animal and primal we both needed to remind ourselves of our own mortality. We were still alive. We were the lucky ones.

Afterwards I lay in the crook of his arm again, sweat drying against my skin.

'I just can't believe he did it in front of me,' Ethan said so quietly I had to strain to hear him. 'Why would he do that? And did he even know what he was doing in the end or was he just confused? That . . . that moment when he looked at me, it was like there was an apology in his eyes. In that split second before, he seemed so clear, so alert, like he'd made the decision and he was saying a silent goodbye. And then he was gone.'

'I'm so sorry, Ethan. It's awful.' I squeezed him close to me.

'He must've blamed me for what was happening. How can I live with that? How can I live with the thought that if we hadn't dug up that bloody garage he'd still be with us now?'

But I knew what he was really saying to me. *How can you live with yourself, Olivia? This is all your fault.*

'I'm sure he didn't blame you. It's not your fault, it's m—'

He cut me off. 'I don't want to talk about it.'

'It might help.'

'I don't even know what I'm thinking right now so I can't talk about it.'

We were both lost in silence, trying to deal with the shock and sadness. Eventually I listened to his breathing slow as he drifted under the blanket of sleep. It took me a long time, but when I finally joined him, I was haunted by images of Katie. A faceless person dressed in black carried her unconscious body through the dark woods and into our garage. He paused at the wooden door, looking over his shoulder, but I couldn't make out any features. He carried her towards a hole already dug into the ground and gently placed her in its depths, shovelling soil over her. When he finished, he walked over the earth, flattening it down, and I could hear Katie's voice, muffled and distraught, from beneath. *Help me. Help me!* She was still alive down there, trapped in a dark place, unable to claw her way back out.

I jerked awake the next morning, gasping for breath, covered in a sheen of sweat with the sheet knotted in my clenched fist. The bed was empty. I reached out and touched Ethan's side but it was cold.

Running a list of things to do over in my head, I got dressed. I needed to call Elaine and see if she'd cover my shift that afternoon. I'd always thought work was a great distraction, and it would stop me sending myself mad with thoughts, but I wanted to stay home at least for one day so I could be with Anna. Nadia had said she was going to make arrangements with work to cover Ethan's schedule so his meetings for the next couple of days would be rearranged and he wouldn't have to go in. She had probably been up at 4 a.m. sending emails to people. Even though Tom hadn't worked at Tate Construction for more than ten years since his retirement, a lot of people would be in mourning for him. Would they still be mourning when they heard what he'd confessed to, though?

I avoided the creaking floorboard outside Anna's room so I didn't wake her and went downstairs. Chris was nowhere to be seen and neither was Ethan. Poppy shot out of her bed in the corner of the kitchen and greeted me with a lick on the back of my hand and a funny little noise that would usually make me laugh, but not today. I noticed a note from Ethan left on the island as I stroked her.

Gone for a walk. Don't know when I'll be back. Need to get my head straight.

xx

Poppy butted my hand with her nose, dog-speak for *Stroke me more.*

'Good girl. I'll take you out later.' I eyed the clock on the wall and wondered if Elaine would be up yet. It was quarter past seven and surgery started at eight so she should be.

I dialled her mobile number and avoided looking out of the window. Yesterday, the pull to look at the garage had been so strong I couldn't ignore it. Today, I wanted to obliterate it from my vision.

Elaine was very sympathetic and kind and immediately agreed to cover my shift for as long as I needed it, although I told her I'd be back the following day. And Ethan would be here for Anna.

Next, I brewed a cup of tea and made myself eat a slice of toast before I passed out. Yesterday I'd hardly eaten a thing, and with all the whisky on top, my stomach felt like it was eating itself.

I tried to block out the scene from Tom's bedroom yesterday, but it kept drifting into my head. I also had a vision of his body at the foot of the cliffs, broken and destroyed, his lifeless eyes staring out into nothingness. When Tom was diagnosed with Alzheimer's I'd read up on it in medical journals, websites, blogs and chat rooms. A lot of Alzheimer's patients were clinically depressed and considered taking their own lives while they were still well enough to do so, but suicide rates were actually quite low, because although people may want to do it before the disease got too debilitating, very few went through with it while their lives still retained meaning and happiness. It's hard to kill yourself because of the *prospect* of future suffering, when things in the here and now aren't that bad yet. So time stretches on with a desire to hold on to life, and before they know it they've lost the cognitive ability to actually end things. One woman had written herself a letter with instructions on how to take a bottle of tranquilisers she'd been keeping for the occasion. She'd kept the letter pinned to her fridge to remind her what to do when the time came. But in the end, she'd left it too late for her to understand, and she thought it was written by someone who was trying to kill her.

Tom had never mentioned suicide, though I didn't think that was unusual. If he had thought about it, he'd want to spare his family the knowledge that he intended to take his own life, even though I still thought it would be the kindest option to Tom. A final respite from years of degradation, destruction, frustration and pain. But he had always maintained he didn't want to be a burden on anyone, and he hadn't wanted to prolong his life when the disease progressed, hence the DNR order he'd insisted on. So had he been so confused and agitated up there on those cliffs that he didn't know what he was really doing? Or was he lucid in those final moments, not wanting to carry on any longer? Had he just made a snap decision to end it all before life became too much? Or had he killed himself because of what he'd done to Katie? After he'd confessed and the truth had begun slowly coming out, had it been too hard for him to bear anymore? On some level did he fully remember what he'd done and felt so guilty that this was how he'd dealt with it?

The phone rang as I was wiping the worktop, questions running over and over in my head. It was Nadia.

'How are you?' I asked.

'Not great. You?'

'Probably better than Ethan. He's devastated. But you know what he's like. He doesn't like to talk and keeps things bottled up inside. I don't think it's healthy, but he's not going to change now, is he?'

'No, I suppose not. I've been trying to get him on his mobile but he's not answering. Is he there?'

'He's gone for a walk. He probably doesn't want to be disturbed. How's Charlotte handling it?'

'She feels guilty that she hadn't seen Dad for a while because she was busy with her exams, and in her spare time she wanted to see her friends. You know what teenagers are like,' she said bitterly. 'One minute they love you and the next they're screaming how much they hate you.'

'Anna hadn't visited Tom that often in the last few months, either. He didn't know who she was most of the time, which was upsetting for her, plus when he got agitated and angry, he scared her. I was torn between wanting her to see him because I knew he wouldn't be around much longer and not wanting her last memories of him to be bad ones. But now, of course, she's angry at me, saying that I didn't let her go and see him before he died.'

'Charlotte's acting the same. God, sometimes being a parent is the hardest job in the world.'

'I know. I never know if I'm doing the right thing. And now it's too late to worry about whether that was the right thing for them or not, I suppose.'

'Yes.' She sighed. 'Can you tell Ethan when you see him that I've rearranged his meetings for the next few days so he doesn't have to go anywhere? I've organised the York project to be overseen by Kevin until early next week so he won't have to rush back up there.'

'I will, thanks, Nadia. I don't know what we'd do without you.'

'I'm just glad to help. Anyway, it keeps me busy. I don't want to think about it.'

'You sound like Ethan. You have to let yourself grieve, though. Repressing it will only manifest in other problems later on.'

'Spoken like a true member of the healing profession,' she said with an edge to her voice.

'OK, I'm sorry.'

'No, I'm sorry. I know you're only trying to help. This is just so difficult.'

'Have you spoken to Chris yet this morning?'

'Yes, I just rang him to say I've organised another guy to stand in as project manager on the Weymouth supermarket he's working on. He was in a bad way with a hangover.'

'I'm not surprised, the amount he polished off last night. Still, we all grieve in different ways.' I heard Anna's bedroom door open and the sound of her light steps on the stairs. 'I've got to go – Anna's up. Speak soon, OK?' I hung up as Anna walked into the room. Instead of her graceful posture, her shoulders were rounded, her feet dragging on the floor.

'Hi.' She said glumly, sinking onto the stool next to me at the island.

Her eyes were puffy and red, her nose blocked, making her sound like she had a cold.

I slung my arm around her shoulder. 'What would you like for breakfast? There's Rice Krispies or toast. I need to go shopping.'

'No change there, then.' The corners of her lips lifted in a cheeky smile, and I thought maybe Anna really was more resilient than I gave her credit for. But how would she react to finding out there'd been a body under the garage all this time?

I banished the thought from my mind and stood up. 'Do you want to walk Poppy with me? It's a beautiful day; we could head through the woods to Abbotsbury if you like.'

'Is Dad coming with us?'

'No, he needs some time to clear his head.'

'I don't feel like going out anywhere. I'll just watch TV.'

Normally, I'd have a moan about her being inside holed up in front of the flat screen all day in the summer holidays when it was such fabulous weather outside, but I was treating her with kid gloves.

'Well, I'm not going to work today so you don't have to go over to Nadia's.'

Since Nadia worked from home doing the accounts and office admin, Anna had always spent the holidays at hers when I was at the surgery. It worked out great for both of us since it also kept Charlotte occupied.

'I'm old enough to be left on my own now, anyway. I'm going to be thirteen soon.'

'Mmm, so you keep reminding me.' I swatted her backside.

She poured out some Rice Krispies, leaving a trail of them on the worktop which she stuck to her finger and popped in her mouth. With great concentration she poured out some milk over the top. They fizzed and crackled as she brought the bowl over to the table.

'When is the funeral going to be?' she asked sadly.

'I don't know. The coroner has to release the body first. There will be an inquest but that probably won't take place for ages.'

'What, do we have to wait until the inquest before we can bury him, then?'

'No. As soon as they let us know, we can organise things. He wanted to be cremated.'

'I want to be cremated,' she said morbidly.

'Oh. Why?'

'Because I don't like the thought of being eaten by bugs.'

A picture of Katie in the ground underneath the concrete flashed in my head, her hollow eye sockets writhing with beetles and worms and larvae. I shook it away.

'Yes, well, you won't have to think about that for a long time yet.'

'How do you know? I could get hit by a bus tomorrow. I could fall off a cliff, just like Granddad.' She stopped eating and stared at her bowl, blinking to stop the tears. 'Or you could. Or Dad. What if something happens to you both?'

'Sweetheart, nothing's going to happen.' I reached out and squeezed her forearm.

'You can't say that, though, can you? You don't know what's going to happen. I didn't even get to say goodbye to Granddad!' She slid the stool back with a scraping sound that made Poppy cower, leaped up and ran out of the room.

And that was how the next few days in the Tate family went. Anna was up and down; Ethan was pretty much silent and didn't want to talk; Nadia was efficient, organising everything and bringing round casseroles and pasta bakes she'd made for us. Lucas was somewhere in America on a flight he couldn't find cover for, probably shagging his bit on the side, and Chris was drunk.

Our once-happy family was unravelling.

Chapter Twenty-One

I was walking home from work three days later past Chris's
house when I spotted DI Spencer and DS Khan about to
get into their car, which was parked outside. From the path,
I glanced up at Chris's open door and saw him leaning against the
frame watching me. He was in paint-splattered jeans, work boots
and a black T-shirt. His face was pale and drawn, his eyes sunken, as
if sensitive to the sunlight.

'Is there any news on the . . . um . . . body? I mean, skeleton,'
I asked DI Spencer. 'It was Katie, wasn't it?'

He gave me a pensive look before he said, 'We checked the
dental records, which confirmed the remains were from Katie
Quinn.'

'Oh, God.' I blinked as his words slammed into me, my hands
flying to my cheeks. An overwhelming heaviness made my limbs
feel like lead. 'Don't you have to do a DNA test?'

'There were viable bone cells and teeth pulp collected from her
remains, but a DNA test would've been tricky. Rose doesn't have
anything left of Katie's to compare it with, such as a hairbrush with
strands of hair. And Jack is no longer alive. To be sure it really was
Katie, we'd need a sample from both parents for a true analysis.'

He glanced briefly at DS Khan. 'Actually, we were going to come and speak to you later. Are you free now?' he asked.

I thought of Anna at home, parked in front of the TV, and Ethan off God knows where walking for miles again. He'd barely been in the house since Tom's death and finding Katie. I didn't want to hear what the police had to say. Not yet. I wanted to bury my head in the sand and forget. Switch the clocks back a few days to before Tom chose to spill his ghastly secret to me. Go back in time and protect my childhood friend. But I didn't think I'd have much of a choice in the matter. There was no way back now.

'Um . . . yes. But we haven't said anything about this to Anna yet so I don't want to talk at home. Can we go somewhere else?'

'Of course. Let's go for a drive.'

DS Khan parked in the car park overlooking Chesil Beach, and they both spun around in their seats to look at me. I felt nervous and cramped in the small space, like a prisoner trapped in a cell.

'I'll get us a coffee, shall I?' DS Khan nodded her head towards a van parked in the corner, selling ice creams and hot dogs. 'What would you like?' she asked me.

'What?' I said, trying to concentrate while my mind was reeling.

'Do you want a tea instead?'

'Oh, um, coffee's fine, thanks.'

'Back in a minute.' Her lips pursed into a flat, serious line.

'How did she die? Could you tell from . . . from what was . . .' I trailed off.

'She had a fractured skull.'

'Oh.'

'You mentioned before that Katie had said something you thought was odd before she left home. Can you tell me again what it was?'

'Um, yes. She said "If he thinks I'm going to fuck him again, he can fuck off", and then she said, "I've got something he wants and I'm going to make him pay".'

'You're positive about that? After all this time?'

'Yes.'

'Did Katie ever mention to you sleeping with Chris after he broke off their relationship?'

'No.'

'Did Chris?'

'No. In fact, he told me the other day that he definitely hadn't.'

'Did Katie ever mention sleeping with Tom?'

'No.'

He was silent for a while before adding, 'Katie was pregnant when she died. About six months.'

I sat back, stunned, as if he'd slapped me. 'Well, I wasn't expecting that.' I thought about Anna and all the miscarriages I'd had. How badly I'd wanted a child of my own. Katie had been about to become a mother, too. Why hadn't she said anything? Then it hit me. The baggy tops she'd been wearing, the toned-down look. She wasn't trying to reinvent herself as someone dowdy and frumpy at all after her break-up with Chris; it wasn't a sign of depression. She'd been trying to hide her pregnancy.

DS Khan returned with two cardboard cups and a bottle of water. She handed me the coffee and I took it vacantly.

'Is that was she was talking about, then, when she said she had something he wanted?' I said. 'She was going to make him pay for the baby? She hadn't really stolen something – she was talking about the baby?'

'It's likely.' DS Khan unscrewed her bottle of water and took a sip.

'Six months? Wow. But Chris can't have kids, anyway. It's why his wife left him. They were trying for ages, but . . . well, his sperm count is too low.'

'That could've changed over the years. We still need to be sure. To rule him out as the father we'll be running DNA tests on a sample he provided earlier, along with a sample recovered from Tom's body.'

'Right.'

'Chris was apparently the last person to see her alive.' DI Spencer took a sip of his coffee and watched me carefully. 'If the baby is his, that could point our investigation in a new direction.'

A sudden chill sliced deep inside of me. 'You think Chris could have killed her?'

They didn't answer.

'But if that was the case, why did Tom confess? He knew where she was buried – he told me!'

'He also told you he was protecting his family. It's possible that meant he was covering up for somebody. We need to explore all possibilities at the moment. We can't trust Tom's confession because of the Alzheimer's. We've checked his medical records and, as you know, he suffered from a considerable amount of confusion in the end. We need to follow certain procedures. Dot all the i's and cross all the t's.' DI Spencer shifted in his seat.

'But what about Jack? If he was abusing Katie, could the baby be his?'

'We spoke to Rose, who denied any knowledge of any abuse going on.'

'Well, I suppose she would, wouldn't she?'

'We have no DNA of Jack's to compare any sample to. And the only two people who know for certain whether any abuse happened are dead. But we think if it was Jack's baby, Katie would've more than likely had a termination.'

I nodded vaguely. 'Yes, I suppose.'

DS Khan said, 'Chris has admitted he was working on the barn renovation with Tom at the time so he had access to the site.'

I opened my mouth to speak but my mouth felt rubbery. 'But he saw her walking towards the barn and then he got on the bus to go to the gym. And lots of people must've had access to the site.'

'That's what he said, but we have no proof he went there or not. We spoke to his trainer, who still works there, but he can't remember after all this time whether Chris actually showed up that day or not. They don't keep any clocking in and out records there. And we don't know for certain she was even killed then. It could've happened any time after she was seen apparently walking towards the barn.'

'Or maybe she never did walk towards the barn like Chris said,' DS Khan threw in. 'Maybe something else happened later.' Her words hung in the air for a moment before I grasped the meaning.

'You think Chris is lying?!'

DS Khan shrugged. 'We're not sure of anything at the moment. That's why we need to investigate. We're trying to trace anyone else who remembers seeing her that day.'

I stared out of the window at a couple walking past with their dog, oblivious to the macabre conversation going on in the car. *Oh, yes, don't mind us. We're just talking about a dead body here. Carry on about your business, folks.*

'Do you happen to remember seeing Tom the day Katie wrote the letter and left home?' DI Spencer asked.

I shook my head. 'No. After PC Cook came and asked me if I knew anything about where Katie had gone, I thought I'd try and look for her myself. I checked the pub, but she wasn't there, and I borrowed Mum's car and drove to Abbotsbury because she was last seen by Chris heading in that direction. Then I went to Dorchester. We used to like hanging out in one of the parks there when the weather was nice. Just lying on the ground and staring at the sky, chatting, you know. Well, this was before she got upset about Chris breaking up with her. After that she didn't want to hang out at all, really. But anyway, she wasn't there, of course, so I drove to some other places that were our usual haunts over the years. Here,' I pointed out to the beach, 'and then on to Weymouth. It was getting dark by the time I got back and I went to Tom's house to see Ethan. The other house, I mean, their old one on the other side of the village. At that time I just thought she'd come back in a few days' time. I didn't think she was serious about running away, even though PC Cook told me about the letter, so I wasn't that worried at first. But . . .' I trailed off, remembering how I'd followed Ethan up the stairs to go to his room and seen Chris coming out of the bathroom, obviously upset, with a flushed face and tear-stained cheeks.

'She's gone. Katie's gone.' Chris had gripped my arm so tight his fingernails had dug into my flesh. 'PC Cook told me.'

'I'm sure she'll turn up soon. She's probably had another row with Jack and Rose and she's just gone to cool off. She'll be back in a few days.' I pulled my arm away. 'Chris, that's hurting.'

'What?' He looked at my arm with confusion. 'Oh, sorry.' He let go.

'She's just looking for attention.' Ethan was sitting on the top step, folding his arms. 'She's a drama queen. She's probably only done it so you go running back to her.'

Chris shook his head adamantly. 'She's gone. She's gone and she's not coming back.'

DS Khan's voice brought me back to the present. 'But, what?'

'Pardon?'

She watched me carefully, her eyebrows pinched together. 'You said you weren't worried at first "but".'

'Oh, Ethan thought the same as me – that it would blow over and she'd come back soon. Chris was adamant she was already gone for good.'

DI Spencer caught DS Khan's eye.

'What did the rest of the family think when they heard Katie had run away?' DI Spencer took a sip of coffee.

I stared into my drink, trying to remember. 'Well, Nadia wasn't there that night when I got back, I don't think. She was probably with Lucas. And I don't remember seeing Tom, either. I stayed at their house that night but Ethan and I were watching a film or something in his bedroom, and I don't think I saw Tom until the next morning when Ethan and I got up for uni.' What an awful friend I was. I'd been watching TV or having sex with Ethan while she'd probably been dying.

'What happened as the time went on and Katie didn't come back? How did Tom and Chris react?' DI Spencer finished his coffee and placed the cup in a circular holder between the front seats.

'Chris was just really upset all the time and kept wanting to talk to me about it because I was her friend. He said he felt guilty. That it was his fault she'd run off. It took him a long time to get over Katie. Even though he was the one who ended things with her, he was clearly still in love with her. I think it took about four years for him to start seeing Abby – that was who he married, eventually. Tom . . .' I shrugged. 'I don't really remember. I don't remember him saying very much about it, although Ethan thinks Tom was happy they'd split up.'

'We've just spoken to Lucas but he doesn't remember anything helpful. We'll need to speak to Ethan again, although he wasn't answering his mobile phone earlier.'

'No, he's off walking somewhere again. He's very upset about everything that's happened.'

'I appreciated this is very raw for you all.' DI Spencer was silent for a moment. He glanced at a seagull that landed briefly on the side mirror before flying off again with a piercing screech. 'Did Tom pressure Chris to end his relationship with her?'

'I don't think so.'

'Do you think Tom was having an affair with Katie?' DS Khan asked.

I swallowed back the lump in my throat. 'It's possible.'

There was silence for a moment before DS Khan asked, 'Do you have any other ideas of who could be the father of Katie's baby?'

I stared out of the window again. That was the million-dollar question, wasn't it?

Chapter Twenty-Two

I was torn between going to Chris's and asking him again whether he'd slept with Katie and going home for Anna. Anna was my priority. He'd already told me twice he hadn't slept with Katie in the seven months after they'd split up, which meant he couldn't be the father – even if his sperm had started out life as Olympic swimmers – so there was no point asking again. But Tom? Was it really possible he'd got her pregnant? Was Katie using that as leverage to get money from him? Had she, in fact, planned the pregnancy to trap one of them all along? When it didn't work with Chris because he was infertile, she tried to sleep with Ethan, and when that didn't work, either, because he turned her down, had she then resorted to Tom?

I had always defended her over the years, but had Katie been more conniving and sly than I'd ever realised before?

When I got to the barn, it looked like Anna hadn't budged from the TV all day. An empty bowl sat on the floor by her feet with the remnants of one of those packet cheesy pasta dishes that take five minutes in the microwave.

'It stinks in here.' I opened the French doors that faced the front garden to let in some air. I was about to tell her off for not putting the bowl in the dishwasher but had second thoughts. I didn't want to upset her and start off a crying fit again. I picked up the bowl, along with an empty glass of orange juice.

She turned the TV off with the remote control and looked at me, her mouth turned down in a serious expression. 'Do you believe in reincarnation?'

'No.'

'Why not?'

'Because I think it's impossible. And if you were reincarnated as someone else or something else, how would you even know you used to be someone else in the first place?'

'Huh?' She frowned.

I shrugged. I didn't know what I meant, either, but I knew she wouldn't let it lie until we'd talked about it. 'If you came back as a tree, for example, trees don't have brains, do they? So they won't remember they used to be you before, so how would you actually know you were reincarnated? If you were a tree. Or something equally brainless.'

She ignored me and drew her knees up to her chest. 'I've been thinking about it a lot, though,' she carried on. 'And I think it's a really nice idea. Poppy could really be someone we know, couldn't she? She could actually be Granny Tate. I mean, how do you know her spirit didn't come back inside Poppy when she died?'

I bit back a remark about how crazy that sounded. But if Anna wanted to believe in reincarnation, maybe it was a good thing. Anything that helped her get over Tom's death was a good thing, especially since Ethan and I would now have to break the even worse news about the skeleton being Katie. Anyway, Poppy hadn't even been born when Eve died.

'Yes, maybe she is,' I agreed, hoping to make her feel better about things.

'Which means that Granddad could come back as something else or someone else, too. Which means he's not *really* dead, is he? He's just kind of . . . in limbo, waiting to return.'

'Well, when you look at it like that, I suppose so, yes.' I tried to raise a smile in agreement.

'And the people on death row, they'll come back as something else, won't they?'

'Hopefully not as psychotic murderers again,' I said.

'They'd have to come back as an animal or an insect if they'd done something wrong, because I think the Buddhists believe that only people who do good things come back as humans. If you committed a crime then you'd come back as, like, a goat or a snail, or a mosquito or something. I'm not a hundred per cent sure, though. I need to do some more research.'

'Oh, well, that makes sense. Karma and all that. Who wants to be a mosquito?'

'So, say for example, you got pregnant again right now, my baby brother or sister could actually be Granddad. It's weird, when you think about it, isn't it?'

According to what she'd just said, Tom would more likely come back as an ant or a flea, I thought.

She grabbed the laptop from the floor and opened it. 'I'm going to google it some more.'

I kissed the top of her head, thankful the conversation was over and worrying about how to broach the next one.

As I put the bowl and glass in the dishwasher my gaze strayed to the garage again. What had really happened here twenty-five years ago?

I tried Ethan's mobile phone but it was still switched off. He'd done this every day since Tom's death but he was usually back when I got home from work so I was starting to get worried.

I went into my bedroom, shut the door and phoned Nadia, but I didn't even have to ask her the question because as soon as she heard my voice, she said, 'He's here.'

'Oh.' I tried to hide the disappointment that my husband had turned to Nadia for comfort rather than me. I felt excluded. But then I told myself I was being petty and ridiculous. If he needed to talk to his sister to help him cope, who was I to stop him? Still, what about me? I needed comforting, too. I was being left to answer Anna's questions and deal with the police and my own conflicting feelings about what had really happened to Katie while he just distanced himself from me. From us.

'Do you want to talk to him?'

'Yes, please, if it's not too much trouble.' I really tried not to sound snarky, but it didn't work.

'What's the matter?' she asked.

'We've got to tell Anna and Charlotte now,' I whispered down the phone. 'The police told me that it was definitely Katie in the garage.'

'Well, they haven't bothered to phone me and let me know! What if Charlotte saw Rose in the village and she got nasty with her?'

'I don't think they planned on seeing me today, I just caught them leaving Chris's house and they wanted to talk to me. No doubt they'll want to speak to you again, too. There's something else, as well, as if it isn't already bad enough. Katie was pregnant.'

She was silent on the other end for so long I thought we'd been cut off.

'Nadia? Are you still there?'

'Um . . . yes. Um, that was a shock.'

'That's what I said. They asked Chris to do a DNA test. And they're testing one from Tom, too.'

'Chris? He can't have kids.'

'I already told them that.'

'It could be Jack's baby, I suppose, if something was going on.'

'The police think she would've terminated it if it was Jack's, and I think they're right. But, anyway, I agree with you about Rose. She can be pretty volatile, and I wouldn't be surprised if she turned up here drunk and upset. Maybe we should go round to see her and apologise.'

'We don't even know that Dad did anything yet so how can we apologise?'

'Even if he didn't actually . . .' I lowered my voice again so Anna wouldn't hear me from downstairs, '. . . *kill* her, then he still knew something and covered it up, so, yes, I think we should go and apologise.'

'I don't know . . . What if she gets violent? Look, talk to Ethan about it.' There was some rustling on the other end.

'Who will get violent?' Ethan asked.

'I'll explain when I come over. I'm going to bring Anna. I think it would be best if we all tell the girls together. And it would probably be better for Anna if we didn't tell her here.'

'Tell them what?' I heard the weariness in his voice. 'What else has happened?'

'I'll be there in ten minutes, OK?'

Nadia and Lucas liked everything minimalist. They'd hired Ethan to design their house on a plot of land on the other side of the village. Some of the locals had protested at the planning meeting, saying it was too modern and not in keeping with the traditional stone cottages that made up a lot of the area. This house was more a cube, made of lots of glass and white concrete. It wasn't my thing – I always thought it felt too sterile, like a show house – but they loved it. And on the upside, at least there was lots of light. There were no photos on shelves. Actually, there weren't any shelves anywhere, just display cabinets with closed glass doors and downlighters. Maybe they had a point about the minimalist thing. No shelves equalled no dusting, which would save time. I made a note to myself to remember that. There were photos on the walls, though, instead of paintings. In the kitchen was a black and white one of Nadia and Lucas taken years ago by Chris, probably about the time Katie went missing. Chris always preferred to be behind the camera rather than in front of it. And he took very good pictures. In this one, they were mucking around in the garden of Lucas's parents' house, pretending to tango, and Chris had caught them as Lucas dipped Nadia backwards, her long hair swishing to the floor, one leg bent in a sexy pose. Lucas's arm supported her around her waist, and they were both staring into each other's eyes with a look of pure adoration and happiness.

Anna disappeared up to Charlotte's room to play on some new computer game. Charlotte had been bugging Nadia about it for months, and Nadia had promised her if she worked hard for her GCSEs, she could have it, along with one hundred pounds for every A-star she got, eighty pounds for every A, sixty pounds for a B, etc. Modern parenting meant bribing your kids to do well at school.

I heard Anna's laugh filter downstairs and felt a pang of guilt twist inside. It was the first time I'd heard her laugh since Tom had died and now we were going to give her a reason to silence it again.

I told them everything that happened with DI Spencer and DS Khan earlier.

Ethan sat on the sofa in the lounge and looked out of the window, which backed on to a view of a field full of black and white cows. He looked like he'd aged about ten years since this all began. 'I can't believe she was pregnant.'

'It's awful.' Nadia's face had turned a deathly pale shade. 'Not just for Katie, but the baby, too. But I don't believe it's Dad's. It can't be.'

'Neither do I,' Ethan said.

'It can't have been an immaculate conception,' I said.

'Could Chris really be the father?' Ethan looked at Nadia, ignoring my comment.

I sank back into the sofa, kicked off my flip-flops and curled up my legs to the side. 'I don't know. Like DI Spencer said, just because he has a low sperm count now doesn't mean it wasn't perfectly OK when he was eighteen. Obviously Tom knew something about Katie's death, and we don't know what yet, but if he knew where her body was, then there are only three reasons why.' I ticked them off on my fingers. 'One, he killed her and buried the body. Two, he killed her with someone else and buried the body. Or three, he knew who killed her, buried her body himself and hid the secret to protect someone.' And that's when Tom's words echoed in my head again.

I was just protecting my family. I was just doing what a parent should.

But what exactly was he protecting the family from, though? What kind of threat had Katie been?

'No. Chris did not get her pregnant and kill her, either.' Ethan scrubbed a hand over the stubble on his cheeks. His voice had lost some of the volatile anger of the previous few days and now just sounded exhausted. 'It's as ridiculous as Dad doing it.'

'Well, someone did,' I said. 'And Tom obviously knew about it.'

'We need to wait for the DNA test before we do any more speculating,' Nadia said. 'In the meantime, what are we going to tell Charlotte and Anna? The police are asking questions. I heard from the office today that they'd been looking through the records to do with the barn conversion, trying to find out who was employed on site at the time. No doubt they've been in the village asking questions, too. And now Katie's been officially identified, Rose will know, and I'm worried how she's going to react.'

'Me, too,' I said. 'That's why I think we should go and apologise to her. Give our condolences.'

'That's not a good idea,' Ethan said. 'It's just asking for trouble with her.'

'Well, I don't agree. How would you feel if Jack had confessed to killing Anna?'

'I'd want to kill him.'

'Exactly, Liv.' Nadia bit her lip. 'She'll be really upset and angry with us. I think we should just leave it.'

'I can't just leave it,' I said.

'You're asking for trouble. But then you always do exactly what you want, don't you?' Ethan snapped.

'Hey, that's not fair! What are you talking about?' I searched his face

'This is all your doing,' he burst out.

'What?' My lips fell open.

It seemed like since Tom had unburdened his awful confession, we were constantly angry with each other. Even though he was sitting just on the other side of the sofa from me, it felt as if he was another continent away. I knew he was grieving, of course, but it felt like more than that. He was distancing himself, shutting me out, blaming me.

'You can never leave things alone, can you?' he muttered. 'It's like you have to pick, pick, pick until you get people to do what you want.'

'What?' I hissed. 'What the hell are you going on about?' I had no idea where this was coming from. What was happening to us?

'Stop it!' Nadia said. 'Bickering amongst ourselves isn't going to make this go away.'

I took a few deep breaths to temper down my annoyance with Ethan and compose myself again. He was upset. He was saying things he didn't mean. I could understand that. It was how he dealt with stress – getting angry instead of talking about his feelings. We were all stressed. And really, he was right. I *was* responsible for all the snowballing heartbreak by not keeping my stupid, big mouth shut.

But could you have kept Tom's confession a secret? Could you really have said nothing? I asked myself the same questions I'd asked a million times since. I still didn't have an answer.

Finally, I said, 'I think we could be vague to Charlotte and Anna about the garage. Obviously, we'll have to tell them Tom knew something, but we can just say that because of the Alzheimer's he didn't know what he was talking about and was confused. We'll say the police are investigating but nothing's clear at the moment, and we don't know how Katie's body got there.'

Which is what we did. Not surprisingly, there were more emotional outbursts.

'I'll never be able to leave the house again! What are all my friends going to say when they see me?' Charlotte screamed.

'Mum, I don't want to live there anymore,' Anna wailed. 'I can't stay in the same place as a skeleton. What about ghosts?'

Anna threw herself down on the sofa in between Ethan and me.

'Darling, there are no such thing as ghosts.' Ethan scooched closer and kissed her forehead.

'How do you know?' she challenged.

'Everyone in the village is going to know that Granddad killed someone. They'll hate us.' Charlotte's lower lip trembled as she tried hard not to cry.

'You'll be starting sixth form college after the holidays; you'll meet new people who aren't from the village or your school so it won't be as bad as you think. And we don't know he did kill someone at the moment.' Nadia reached for Charlotte.

'But it'll be in the papers, won't it? Everyone will know our name.' Charlotte put her hand on her hip, tapping her foot anxiously. 'We'll have to move house!'

'And even if Granddad was confused, how would he know where her skeleton was if he didn't have anything to do with it?' Anna sobbed, her cheeks wet.

'That's what the police are trying to find out, sweetheart.' I wiped away her tears with my hand.

'I'm not going back. You can't make me go back there. I can't live in that house!'

'Nadia will let us stay here for a few days.' I looked to Nadia helplessly. 'But we'll have to go back at some point.'

'My life is ruined now!' Anna jumped up and ran out of the room. The downstairs bathroom door slammed then locked, and she shouted out a muffled, 'I'm staying in here and never coming out!'

Ethan got up and walked out the front door. Charlotte stormed off up the stairs. Nadia gathered some ingredients together to start baking a batch of scones.

Chapter Twenty-Three

I needed to get out of the house and clear my head. The walls were oppressive and claustrophobic, stifling me. I needed to breathe fresh air. Feel the wind on my face. Uncoil my frayed nerves and cramping stomach. Try to outrun the guilt for bringing this upon us all.

I left Anna in the bathroom. I couldn't deal with her at the moment. As soon as I had that thought I immediately felt guilty. Again. The guilt was just piling up by the second. Anna's concerns were legitimate. Well, apart from the ghost bit. She was just being a normal twelve-year-old. Even *I* found it hard eating and sleeping and breathing just metres away from where Katie had been buried. But what choice did we have? We couldn't stay in someone else's house indefinitely. Ethan and I would need to make a decision about selling the barn now, but who would want it? A body buried underneath it would completely put off any prospective buyers, unless they were someone like Fred West.

No, the whole thing was a mess, and at that moment I hated Tom. How could he do this to us? How could he put us all through it? Put me in such an impossible position. I was damned if I didn't tell someone about it and damned if I did. He'd said he wanted to protect his family but he was just poisoning us all, breaking up the thing he valued the most. He had us all fighting and crying. Part of me wished Tom had kept his horrific secret until his death. Some things are better not known.

My first thought was to go to Durdle Door and walk along the cliff edge, but it would only remind me of Tom and I wanted to forget about him for a while. Even if Nadia and Ethan didn't approve, I still needed to give my condolences to Rose. I tried to put myself in her place as I'd asked Ethan to do. How would I feel if Jack confessed to killing Anna and Katie came round to apologise? How could I hold it against her, his daughter? The sins of the father are not the sins of the rest of the family. In my scenario, Katie wouldn't have been any more responsible for Anna's death than I was now for hers. So I absolutely had to go. It was the right thing to do.

I almost wished I was invisible as I hurried past the primary school, which was thankfully now closed for the summer holidays. The mums dropping off their kids were always the worst for village gossip. 'I heard that so and so's dad was off shagging so and so's mum'; 'Did you see how much weight so and so's put on? She's enormous! What are the parents feeding her?'; 'Well, I heard so and so forgot her kid's sports day. Poor little thing had to do the village fun run in her skirt!' (That had probably been me they were talking about, actually.) It was one of the few things I hated about being a parent. That many women together in one place could never be a good thing, I always thought.

I passed a grungy teenager sporting a black Mohican with bleached tips, dressed in black jeans, a long-sleeved black T-shirt and black Doc Martens (in the height of a sweltering July day, seriously? Hadn't anyone told him black absorbed the sun the most?). He chewed on some gum and blew a huge bubble with it as I walked by.

As I headed past the surgery, I saw Emily Carver, a widow whose husband had died of bowel cancer last year.

Don't let her see me. Please don't let her see me.

I increased my pace, head down, hoping she'd be turning off before she got to me, but no such luck.

Oh, God! Please don't let her have heard the news.

I beamed at her brightly and asked how she was, the words coming out automatically. Even my professional nursing smile was fixed firmly in place. Hopefully she didn't notice me holding my breath, bracing myself for her to ask what was all this she'd heard about Tom and Katie and our garage. Luckily for me, she'd been stuck in the house for weeks because she'd had that horrible virus that was going round, so she hadn't heard what was going on. I shuffled from one foot to the other, trying to listen politely as she raved on about how it was the hottest July day for twenty-eight years, and wasn't that amazing, just in time for the kids breaking up, too. *Blah, blah, blah, who gives a shit?* I thought.

After I managed to get away, I carried on past the duck pond, pausing in front of it. There was a mother duck swimming with four ducklings riding the fanned ripple of water close behind her. A memory of Katie flashed into my head. We were probably about ten and we'd brought some bread to feed the ducks, which I've since discovered is the worst thing for them. Actually, I'd brought the bread and was *trying* to feed them. Katie kept nicking it and stuffing it in her mouth like she hadn't eaten for a week, which, on reflection, she probably hadn't. I should've guessed something, I supposed, even then. The bread was stale and mouldy in parts, but she just picked those bits off and carried on. I was having a go at her for stealing their food, but instead of telling me she was starving, that Rose and Jack didn't bother to feed her because they spent their unemployment benefit on booze, she just stared out at the pond, chewing quickly and swallowing so loud it frightened a mother duck on our side, causing it to jump into the water and quickly swim across the pond in the other direction to get away from us.

'Look, she's forgotten one.' Katie pointed to a tiny lone duckling tottering around the surrounding grass on wobbly webbed feet. A ginger tom cat was right behind it, crouched low in the grass, all muscles taut and ready to launch itself in an attack on the poor little thing. Katie had dropped the bag of food, shooed the cat away and picked up the duckling in her hand. Taking it round to the other side of the pond, she'd placed it gently in the water next to its mum, saving the day and reuniting them.

Katie could be cruel and a bitch. She could be selfish and lie and steal and betray me. But she could also be kind and warm and funny and caring. And no matter what, she didn't deserve to die.

I swallowed back the tears and carried on to Rose's house. The curtain at the front window was closed again. I knocked on the door as the moisture evaporated in my mouth and the sweat chilled against my skin.

No answer. I knocked again.

I glanced around, looking up and down the street. When I looked back I thought I saw the edge of the curtain drop back into place. I knocked again but there was still no response so I walked home, head down, palms sweating.

I collected Poppy from our house and walked along the path at the side and into the woods, trying to rid my mind of everything that had happened. But every time I forced the thoughts away, they hurtled straight back. Katie's baby would be twenty-five years old now if it had lived. What was Katie thinking when she had the idea to run away? She couldn't support herself financially on her meagre earnings from the shop, and it would be even worse with a baby on the way, but she'd still had the intention to leave the village. She must've had a plan, and that plan would involve getting money from somewhere to support herself.

I've got something he wants and I'm going to make him pay.

She was going to blackmail the father, I was sure of it. Her words made total sense now. She must've pre-arranged to meet her killer at the barn. But was that person Chris or Tom? We wouldn't know until the results of the DNA test.

It was a Sunday when she wrote the letter to Rose and Jack and then disappeared, which meant none of the contractors would've been working on site so there would've been no witnesses. Tom always insisted on having Sundays off so he could spend time with his family, and he'd made sure his employees didn't work then, either. I tried to picture what stage the renovation was at then, but only vague images came into my head. Because of its historic importance, the barn was a listed building, so the original walls made of local stone had to remain in place and couldn't be knocked down, only repaired. I remembered them all being *in situ* throughout the renovation work. Since Katie was buried under the garage floor, the foundations for it would have surely already been dug out at that stage. When we bought the property from Tom he'd told us he'd made the foundations in the garage suitable to take a two-storey extension in case he ever wanted to build a studio or office over it. And all that time her body had been rotting away underneath it.

As I opened our front gates, I saw Chris sitting on our doorstep, his head in his hands. He glanced up, looking dishevelled and ravaged. His hair, usually kept closely clippered, was sprouting out in all uneven directions, like patchy grass. His sallow cheeks were covered in several days' worth of stubble. There were dark hollows beneath his eyes.

'Hi,' I said as Poppy struggled on the lead, trying to run off and greet him.

'Hi.'

I walked towards him. 'Are you OK?'

He shook his head, ignoring Poppy nuzzling her snout into his hand. 'I . . . I just wanted to sit here for a while.'

I frowned. 'Why?'

'I wanted to say goodbye to her.' He clasped his hands behind his head, elbows sticking out in the air. His T-shirt lifted, revealing a tanned, toned stomach. He stared at the ground. 'I can't believe she was pregnant.'

I didn't know what to do. What if Chris was the father? What if he had something to do with Katie's death? But then a tiny inner voice told me to stop being crazy. Of course he hadn't. I knew him. He was kind and funny and sweet. The shy, quiet one.

Yes, but isn't it just as crazy to think that Tom did it? You knew him, too. Or thought you did. And what is it they always say about the quiet ones?

Had Katie made fun of Chris, taunted him, and he lost his temper and snapped? Is that what got her killed in the end?

Don't be ridiculous!

I settled for, 'Do you want to come inside?'

'No.'

'Do you remember what was happening here with the renovation when Katie went missing?' I asked. 'Do you remember working on the garage floor with Tom? Or was there another builder working on them?'

He shook his head in response, his gaze drifting to the garage. An expression passed over his face for a brief second and then it was gone, too fleeting for me to work out what it was. 'When you're that age, you think you know everything, don't you? Think you're capable of anything. If she wasn't running away it wouldn't have happened.'

'What are you saying, Chris? How can you know that?' A feeling of dread crept up my spine, as if in anticipation of a confession. 'Do you know what happened to her? Why Tom confessed? You can talk to me, Chris, you know that.'

He looked at me, but I don't think he was really seeing me. Before he stood up and walked away, he said, 'The others, they didn't like her. You're the only one who understands.'

Except I didn't understand anything. Not then.

Chapter Twenty-Four

The logistics of staying at Nadia's were fairly easy since she had two spare rooms. It was the atmosphere that was hard to take. It wasn't just Ethan and I that were showing signs of cracks in our relationship. When Lucas returned, he and Nadia bickered like crazy. Nadia was also angry with me about going to the police and heartbroken about Tom's suicide, but she was trying to hide it. Anna didn't want to talk much, which was completely unlike her usual chatterbox self. Most of the time she stayed in the spare bedroom on her laptop or was in Charlotte's room watching DVDs. When I went upstairs, I could hear their hushed tones as they whispered secretly to each other behind closed doors. Charlotte had complained about being a 'prisoner in her own home' at breakfast that morning and Anna had replied, 'Did you know prisoners on death row only get about an hour out of their cells every day?' to which Charlotte had countered, 'Yes, but they're guilty. We haven't done anything wrong.' Anna shook her head and added, 'They might not be guilty, though. Do you know how many innocent prisoners get convicted each year?'

I'd slammed my hand on the dining room table. 'Stop talking about death row prisoners! This is not the same thing at all. And until we find out what *really* happened at our house, we just need to get on with things as best we can. This is difficult for all of us, and Granddad may very well be innocent, too.' Although I didn't believe that last part.

'He can't be!' Charlotte pushed away her untouched American-style pancakes that Nadia had made. 'He confessed. Why would he confess if he didn't do it? I'd never confess to murdering someone if I didn't do it. It's mental.'

'He confessed to a crime he didn't commit because he's confused. Eat something, please. You're not eating anything lately.' Nadia pushed Charlotte's plate back.

'I'm not hungry. How can I eat at a time like this?'

'Yeah,' Anna again to me. 'Why *would* he confess if he didn't do it?'

How could I say that I now believed the only possible reason for Tom's confession was because he was trying to protect someone? Because then I'd have to voice the horrible thought that was welling up inside, throbbing away like a nervy toothache. If Tom really *was* protecting his family like he'd told me, it meant one of us was the person who had really killed Katie. And the only thing I could be completely certain of was that it wasn't me.

'How can you be so stupid, Mum?' Anna glared at me. 'Of course he must've done it. And my friends will never speak to me again. Neither will my teachers. I don't want to be here! I want to move!'

'Now, just a minute! There's no need to be rude,' I snapped.

'Oh, shut up!' Anna yelled before she ran out of the room and stormed upstairs.

And so it started all over again. Lucas, back from a long-haul flight, hovered at the worktop, drinking coffee, staring out of the window and not offering anything remotely helpful to the conversation. Ethan had disappeared somewhere before I'd even woken up, probably on another one of his solitary walks. I left for work feeling like I'd done a day's hard slog in a boot camp before I even got out the door.

It was a relief to be away from the house and the family as I took patients' blood pressure, checked dressings and did blood glucose checks for the diabetic clinic. While I was working I could forget for a time and the morning passed quickly. After Elaine arrived to carry on the afternoon shift, I walked home to Tate Barn to put some washing on and get some new clothes for all of us.

This had to stop. We couldn't carry on living at Nadia's. Late last night Ethan had said he was going to move back into the barn at the weekend and go back to work on Monday. I didn't want to split the family up, but I was dreading Anna's reaction. She'd have nightmares, I knew it. Even I was having horrible, haunting dreams. What if she refused to come back here? What should I do then? Should I force her?

I noticed DI Spencer's Mondeo parked on the road in front of our house but neither he nor DS Khan was sitting inside it. As I opened the gate I expected them to be checking something in the garage, but the door was closed and bolted from the outside, like always. Odd.

I opened the front door and heard their voices, along with Ethan's.

I walked into the kitchen and they were sitting at the oak table, empty mugs in front of them and a plate of digestives that were probably stale by now. I thought about adding digestives to my mental shopping list but then thought, Sod it. I didn't care anymore.

'Oh, hi.' I put my bag on the island. 'I didn't know you were all here.' I smiled tentatively at Ethan, who gave me a brief tight smile in return and looked away.

'Have you got some news? About the DNA results?' I asked hopefully.

'I'm afraid not yet. Any time now we're expecting it.' DI Spencer stood and glanced at DS Khan, who followed his lead. 'We've got more enquiries to make so we'll leave you to it.' He nodded briefly before they showed themselves out.

An oppressive silence settled over the room after they'd left, buzzing in my ears, and I had to fill it.

'What did they want?' I asked Ethan.

He shrugged. 'They just wanted to talk to me about where I was that Sunday when Katie left home.'

'Right.' I sat down next to him. 'Where were you? They asked me if I remembered what you were doing but I couldn't remember. I mean, I know we saw each other in the evening, after I'd come back from looking for her, but—'

'I don't remember, OK? How am I supposed to remember what happened twenty-five years ago?'

I was momentarily stunned by the anger in his voice and the look in his eyes. 'I remember.'

'You only remember some of it. And that's because you kept going on and on about it after she left. Just like Chris did.'

'She didn't leave, Ethan. She was murdered.' I surprised myself by keeping my voice on an even keel.

'We don't know that yet.'

'She had a fractured skull. She's hardly unlikely to bash her own head in, is she? What's wrong with you? I know you're grieving about Tom's death and frustrated and upset about his confession, but what's happening to us? It's like you don't even want to be in the same room as me anymore.' He was silent so I carried on. 'You don't want to talk about anything—'

'Of course I don't! Dad talked to you and looked what happened! That's *your* job, the talking. And you go on about things until we have to *talk*.' He said the word mockingly. 'I don't want to bloody talk!'

I counted to ten, trying to think of something nice to say. I carried on to twenty, but niceness had upped and disappeared somewhere. 'Look, this isn't my fault, so why are you blaming me? I had to do something. I had to tell the police. Stop distancing yourself. We're supposed to be a family – bloody well act like it, instead of leaving me to deal with Anna and going off on your own all the time, brooding. You're not the only one who's upset by all of this. You're not the only one grieving.'

He rested his elbows on the table and put his head in his hands. I didn't know he was crying at first. I'd only ever seen him cry once before, and that was when Anna was born, so it seemed so alien that I didn't understand. It was only the shaking of his shoulders that gave it away.

I sat next to him, arm around his shoulder. 'I'm sorry.' I leaned my forehead against the side of his, feeling his heat through my hair.

He turned towards me, his face a mass of anguished wrinkles. 'I don't know how to deal with something like this.'

'Together. We'll deal with it together.'

Whoever was up one minute was down the next and vice versa. Ethan was happier at dinner that night, but I couldn't shake the feeling of impending disaster. Lucas was quiet and withdrawn, and Nadia was almost manic in her liveliness. Anna was back to asking a million questions, this time about the entomology of insects on buried human bodies. Not a very appetising conversation for the dinner table. Charlotte obviously agreed because she ran to the bathroom a few minutes later and vomited up Nadia's roast beef. How Nadia had the time or inclination to cook a full roast dinner in the midst of everything going on beat me, but it was Lucas's favourite, and since he was only home for one night before jetting off again, she somehow found the time, as she always did. Maybe that's what Ethan needed: a nice roast dinner to make everything OK again!

DI Spencer and DS Khan appeared an hour after we all finished eating. Nadia poured red wine into large, almost bowl-shaped glasses. I looked at it as she handed one to me and thought that definitely wasn't going to be enough to blot out what was going on. Lucas was on beer. Ethan hit the whisky. DI Spencer and DS Khan declined anything.

'We just have a few more questions for you and Nadia, actually,' DI Spencer said to Lucas. 'You don't all need to be here.'

'Right.' I stood up.

Ethan and I went into the lounge to wait, avoiding each other's eyes. There was one of those awkward, fidgety silences that you get on a blind date when you find out you've got absolutely nothing in common with the other person. I chewed on my lip and stared out into the garden.

A little while later I heard Nadia talking in the hallway outside as she showed them out.

'So, we're no further forward, then?' Nadia asked them.

'Oh, I wouldn't say that,' DI Spencer replied before they left.

Nadia poked her head round the door. 'Come into the kitchen. I need another drink.'

'What did they ask?' Ethan asked her as he sat at the sparklingly shiny glass dining room table.

Nadia set her glass on the worktop and uncorked another bottle of wine. 'They wanted to know if I remembered where Dad was that Sunday when Katie left home, but I don't know. It was a long time ago. Apparently Chris told them that Tom mentioned he had something urgent to do that day and couldn't give him a lift to boxing, and they wanted to know if he'd mentioned what might've been so urgent.' She poured some wine into her glass and topped up mine, then sat in between Lucas and Ethan.

Lucas sighed. 'They wanted to know if Tom could've been working at the barn, but he couldn't have been, could he? He never worked on Sundays. Ever.'

Nadia took a sip of wine, and when she set it back down, the base of the glass clipped the edge of the table and the glass tipped over. She leaped back as red wine splattered across the glass and dripped onto the laminate beech floor.

I shot up and grabbed the tea towel resting on the back of the oven door as Nadia reached for the kitchen roll, and between us we mopped up the spilled mess.

'Sorry. Sorry about that!' Nadia sat back down, face flushed, wiping her hair away from her forehead.

Ethan took Nadia's glass and silently refilled it. Lucas stared at the floor, looking blank. Or bored. I wasn't sure which. Probably wishing he was a million miles away, just like all of us.

Chapter Twenty-Five

That night in bed it felt like I had the old Ethan back at first. After I'd seen a sullen and uncommunicative Anna to bed, we went upstairs to avoid Nadia and Lucas's jibes to each other.

'It's only nine o'clock.' Ethan lay on top of the bed, rigid, like a corpse. 'I feel like a prisoner here, too. It's like we're in limbo. I can't stay here anymore. I need my own space.'

I felt the same. The only one who was enjoying being at Nadia's was Poppy.

'What about Anna, though?' I asked. 'You said we'd stay until the weekend. This is a lot for her to handle. Just give it a few more days.' I lay on my side facing him, propping my head up with the palm of one hand.

I twined my fingers through his. He stared down at them as if they were something foreign.

He sighed. 'OK.'

I stroked the stubble on his cheeks. He hadn't shaved in days, and it was flecked with grey now.

'Are you growing a beard?' I laughed, trying to lighten the mood. 'I hate beards. Especially grey ones.'

'What about Sean Connery? He's got a grey beard and you fancy him.'

His words catapulted me into the past, sparking off a memory. I gasped. 'I don't think it was Tom's baby.'

He glanced at me sharply. 'Why not?'

'Because I just remembered something. One day Katie and I were having a conversation about older men, and she'd said they were disgusting and they made her feel ill. I mean, I was talking about good-looking older men at the time, and I was listing my top five actors who I fancied.' I waved my hand around. 'Anyway, I said Sean Connery and Jack Nicholson and – God, I can't remember who else – but she got . . . I don't know, really angry about it, and upset. Saying it was sick and twisted to have some old man pawing at young girls and they had no right to do it and why didn't anyone listen to them.' I shook my head. 'I mean now, suspecting Jack might have sexually abused her, it puts all that into context, but at the time I just thought she was overreacting.'

Ethan watched me without saying a word.

'So, you know, she wouldn't have slept with Tom, would she, if she felt like that? Did you ever see Tom looking at her in that way when she was at the house with Chris or us?'

'In what way?' He pronounced every word slowly like I was stupid, and it was clear he was only humouring me.

'You know. A sexual way.'

'I can't believe you're even saying it. No, I didn't notice that. Of course not.'

'Neither did I. Unless . . .' Another horrible thought hit me. 'What if he raped her?'

Ethan dropped my hand and sat up. 'He did *not* rape her.'

'How do you know?'

'Because no one needed to rape her. She would've dropped her knickers for anyone.'

A fire sparked in my head, molten anger bubbling to the surface. I sat up. 'I can't believe you just said that. How can you trivialise being raped?'

He rolled his eyes. 'Oh, for God's sake, here we go again.'

'What?' I blew out an angry breath.

'I can't say anything right these days, can I?'

'Well, neither can I!' I hissed, hyper-aware that the walls were very thin and we were in someone else's house. 'Victims of abuse come in all shapes and sizes. Even the strong ones can be abused, you know. I once worked with this surgeon whose husband was beating her up. You'd never have guessed this composed, confident, competent woman was a victim of domestic violence.'

'How do you know Jack wasn't the one who got her pregnant?' He bit back.

'If Jack raped her, she wouldn't have kept the baby, would she?' I muttered.

'What?'

'DI Spencer said she was almost six months pregnant. Why would she have kept it, if it was Jack's baby? She would've had a termination, wouldn't she? I mean, no one in that situation would want to have their father's baby.'

'How the hell do I know what she thought? Maybe she couldn't afford an abortion.'

'She could've explained what happened and got it done on the NHS.'

'Maybe she didn't want to explain anything. She didn't even tell you at the time how bad Rose and Jack were and you were supposed to be her best friend. She didn't tell you she was leaving. And she didn't tell you she tried to sleep with me!' He had a defiant glint in his eye. 'You didn't really know her at all. All you've got is speculation and pieces of a puzzle that don't fit anywhere. We're just going round in bloody circles here!' he spat out, trying to keep his voice down and failing miserably. 'There's no point in going over and over this until the police tell us the results of the DNA test. And even then I don't know what that proves. No one saw anything, and the only people who remember much are you and Chris. Maybe we'll never know what really happened. The police investigation is going nowhere. They're not going to find out exactly what happened. Not after all this time. I don't know why they're even bothering. But just remember that if it wasn't for you, none of this would've happened! Dad's dead because of your actions. I just hope you're satisfied now.' He lay down and turned away from me onto his side so hard the bed bounced up and down under his weight. He stayed in that position, ignoring me, for the rest of the night.

I stared into the darkness, tears silently falling down my cheeks, wondering again if I should've done things differently. But then wondering just what I could've done instead. Whether I could've lived with myself if I hadn't shared Tom's terrible secret.

I waited for sleep to claim me, for some sort of reprieve from the blame I shouldered, but all I got were more tormented images of Katie in my dreams.

The next morning when I was heading to work, I bumped into DI Spencer outside Chris's house again.

'Morning,' he said.

'Morning. Is everything OK?' I glanced at Chris's front door. It was shut and the curtains were still closed. His pick-up was on the drive.

'We were just giving Chris an update. It appears there's no DNA match between the foetus and either Tom or Chris,' DI Spencer said.

I didn't know whether that was a good thing or a bad thing. 'What does that mean, then – that you can rule out the baby as a motive for murder?'

'We're not sure at this stage.'

'And we won't know who the father was until we have a suspect we can compare a DNA sample with,' DS Khan said.

I felt terrible for not believing him when he said he hadn't slept with her. How could I have suspected he had anything to do with Katie's death? And if the baby wasn't his, surely there could be no reason for him to have killed her.

But then I thought about jealousy, and how that could be a motive, too. What if Chris knew Katie was pregnant by someone else and he'd become insane with jealousy? Had he lashed out and killed her by accident? Had he enlisted Tom's help to cover it up?

I'd hoped the results would prove something but all they'd done was give me yet more unanswered questions.

'How did Chris take it?' I asked.

'He was . . . subdued,' DI Spencer said.

'Where do things go from here, then?' I stared into space, chewing the inside of my cheek, deep in thought.

'We're still making enquiries. We'll be in touch.' DS Khan did her signature frown.

After they'd gone I walked past the shop and saw a couple of parents whose kids went to Anna's school. They nudged one another and stared at me, whispering like five-year-olds. I could just imagine what they were saying. *Did she know? Daughter-in-law of a murderer! Someone must've known there was a body in there.*

It's not my fault! I wanted to scream at them. A hot flush crept up my neck into my cheeks and I kept my head down, thankful that my phone was ringing to distract me. It was Mary from Mountain View Nursing Home. After she'd given me her condolences she apologised for calling but said they'd put together

Tom's things and she wanted to let me know we could come and collect them.

I drove over to the nursing home when I finished my shift, wondering what was left of Tom's belongings. When we'd moved him in there they'd told us not to bring any valuables, so those were still in boxes in our loft somewhere. All he really had were minor things that signified his existence in the world. Apart from Katie, of course: she would be the major legacy Tom would leave behind. Thanks, Tom, for your generous contribution to society.

There were more condolences from Kelly on reception, who said she was sorry for our loss. I know it's what you're supposed to say, but I'd always hated it when people said that. It sounds as if you've just misplaced something trivial. As she asked me to sign for Tom's belongings, which had been packed up in two square card-board boxes, it reminded me again of being in prison – anyone would think it was *me* who had a guilty conscience! – and having your belongings returned when you were released back into society. There'd be no chance of Tom going to prison now. No chance of justice for Rose for whatever part he'd played in Katie's death. No chance for redemption. Not that the Crown Prosecution Service would've even tried to convict for murder with the condition he was in, anyway.

I wanted to take the boxes and throw them off the cliffs at Durdle Door after Tom. I imagined them hurtling through the air, hitting the water, slowly sinking. It would probably feel good for a minute or two – that momentary release of anger and frustration.

I didn't, though, of course. Instead, I hauled them out to the car and dumped them on the passenger seat. I took the lid off the first one and rifled through. I didn't know what I was expecting to find. A suicide letter explaining everything that had happened to Katie – something that said how she came to end up buried under the garage? Something that said how remorseful he'd been? That was obviously too much to ask, because all I found were folded-up pairs of trousers, shirts, a couple of cardigans, slippers, one odd shoe – where had the other one gone? – and the magic wooden box. I picked the box up and tried to open it. I remembered Tom telling me he'd carved it for Eve as a wedding present. Nadia had told me her mum loved it, and it had always kept pride of place on the mantelpiece. Apparently, she never put anything in it because she could never open it. Tom and Anna were the only ones who ever remembered the weird combination routine thingybob to it.

I threw it back into the cardboard box before my anger got the better of me and I chucked it out the window or something.

When I got back to the barn the place was deadly quiet without my family and Poppy. Normally, I loved this place. It had always felt warm and alive. Now it was oppressive and cold and evil. Was it a good idea moving back into the barn like Ethan wanted? Would I see Katie's ghost in everything that happened here? Would it taint us? I wondered how long it would take to sell.

I put the boxes in a cupboard in the utility room out of sight so I could stop thinking about Tom and everything he'd done, or might've done, and trudged upstairs into my bedroom. Reaching into the back of my wardrobe, I retrieved an old shoe box where I kept my mementoes and old photos. Dumping everything on my bed, I picked out ticket stubs from the first concert Ethan had taken me to. His Valentine's cards from before we got married. Stupid little notes he'd left me around the house when we moved in together. I smiled as I flicked through them. There were old pesos from the Dominican Republic where we'd been on our honeymoon. Train tickets to London – Christmas shopping trips Ethan and I and

Anna had taken when she was little. A poster from a Christmas panto we'd seen in Weymouth. Anna's baby teeth in a clear box, a lock of her hair, her hospital bracelet from when she was born. A lifetime of memories.

I searched through the photos inside, wanting to find a picture of Katie as she really was, not as the grotesque images that had been haunting my sleep and piercing my wakefulness. And then there she was. Standing next to me on my fourteenth birthday as both of us blew out my candles. I knew her parents never made a fuss for her on her special day so I had always let her share mine. We were caught on camera mid-blow, goofy-looking expressions on our faces. The next one was from about a year later. Katie and I had been in our favourite park in Dorchester in the school summer holidays, hanging out, sunbathing, eyeing up the boys, making stupid plans for the future and sharing our dreams. We posed on the grass in skimpy tops and short skirts. She was pouting for the camera, her long hair falling down on one shoulder, her eyes half-closed in a sultry look.

There were more. Katie and I on holiday when my family took her with us to a caravan park in Devon one year, standing against the railing in front of the sea, arms wrapped around each other, my head resting on her shoulder. Katie at our school disco on our very last day at secondary school. Katie on the village green outside the pub with a cigarette in her hand.

I put the photos back, a heavy sinking feeling in my heart. For a long time we'd been so close, but when she vanished from my life I'd abandoned her when she needed me most and slowly erased her just like everybody else had, as if she was inconsequential. As if she was nothing.

I had to try to apologise to Rose again.

I knocked on Rose's door a few times but the place looked the same as every other time I'd been there, neglected with the curtains closed. I was about to turn away and walk back up the road when the door opened and she stood there, pale and skeletal, her short hair flattened and stuck to her head.

'You've got a bloody nerve coming round here,' she rasped.

'I just wanted to come and tell you how sorry I was. I . . . I know you probably don't want anything to do with our family, but we didn't have a clue. We didn't know anything. I mean, we still don't really know anything.'

'*I* know!' She swayed a little before leaning on the door frame for support. I could smell the alcohol permeating the air between us, thick and heavy. 'Tom Tate killed her and that's that. He's a murderer. A monster!'

'I'm so sorry. I . . . I don't really know what to say. I feel terrible. She was my friend and I let her down.'

'Don't come here again. I don't want to talk to you. Any of you. You think you're so much better than me, don't you, with your big house and your fancy cars? But your family's a damn sight worse,' she spat. 'Don't come round here again!' As she closed the door, I stuck my foot in it and put my arm out, hand pushing against it. She glanced up, surprised.

'Rose, what did Katie mean in her letter? When she said you know what you've done and that she hoped you'd rot in hell? What did she mean by that?'

'What? You trying to put the blame on me now?' She let out a deranged cackle. 'Oh, that's rich. That's fucking rich.' But there was something in her eyes that I recognised. Fear.

Maybe I shouldn't have said anything. Maybe I should've just left things rather than stirring up trouble. Rose was grieving, too, after all. But I couldn't let it lie. I still needed to know the truth. Needed to know why it happened.

'Was Jack abusing her? Did you know about it and not do anything? Is that what she meant? Or did Katie tell you and you didn't believe her?'

'Don't you dare go round spouting accusations against us! Sullying Jack's memory. Making up lies!' She glared at me. 'You don't have a clue. You don't have a bloody clue.'

'So tell me. Why did she want to get away from here so badly? Why did she want to run away from all of us? What did you and Jack do to her?'

She tried to push the door closed but I was stronger, and I wanted an answer. No. *Needed* an answer.

'We didn't kill her! Your bastard father-in-law did.'

'But if she hadn't been running away that day maybe none of this would've happened. What did she mean in the letter? What happened to her?'

She scowled in return, her facing turning a mottled red.

'She just wanted to be loved. What's wrong with that? You and Jack didn't care about her, did you? All you cared about was the drink. You neglected her, let her fend for herself. You can't deny that, can you?'

'Don't you dare try and pin this on me,' she screeched. And with an almighty push using both hands, she shoved the door closed. I just managed to retrieve my foot before it got crushed in the process.

Well, that apology had gone swimmingly well.

Chapter Twenty-Six

The Tate family was cursed. It was as if Tom's confession had unleashed something dark and destructive. Some foul black ripple effect that kept coming at us, leaving us spluttering and gasping for air, threatening to drown us all in it.

I stared at the computer screen in the nurses' room, totally unprepared for what I was seeing. With everything going on I'd completely forgotten about her appointment. I scrolled backwards to the main menu and went into her records again, just to make sure I was looking at the right ones.

Yes, there it was.

The blood test results had come through earlier that morning.

Charlotte. Too many white blood cells. Not enough platelets. Not enough red blood cells. But the real kick was that there were blasts – immature cells that aren't normally found in blood. It was highly suggestive of leukaemia. She'd need a sample of her bone marrow cells examined to make sure, but the blood test seemed pretty conclusive. It explained all her symptoms, too. The nosebleeds, fatigue, pale skin, loss of appetite, being unable to shake that virus. How had I missed it all? Taken individually, maybe they didn't add up to much. Nadia had been adamant the nosebleed was an accident. And weren't all teenagers stressed and run down during exam times? None of it had seemed that drastic on its own. But in context, it was glaringly obvious. And I'd missed it all. I'd been so busy worrying about everything surrounding Katie's murder that I'd overlooked something so vital. I was a disgrace as a nurse, and an aunt.

Charlotte. Leukaemia.

I rested my forehead on the desk and closed my eyes, too shocked to even cry. My beautiful niece had leukaemia.

Was she going to die? Was this all some kind of family karma? Redemption? A life for a life?

How much more could we all take? It was cruel and unfair and . . . why? Just, why? What had Charlotte ever done to deserve this?

The only thing that helped me was doing something proactive, and that meant sorting out the immediate next steps for Charlotte with her GP, Doctor Palmer, who called Nadia to arrange for them all to come to the surgery later that afternoon.

As I waited for their appointment time, my mind was all over the place. I tried about six times before I managed to finally draw blood from Sam Caldwell's vein, something unheard of for me. And I forgot to tell Jimmy Dawson to come back in two days to get the abscess on his back lanced if the cream I gave him didn't draw it out. I had to call him later to let him know.

I hovered outside Doctor Palmer's office while they were inside, wringing my hands, waiting for them after they'd been dealt the life-shattering blow.

Nadia had tears in her eyes as she led Charlotte back out with an arm protectively around her shoulder. Charlotte's eyes were blank, her mouth hanging open, lips trembling. She was in shock. Lucas's colour had faded to a sickly pallor, pinpricks of sweat on his forehead.

'Come into my office.' I took Charlotte's hand and we all walked along the corridor. I sat her down in a chair and crouched in front of her, clasping her hands. 'Do you want something to drink?'

Charlotte shook her head vaguely.

'I'm so sorry, sweetheart.'

'Doctor Palmer said the results are highly suggestive of leukaemia,' Nadia said. 'But that doesn't mean it's certain, does it? It could be just a mix-up, couldn't it?' She shook her head violently.

Lucas took a deep breath, blinking rapidly up at the ceiling, trying to be strong and hold it together.

'No, I don't believe it.' Nadia carried on with her denial. 'The tests must be wrong.'

I gave her a pained smile, digging my nails into my palm hard to stop myself crying. 'I'm sure Doctor Palmer explained that the *blast* cells shouldn't be there. The oncologist will take some bone marrow samples to examine, but I'd say it was almost certain. I'm so, so sorry.'

Tears fell from Charlotte's cheeks, dropping onto her dress.

'There's a high chance of remission.' I rubbed her tears away as Nadia carried on shaking her head, unable to take it in. 'That's what you need to concentrate on, Charlotte.'

'Doctor Palmer talked about chemo. Or possibly stem cell treatment,' Lucas said, rubbing Charlotte's back.

'Yes, the oncologist will be able to give you more information at your appointment tomorrow, but I think you've caught this early and you're going to respond well to treatment.' I forced a bright, positive smile at Charlotte.

'God, why didn't I take her for a blood test sooner?' Nadia muttered. 'It's all my fault. All my fault. I thought it was just a virus. That she was tired from all her exam revision. I thought—'

'You can't blame yourself,' I said lamely, knowing that every parent in the same position would find a way to blame themselves for something like this. I was a nurse and even I hadn't put her symptoms together sooner. I was equally to blame. 'The paediatric oncologist in Dorchester has got a great reputation. It's likely she'll do the bone marrow aspiration and biopsy tomorrow at your consultation, to speed things up. Look, I think I should get out of your hair so you can have some private time alone to prepare for the appointment. Anna and Ethan and I should move back home.'

'Anna really doesn't want to go home. It'll upset her,' Nadia said.

I wanted to hug her. Even in the midst of her own crisis she was still thinking about others.

'We can't stay with you forever. And besides, you need to . . . you know, we're not going to impose right now. I'll phone Ethan and tell him to come back to ours when he's finished his planning meeting. We were going to move back after the weekend, anyway. You just do what you need to do.'

We all walked back to their house together in silence, trying to make sense of something so awful, each of us lost in our own worrying thoughts.

I left them in the kitchen and went up the stairs to Charlotte's room where Anna was still watching a DVD. She lay on her stomach on the carpet. At least she'd bothered to get dressed, which was an improvement. But the room smelled of unwashed kids and curry-flavoured crisps.

I bit back the tears, blinking fast, holding off the point when I couldn't control them any longer. I managed to force a smile but it felt as if my face was about to crack. 'Hi.'

She ignored me for a moment, engrossed in *Norbit*. I don't know why; she'd watched it at least twenty times – could even recite the words.

'Oh, hi,' Anna finally said without looking at me.

'Anna, I need to talk to you.'

'Yeah, this will be finished in about half an hour. There's a really funny bit coming up.'

'No, I mean now.'

'Huh?' Her gaze didn't stray my way.

'NOW!' I said.

That got her attention. 'Oooh, you're so snappy at the moment,' she snapped. I might've found the irony of that funny in any other circumstances.

'Anna, I don't want any more arguments from you. Get the laptop and your bag of clothes and meet me downstairs.'

'What? Where are we going?'

'We're going back home.'

She pushed herself up to a sitting position. 'We can't go back there. There's a dead girl,' she whined, her eyes imploring me.

I felt like a bad mother. A horrendous mother. And maybe I was. Maybe I was paying for every mistake I'd ever made. Maybe we all were. I wanted to hug her. Squeeze her tight. Squeeze Charlotte tight. Cradle them both in my arms, as I'd done when they were babies, and promise them that everything was going to be all right. That I was there to look after them. The whole family was. I had a duty to protect my daughter and Charlotte from harm. From evil things happening in their world. Rose had failed to do that with Katie; I couldn't fail to do it with my miracle child and my niece. And yet here I was, powerless. Powerless to change the direction of their lives or the hands that they had been dealt. Powerless to take the fear and grief away from my daughter and the pain and disease away from Charlotte. I had to be strong – strong for everyone. Nadia and Lucas would need us now, too, more than ever. But all I wanted that second was to fall apart.

I took a deep breath. 'Let's go and take Poppy out for a walk on Chesil Beach and then we can talk about things, OK? You haven't been out of the house for days. It will do you good to get some fresh air.' I was expecting a drama, another tantrum like the ones she'd suddenly succumbed to since Tom's death, but she just looked tired. Weary with it, as we all were. 'I'll buy you an ice cream,' I said lamely, every mother's best bribe.

'And then are we coming back, though?' Her lower lip trembled and she was about to burst into tears. 'I want to come back.'

'Come on. We'll get that ice cream first.'

I left a message for Ethan to come home as soon as he could and drove Poppy and Anna to the beach.

Poppy barked excitedly as we pulled up in the car park, her head poking through the unwound window. I opened the door and she shot out just before I managed to undo her lead. She bounded towards the sea, barking at the waves.

'I know you don't want to go home at the moment, Anna, but Charlotte and Lucas and Nadia need their space.' I put my arm around her as we walked along.

'No, they don't. We're family. Me and Charlotte are like sisters.' She shrugged me off.

'Yes, I know that, darling, but . . .' I glanced at a green piece of glass nestled in between the pebbles that had probably started off life as a bottle but been smoothed away by the sea to an odd shape, like a bone.

I shuddered, a vision of Katie's bones lying under the garage flashing into my head, but pushed the image away.

'We can stay with Nadia and Lucas until we sell the barn, then. They won't mind,' Anna said.

'I have some bad news.' I stopped, my hand resting on her shoulder. 'It's almost certain that Charlotte's got leukaemia, sweetheart. I found out today. They need their space to deal with this. She's going to have some pretty hard treatment and she'll be feeling very ill with it, and probably very down. It's going to be a terrible time for everybody.'

Anna's eyes grew huge. 'What do you mean, *leukaemia*? You mean, she's going to *die*?' Her cupid bow lips opened in a gasp.

I took her hand and we sat on the pebbles, looking out to sea while Poppy turned her attention to chasing after the seagulls, which took flight in a blur of white.

'Hopefully not. She has a good chance of going into remission.'

'So she'll definitely live, then, won't she, Mum?'

'Unfortunately, no one can make those promises. It depends on how she responds to the treatment. It's going to be a long, painful road.'

'But you said she'd go into remission. That means she'll survive.'

'She could do, but she could also . . . die.' I wanted to sugar-coat it but at the same time I wanted to be honest. I didn't believe in lying. Anna was old enough to know the truth. And what I didn't tell her she'd only google, anyway.

She burst into tears. 'Everyone's dying around me.'

'Come on, now, Anna.' I blinked back my own tears. 'You need to be a strong girl for Charlotte. We all need to be strong for her.'

'You'll die soon, too. And Dad. And what if I'm left on my own?' She wiped her snotty nose with the sleeve of her T-shirt.

'We're not going to die.'

'How do you know? You don't know anything. You said that the other day and now Charlotte could die!'

I wished I had the magic answer to make everything better, but last time I consulted the perfect parents' handbook there must've been some pages missing. The truth was, I didn't know what to say.

'Well, if I do die, I'll come back as your stepmum so I can still look after you.'

'Oh, don't be so stupid!' She jumped up and stomped away from me.

Right. So obviously I shouldn't have said that, then. Magic answer still sadly lacking. I leaped up and rushed after her. Poppy, thinking this was all good fun, ran along in between us, getting beneath my feet, almost tripping me up.

'Come back here, Anna!' I expected her to ignore me but she didn't.

She stopped abruptly, as if she'd hit an invisible brick wall. By the time she turned around I'd caught up. Her eyes were downcast and teary. She ignored Poppy nuzzling into her hand for a stroke.

'Sometimes in life we have to put other people first.' I bent my knees a little so I was in her sightline. 'We're upset and scared about Charlotte, but we have to put that aside and be here for her right now. And Lucas and Nadia. And that means giving them space and moving back into our house. We'll sell the barn when we can, but I need you to be a big, strong girl and help us out, OK?'

'But Katie's in there.'

'She's not, darling.' I pressed my fingertips to my eyelids, trying to keep the tears inside. If I started, I didn't think I'd be able to stop. I dropped my hands and took hold of hers. 'The police took her away. There's nothing left. She's not there.'

'Her ghost is still there.'

'Darling, we've had this conversation.'

'I don't care – it's still there!' She stamped her foot. I felt like doing the same. If only it would solve everything. 'And Granddad killed her!' she yelled the last part at me. I glanced around to see if anyone had overheard, then thought *What did it matter?* Everyone in the village probably knew by now, anyway.

'We're not going to be there for long – just until we can sell it, like I said. And we don't know that Granddad did have anything to do with her death yet.' I tried to hold on to that thought, like I'd been trying to all this time, and yet I was still struggling with it. 'It might've been an accident for all we know,' I said lamely. 'In the meantime, we have to leave them all be and let them get through this traumatic time as best they can. We can visit Charlotte whenever she wants to see us, but we can't stay in their house. It's not fair of us to burden them with how we're feeling when they have to cope with her illness.'

She sullenly stared down, kicking at pebbles with her feet. 'Can I go with her for her treatment? Hold her hand and keep her company?'

'If she wants you to, darling, of course you can. I think that would be a very brave and loving thing for you to do. Concentrating on helping her get through this will give you strength to deal with it, too.'

She pulled at her lip with her thumb and forefinger, thinking about that for a few moments, and then nodded. 'OK. I'm going to be the best cousin I can so I can help her, and I need to be grown up to do that, don't I?'

'You do indeed.' I smiled with relief and looked up at the sky, blinking rapidly to clear my blurring vision. I hugged her towards me, feeling an overwhelming rush of pride. 'You're a good girl, darling. I'm very proud of you.'

'But can I sleep with you tonight? I don't want to be alone in my own bedroom. I might have a bad dream thinking about Katie and Charlotte and everything.' She looked at me, lost and forlorn.

'Of course you can.' I gripped her hand as tight as I could without hurting her.

'And can Poppy sleep with us, too? She'll help chase the ghosts away.'

'Yes.'

Poppy sat down and barked at us, knowing we were talking about her.

'She wants her dinner,' I said.

My stomach rumbled and I realised it was way past our dinner time, too. I thought about the meal Nadia would've been cook-ing when she got the call from Doctor Palmer, which would sit there untouched now. You always take life for granted, don't you? You think you've got years and years ahead of you so you plan all this stuff you're going to do in the future. I wonder how much time we waste being unhappy, doing things we don't want to, never fulfilling ourselves, because we think there's all this time left when we'll finally get round to doing what we want. Except there isn't. Life can change in a split second. It can all go wrong in one shattered moment. And then it's too late to do the things we put off. Too late to live the dreams we've been dreaming of all this time. It was too late for Katie and it could be too late for Charlotte. We had to do everything in our power to make things as wonderful for Charlotte as possible while we still could. While she still could appreciate life.

'I'm hungry, too,' Anna said. 'Nadia was making Thai green curry and apple sesame fritters for pudding.'

I squeezed her hand, wondering what the hell I still had left in the kitchen cupboards that I could feed her. 'Well, I could probably rustle up a Chinese or something.'

'You're going to cook a Chinese? What, from scratch?' she said disbelievingly.

'No. But the Peking Kitchen will, and as a bonus they'll even deliver it. Are you ready to go home?'

She looked at me. 'Will you make me waffles for breakfast with ice cream and chocolate sauce?'

Oh, to be twelve again, where the lowest lows are followed by an overdose of ice cream and chocolate. Anything sugary, in fact. Roll on a few years and the ice cream is replaced by wine. Which reminded me, did we have any in the house? It was going to take a hell of a lot to make me sleep tonight.

I forced a smile. 'Absolutely.'

'You promise?'

I held up my little finger. 'I pinky swear my promise.'

She entwined her little finger with mine and gave me a brave smile.

———⌣———

When we got home the sky was turning to dusk. Ethan's car still wasn't there. Anna stuck close by me, walking stiffly up the front steps, pointedly avoiding looking at the garage.

I took her hand and led her into the house, flipping on the lights as we went. She followed me into the kitchen and bumped into the back of me when I stopped walking. My Klingon had returned.

'Do you want a drink?' I asked her.

'Yes, wine.'

I actually laughed at her joke. I don't know where it came from. I was probably hysterical. Or having a breakdown. No, I actually think it was a way to get rid of all the nervous tension and worry and stress that had built up like a pressure cooker, waiting to explode. It had to go somewhere, I guess. I laughed and laughed and couldn't stop. Then Anna was laughing, too, until tears streamed down her cheeks. I clutched my stomach, bent over double and howled. We were making so much noise that I didn't hear Ethan coming in. It wasn't until I saw him hovering in the kitchen doorway that my laughter faded to a dull tinkle.

He looked at us both with a confused, pinched frown. 'What's so funny?'

'Charlotte's got leukaemia,' Anna and I said in unison.

Chapter Twenty-Seven

I needed to stay busy. I wanted something to take my mind off Charlotte, and going to work would've been the best solution, but leaving Anna at home on her own in a house she was scared of while dealing with Charlotte's leukaemia was out of the question. Luckily, the practice arranged for a locum nurse to come in and take over my shift for the next week.

I slipped out of bed, unable to sleep, just as it was getting light the following morning. Ethan was in Anna's bed because she was in with me, but I didn't want to wake him. He'd taken the news about Charlotte really badly on top of everything else. He'd cried. A lot. Head in his hands, shoulder-shaking sobs, I'm talking about. He was trying to be strong for us, I knew that. But inside he wasn't dealing with things well. It felt like all of us were falling apart.

How did you get through something like this? Tom's confession. His suicide. Katie's murder. Her pregnancy. Charlotte's illness. The secrets and lies and unanswered questions.

One step at a time. That's how we'd get through it. One tiny step at a time. We'd be all right. We had to be. Had to.

I walked into the kitchen, dug the waffle maker out of the cupboard and switched it on to heat up. Nothing happened. I flipped the switch a few times, waiting for the light to come on but it didn't make any difference. There wasn't a power cut because the fridge was still on. The fuse had blown, then. Well, I wasn't about to ask Ethan to replace it like he normally did, not at the moment with all he had on his mind, but I couldn't go back on my promise to Anna. Not now I'd managed to get her back here. Although I didn't really want to venture into the garage, either, where I knew Ethan's toolbox was kept.

My gaze flicked out of the window to the garage. I'd have to go in there sometime. I was being pathetic. Katie wasn't there. Her ghost wasn't there. I had to get this over with and face my fears.

Plus, I hate to admit it, but a little morbid part of me was curious.

I unlocked the back door and squeezed my feet into a pair of Anna's ballet-style flats that were two sizes too small. It was only about six metres to the garage door but it felt like two miles, as if I was walking down some kind of Alice-through-the-looking-glass tunnel and the closer I got the further away it seemed.

I stood outside it, my pulse hammering hard against the base of my throat. I undid the bolt and slowly pulled opened the door. The wood creaked, sounding like a painful, high-pitched cry, which made my hand drop abruptly to my side with a slap.

I pressed my other hand to my chest and took some deep breaths. The morning sun streamed through the double window on the opposite side of the garage, illuminating the scene. Along the wall to my left were shelves full of Ethan's tools and odds and sods. Sanders, drills, half-used tins of paint, boxes full of old leads and adaptors, dust sheets and rags. The bottom shelf was used as a workbench with a vice attached. Leaning against the opposite wall were ladders, fold-up chairs, a couple of sun loungers, Tom's old ping pong table, Ethan's and Anna's bikes, and probably a load of old junk we should really take to the rubbish tip. We'd have to sort that out before we moved.

In the centre of the concrete floor was a big, gaping hole that went down into the earth like an open wound. A hollowness opened up in my chest and I found it hard to breathe. This was my best friend's grave.

Was it really an accident or had it been planned? Had she begged for her life, or was she unconscious when she was killed? Was she trying to save herself and her baby? Did she fight back? Scream?

I made an involuntary noise that sounded like a cross between a sob and a squeak.

My poor, poor friend.

Anxious to get out of there, I rushed towards the bench where I saw Ethan's toolbox. It was metal with two upper compartments that were double hinged on each side and rotated outwards to expose the main tool storage underneath. The upper compartments were already open and I could see some tools in the bottom section, so I searched for a screwdriver to poke in the fuse cover on the waffle maker's plug. Next, I picked out a hammer and pliers and a whole messy, tangled heap of cable-ties, spanners and screws, looking for the small yellow plastic box with spare fuses inside that I knew he kept in there. I rummaged around, my fingers poking into the corners, and that's when I found it.

The discovery hit me like a knife being plunged between my shoulder blades. My heart lurched into my throat and the hairs on the back of my neck prickled. I had a thought then that maybe it really was all my fault. I'd wanted something to take my mind off Charlotte, and didn't they always say to be careful what you wished for?

Chapter Twenty-Eight

I sat at the island in the kitchen, the room silent apart from the ticking of the clock. On the worktop in front of me was a silver necklace. The chain was a flat curb-link pattern. Pretty ordinary and nondescript, really. Nothing strange about it at all. The strange thing was the charm on the end of it. A sun with wavy rays fanning out in a circle around it. Underneath the sun dangled a smaller star with a clear sparkling stone in the centre, probably cubic zirconium or something like that. On the back of the sun was inscribed *You're my sun and stars*. I'd never seen it before in my life but I was pretty sure I knew what it was. Chris had described it as a necklace with a sun and a star when he'd told me what Katie had worn on the Sunday she was running away from home.

So, the big question was, what was my husband doing with it? Or, more accurately, what the HELL was my husband doing with it?

I stroked the silver chain, which was tarnished with age, wishing it could tell me a story. Was it really the same one, or was it something that just looked similar? How many necklaces were there in the world with a sun and a star on them? Millions, probably. But how many people were wearing one on the day they disappeared and ended up buried in the very place I'd found it?

Still, it could all be a strange coincidence, couldn't it? Just a very odd . . .

Odd what?

Odd coincidence.

Yeah, you said that already. It didn't sound any more plausible the first time. Repeating it won't make it more believable.

Had Ethan killed Katie? Was it his baby? He'd said she'd tried to sleep with him; what if he had? What if he hadn't turned her down, after all? What if she'd threatened to tell me about it and he killed her? Was she trying to blackmail him? Had Tom covered it up?

How do you know it's even the same necklace?

I didn't know, of course, but I had to find out for sure.

Before I could think any more about it, I heard a creak at the top of the stairs. I brushed the necklace into my palm and put it in the kitchen drawer we used for takeaway menus and other crap that we didn't know where to put.

When Ethan came into the kitchen I had my back to him, furiously poking the screwdriver into the fuse cover on the back of the plug to pop it open.

'Morning,' he said. 'What are you doing?'

'Fuse has gone.' My hand shook and I tried to keep my voice light, but it came out sounding sing-songy, as if it was a line from a musical.

'Want me to do that?' He put a hand on mine and I dropped the fuse.

'Sorry, that was my fault,' he said.

We both bent down at the same time and our heads banged together.

'Ouch!' My vision wavered with black and white pinpricks and I rubbed my forehead.

'Sorry.' He put a hand to his own forehead and attempted a smile.

I picked up the fuse, head throbbing.

He gripped my arm and I froze. 'I'm sorry I've been so distant and angry. I . . . this is all really hard. I just . . .' He squeezed my arm hard as his gaze drifted out through the window towards the garage.

'That hurts!' I jerked my arm away.

'Sorry.' He ran a hand through his hair. 'Jesus, sorry. Look, I'm just trying to apologise for how I've been acting.' He crushed me in an embrace, squeezing me to him as if I was his oxygen.

I fought the urge to recoil and confront him about the necklace, but I couldn't say anything. Not yet. I needed to be sure it was definitely the same one before I did that. I didn't think it would go down too well, accusing your husband of murder if he hadn't even done anything. Would you ever get the trust back again? Things were dicey enough between us at the moment as it was.

I rested my clammy palms on his broad back, trying to keep my breathing steady. Is this what he'd done with Katie? Hugged her? Kissed her? Fucked her? Killed her?

'This has just knocked me for six,' he said.

'Well, you were very close to Tom; it's understandable. It's difficult for everyone.'

'And now with Charlotte being ill. It's like someone's got it in for us.'

Or it's reparation for everything this family's done. Payback time.

'Do you think she's going to survive?'

I took a deep breath and pulled back. 'We have to think positively. For Charlotte and Nadia and Lucas. It's going to be a long, hard struggle for all of them.'

'Yeah.' He looked at me and blinked, his eyes shining. He sniffed and stood up straighter. 'Look, I'm not going to be all distant anymore. I'm here for you, OK? And Anna. My girls are the most important thing in the world, and I'm sorry I've been acting so angry. I'm sorry I've been blaming you.'

'You're in mourning,' I said, unable to look at him. 'It's natural to be all over the place.'

He took the fuse from my curled fist. 'Here, I'll do that.' He kissed me on the cheek and I fought the urge to shudder. 'I've got a planning meeting this morning and some other things to finalise but I'll try and get home early tonight. Maybe we can all go out for dinner or something. Save you worrying about cooking.'

'I don't really feel like going out at the moment. I want to know what happens with Charlotte at the hospital.' I watched him screwing the plug back together, wondering if those same hands had killed Katie.

'OK. Whatever you want.'

What I want is to find the truth. What did you do, Ethan? What did you do?

⌣

As soon as he left for work I called DI Spencer and asked if they had any more leads with the investigation.

'Unfortunately not.' He sounded tired, too. 'Because it happened such a long time ago, we don't have many witnesses who actually remember anything. The enquiries we've made have led to no new sightings of Katie on the day she apparently disappeared. I checked with the employees who were working on the barn conversion at the time. There was one labourer helping Tom on site who remembered that when he finished work on Saturday afternoon, the foundations for the garage had been dug out and the sub-base, insulation and rebar were completed, but the concrete lorry wasn't booked to pour the garage floor for another week or so. He was surprised when he came back to work on the Monday and Tom suddenly wanted a rush job on the flooring and a lorry was already on site laying the concrete for it.'

Again, I pictured Tom stuffing Katie's lifeless body into that hole. Her head flopping back as he dropped her down into the cold dirt and covered her up with earth and concrete. My stomach twisted violently.

'At this stage we've found no evidence to suggest that someone other than Tom was responsible for her death and for burying her in the garage. Unless we find anything to contradict that theory, the case will be closed. We can't prosecute someone who's now deceased.'

'Um . . . I just wondered . . . when you found her . . . was there anything with her?'

'What do you mean?'

'Well, did you find what she was wearing? Or was she . . .'

'We didn't find the rucksack Chris said she was carrying. Perhaps Tom threw it away or burned her belongings. We may never know. There are a lot of things we may never know.'

I remembered Ethan saying the very same thing. Is that because he'd hidden the truth so well?

'There were fragments of clothing that hadn't decomposed yet, plus buttons from her shirt consistent with the one Chris saw her in.'

'What about jewellery?'

'We found some plastic hooped earrings.'

'Right. What about the necklace Chris said she was wearing?'

'No. We didn't recover that. It could've got lost in some kind of struggle.'

I stared at the necklace in front of me on the island, tracing the curve of the sun. 'Yes. Maybe.'

Maybe not.

'Or perhaps Tom disposed of it with the rucksack,' he said.

'I suppose so. OK, well, thanks for your help.'

'You're welcome. I'll be in touch if we find out anything else, although to be honest, I don't think there's anything more to find. It will probably be just a courtesy call in a few weeks to let you know we're closing the case.'

I hung up and glanced at the clock. Would Chris have left for work yet? I phoned his mobile.

'Hi. How are you?' I asked.

'Pretty shit. How are you?' His voice was hoarse and he sounded exhausted, as if he'd been up all night.

'Double shit.'

'I can't believe this about Charlotte. It's all gone mad. Our family is cursed. She'll survive, though, right? If it's leukaemia? I mean, people go into remission, don't they?'

'The chances of remission are pretty good. We have to be strong for them all and stay hopeful about the future.'

'Hopeful. Yeah.' And the way he said it let me know he was anything but hopeful.

'Are you at work?'

'Just leaving the house. Why?'

'Can you pop into the barn for a minute? I've got something I want to show you.'

'Sure. Be there in two.' He hung up.

I rubbed my hands over my face and took a deep breath, trying to mentally prepare myself for what was to come. True to his word, Chris was on my doorstep in two minutes. He looked like he'd aged even more since I'd last seen him on the front step. Mind you, we probably all did. His five o'clock shadow was about a week's shadow, but it was his eyes that really got to me. Vacant and blank, as if he'd checked out weeks ago. Or maybe he was still drunk. Or stoned.

'Chris, don't you think you should stop drinking? It's not going to solve anything. It's not going to bring her or Tom back.'

He shook his head. 'Don't tell me what to do, Liv. Don't tell me how I should feel or act.'

I held my hands up in mock surrender. 'OK, OK. You're an adult. I'm just worried about you, that's all.'

'It's not me you need to be worried about.'

'What's that supposed to mean?'

'Nothing.' He sighed. 'What did you want to see me about? I've got a building site I need to be at soon.'

I held my hand out, the necklace resting in my palm. 'Was this the necklace you saw Katie wearing the day she disappeared?'

He took it and held it up so the sun moved on the chain, the star swinging beneath it. 'It looks like it, yeah. Where the hell did you get it from?' His eyes narrowed, dark and turbulent under pale lashes.

'I found it. I . . . I can't say where until I know for certain what's going on.'

A hand went to his hip and he shook his head. 'Tell me, Liv. Where? Where did you find it? Didn't the police take it when they . . . ?' He looked over my head, focusing on the air above me. 'Wasn't it buried with her?'

'No, apparently not. So whoever had it must've killed her, mustn't they? I mean, why would they have the necklace of a dead woman otherwise? The last thing she was seen wearing.'

'Where, Liv?' His voice hardened and something seemed to click in his brain. 'Ethan said you'd picked up Dad's things. It was in there, wasn't it? Was it hidden in that stupid bloody magic box of his? Tell me!'

I opened my mouth to speak but nothing came out.

He took a step towards me, one fist clenching at his side. 'I told you Dad had done it. How could he? How could he kill someone I loved?'

For a moment I felt scared, threatened, as his emotions seemed to ooze through every pore. Fury, hurt, guilt, something else I couldn't quite put a name to.

I took a step back.

'I'm not going to hurt you! What's the matter with you?'

'Nothing, I . . .'

He opened my hand and placed the necklace back in my palm. Then he turned on his heel and stomped back down the path.

I watched him get into his pick-up truck as fear and revulsion did a slow dance in my stomach.

It all made sense now. In his confusion from the Alzheimer's, Tom had confessed to a secret he'd been keeping for twenty-five years. And when the police came to question him about the body buried under his barn, maybe Tom would've been able to tell the truth and give all the details of exactly what had happened. But then he'd suddenly committed suicide while out with Ethan. How convenient for Katie's killer. Ethan had insisted on being the only one to take Tom to Durdle Door that day, and we only had his word that Tom actually threw himself off the cliff. What if he'd been pushed? Had Ethan killed Tom, too, to shut him up because he was about to spill everything?

And just look how Ethan had acted through this whole thing. He'd been defensive, angry and obstructive the whole way. I mean, I knew he was in mourning, but still, he'd gone way overboard trying to prove Tom didn't have anything to do with it when you couldn't deny that he must've known *something*.

I was just protecting my family. I was just doing what a parent should.

Yes, it all made perfect sense. Tom had lied to everyone and covered up Katie's death because he'd been protecting Ethan all this time.

Chapter Twenty-Nine

I got through the morning in a kind of daze. I phoned Charlotte to wish her good luck at the consultant's appointment later that afternoon, but there was no answer on the house phone. Both her and Nadia's mobiles were switched off. I texted them each a message instead.

When Anna surfaced at 10 a.m., she thankfully looked like she'd slept OK and hadn't been bothered by ghosts of Katie and nightmares.

'Why don't we make something nice to drop off at Nadia's for dinner?' I suggested to her after she'd had her promised waffles. I needed a distraction to keep me busy. Keep me from thinking. Stop me falling apart.

'Yeah, she's always doing that for other people. That's a great idea, Mum. We should make lasagne. It's Charlotte's favourite.'

'Let's run to the shops and get the ingredients.'

'Can we make cupcakes, too? Emma's mum made some with this wicked icing and decoration stuff we could get.'

'Absolutely.'

And that was how I did it, putting one foot in front of the other like a robot, going through the motions, talking but not really thinking, because if I had to think I'd have to admit to myself that my husband was a murderer. That he'd slept with my best friend, got her pregnant, killed her. And not only that, he'd buried her body with Tom's help in this house. He'd walked over her grave all this time and hadn't batted an eyelid.

He was a psychopath. Or a sociopath, even. Were Anna and I even safe from him once he knew we knew? I'd been too busy suspecting Chris to even contemplate that my own husband could be involved.

———

Hours later, there were perfect-looking cupcakes cooling on the worktop waiting to be decorated; Anna had made them all by herself. She was turning out to be a better cook than I was. Now she was on her laptop with Mr Google again, researching leukaemia. I didn't know if it was a good thing or a bad thing for her to know everything involved, but I wanted her to be aware of what might happen. Forewarned is forearmed. Knowledge is power and all that. Charlotte had a good chance of going into remission, but there was also a chance she wouldn't survive this. There's no easy way to prepare your kids for dealing with death. Hell knows, we'd just had the very worst of scenarios to deal with. But death was very real. It was a natural part of life. Hiding it from her didn't make it go away. Plus, all the research was distracting Anna from her sadness and making her feel helpful and useful, and she desperately needed to cling on to that.

My phone rang and I dived for it. It was Nadia's number that came up.

'How did you get on?' I blurted out straight away. No hello or anything.

'The consultant was lovely. She did the bone marrow biopsy there and then, but we won't get the results until tomorrow.

But . . . um . . . yes, unfortunately, she's pretty sure from looking at the blood test results and the other symptoms Charlotte's had recently that we're looking at acute lymphoblastic leukaemia.'

I exhaled a lungful of air. I'd been expecting it but it still didn't make it any easier. 'Oh, no. I'm so sorry, Nadia.'

She was silent for a moment and I thought she was going to burst into tears down the phone, but that wasn't her usual style. Instead, she acted true to form: calm, in control, dealing with what needed to be done.

'Well, we're just going to take this one day at a time. I've been reading up on it. So have Charlotte and Lucas. We're going to beat this. It's as simple as that. Charlotte dying isn't an option,' she said briskly.

'No, you're absolutely right. Is she up to visitors?'

'Maybe tomorrow. She's a bit sore after the needles, and she didn't get much sleep last night worrying.'

'OK, well, Anna and I have made you dinner. And cupcakes. So you don't need to think about that. I'll drop it off soon. Don't worry, though, we won't stay.'

'Thanks, Liv. That's really kind.'

'It's nothing you wouldn't do for me. What are families for?'

I waited until Anna was in bed. Our bed again, actually. Except it wouldn't be our bed anymore. Not after this. No marriage could survive . . . *this.*

I don't know how I managed to ignore the rising horror and choking panic and act normally until Ethan and I were alone, but somehow I did.

Ethan was on the sofa watching the news, a bottle of beer in his hand, shirt undone at the collar. He patted the seat next to him and smiled.

I stood where I was and held up the necklace by its clasp. It swung gently in my fingertips. 'Do you recognise this?'

His eyebrows rose slightly at my tone. He glanced at it briefly then back to me. 'Should I?'

'It was Katie's.'

'Katie's?'

'Yes. You know, my best friend who everybody thought had run away but it turns out was murdered.'

'Yes, I *know* who she is. What are you doing with it? How did you get it?'

'Actually, that should be my question.'

'What?' He put the bottle of beer on the tiled floor and leaned forward.

'I found this in *your* toolbox in the garage. Katie was wearing it the day she disappeared. How did you end up with it?' My voice sounded surprisingly calm, as if someone else was talking and I was just moving my mouth in time, lip-syncing with them.

He looked at it again. 'I've got no idea. I told you I've never seen it before.'

'Oh, how convenient. You've never seen it before! Well, how did it get in your toolbox, then? By magic?'

'How do you know it's even hers?' He reached out his hand to take it.

I snatched it away so he couldn't. 'I just know, OK? She was wearing it when Chris last saw her but she wasn't wearing it when she was buried under the garage. Then suddenly, years later, I find it in your toolbox.'

'What the . . . ?' He stood up. 'You think *I* had something to do with her death?' He pointed a finger at the centre of his chest.

'Well, how do you explain it, otherwise?'

'I can't explain it! How can I explain it when I've never even seen that necklace before in my life?'

Every part of me seemed to shake with anger, my hand holding the necklace vibrating so the silver shimmered in the ceiling light as if it was alive. 'Don't give me that! You killed her, Ethan. You slept with her behind my back and killed her to shut her up. What, was she threatening to tell everyone about the baby? *Your* baby? Was she blackmailing you to keep quiet? Did you tell Tom and he helped you bury her afterwards? Or was he with you when you fractured her skull? Did you do it together?'

'You've got no idea w—'

'And then, when Tom was going to expose what you'd done, what he'd covered up for you all this time, you killed him, too! How did it feel to push your Dad off the cliff? Was it as good as killing a pregnant woman? Anything to keep your secret hidden, though, eh?'

He stared at me. 'I can't believe what you're coming out with. I . . . how can you accuse me of something like this?'

'Um . . . let me see . . . because no one knows where you were when Katie disappeared. Because you've tried to stall any investigation since it started. Because the one person who could tell the truth died when he was with you. Because you have a necklace belonging to my DEAD FRIEND. Maybe that's got something to do with it.'

'It wasn't me. I didn't have anything to do with her death. I had no clue. This was all as much of a surprise to me as it was to you when Dad started coming out with it.'

'Yeah, right! Everything has just been a lie, hasn't it? From the very beginning of our relationship. You betrayed me with Katie. Got her pregnant and killed her. How did you get Tom to cover it up and keep your secret? What did you say to him? "Oh, hi, Dad, I know you've had a busy day at work, but I've got a bit of a problem I need burying. Can you give me a hand?"' I impersonated Ethan's voice.

He threw his hands in the air. 'There *was* no secret! I didn't kill her!'

'Where were you when she disappeared then, huh?'

'I don't know. I can't remember what happened that day. It was years ago.'

'She was last seen walking towards the barn. Had you already arranged to meet her here that day? Did she want money before she left, or something else?'

He flinched as if my words were a physical slap. 'You're crazy. This is insane.'

'No, you're insane! What's insane is what you did! Come on, tell me. How did Tom find out what happened? Did you panic and tell him? Then you both decided to bury her where you thought no one would ever find her? Is that how it went?' My jaw clenched. 'I don't want you here in the house. Not with Anna. How do I know you won't do it again?'

'I didn't *do* anything!' He held his palms up to me in a 'calm down' gesture. But I didn't want to calm down. I needed to get it out there where it belonged.

'You killed her,' I said. 'And you're too cowardly to admit it.'

'I can't believe you'd think that. Can't believe you think I would be capable of something like this. I thought you knew me better than that.' His words were edged with steel, his once beautiful eyes flashing now with something in their depths that looked dark and dangerous. 'You don't know anything.'

'I obviously don't know *you* at all.'

'After everything we've been through . . . How can you not trust me?'

I held up the necklace. 'Because this speaks louder than words, Ethan. Who else would put this in your toolbox?'

'We never keep that garage door locked. Anyone could've put it there.' His chest rose and fell, a muscle in his jaw pulsing. 'Maybe

Dad put it there when he was living with us. Did you ever think of that? He was always leaving things in weird places. This really is all down to him. His confession was the truth. He was the person who actually killed her and he acted *alone*.' He emphasised the last word. 'You're just looking for something that's not there. Putting two and two together and coming up with nine!' He yelled, the tendons in his neck pulsing angrily against his skin.

'Oh, that's good, isn't it? That's very convenient again. You've been trying to convince me all this time that Tom couldn't possibly have killed her, and now suddenly you're saying he did it just to get yourself off the hook.' My heart beat so hard it threatened to explode out of my chest. My shoulders were taut, rigid bands of muscle.

He stared at me for a long time in silence. Finally, he said, 'I don't know you, either.' And he stormed out of the room.

I heard his heavy footsteps on the stairs. I chewed on my fingernail, wondering what to do, trying to take some deep, calming breaths. Should I go up there and make sure he wasn't hurting Anna? But then, why would he? He'd always been the perfect father.

Yeah, but he's always been the perfect husband and look how that's turning out!

No, he wouldn't hurt her. This wasn't about Anna. It was about sex and lies and betrayal and blackmail.

But what if Tom had put the necklace there?

A thread of doubt unravelled from the tight ball of anxiety curled in my chest. Why hadn't I even considered that? Why did I always shoot my mouth off prematurely? When Tom was living with us before he went into Mountain View, he could've been confused and easily put it in Ethan's toolbox by accident, just like he'd done with the remote control. With many things.

Had I made a mistake? Had I jumped to the wrong conclusion?

An image of Chris popped into my head. When I'd found him on the front step had he actually been here planting the necklace? Was he the one Tom had really been protecting all these years? When I'd shown it to him, he'd seemed genuinely surprised, but was he just a good liar, like Tom? We only had Chris's word that she was even wearing the necklace that day, and he'd been very descriptive about it after all this time. Had he really remembered it that well or had he lied about it so he could plant incriminating evidence to frame Tom or Ethan?

I didn't know what to think anymore. The only thing I did know with certainty was that I didn't want to be in the same house as Ethan at that moment. I needed some time to get my head around this.

I paced up and down. Should I call the police and let them deal with it? But Ethan wasn't just my husband; he was also the father of my child. Anna had been through enough already in the last week; how would she react if her dad was accused of murder in the midst of everything else? It would shatter her already fragile emotions to smithereens. Somehow I had to protect her from the fallout.

I glanced up as Ethan appeared in the lounge doorway carrying a small suitcase, his eyes cold and dark. There he stood, familiar and yet alien at the same time.

'I'm going to stay in a hotel. Tell Anna I'm working in York. I can't . . . I can't be anywhere near you right now.'

I opened my mouth to scream something back – probably 'Good!', which would just sound childish – but my murdering husband etiquette was also apparently in need of some work.

But is he really a murderer?

I braced myself for the slam of the front door but it closed with a soft click and the Range Rover started on the driveway.

Nausea erupted in my stomach and I ran to the bathroom where I was violently sick. My eyes stung and my throat burned as I retched again and again. When I was empty and spent, I sank to my knees on the floor, buried my head in my hands and sobbed. For myself, for Anna, for Charlotte, for Nadia and Lucas, and for a girl whose life had been cruelly snatched away from her.

Chapter Thirty

I lay in bed on my side, examining Anna's sleeping face in the splashes of moonlight that filtered through the window. Her snub nose, the chicken pox scar on her left temple, the beauty spot on her right cheek. I remembered the night she was born. In an attempt to take my mind off the labour pains, Ethan was prancing around in the delivery suite, pretending to be a ballet dancer, doing pliés and pirouettes, singing any songs that were baby related. He started off with Salt N Pepper's *Push It*. And I think he gave Queen's *I Want to Break Free* a go before butchering Curiosity Killed the Cat's *Hang on in There, Baby*. He had me in stitches in the middle of a contraction, although I couldn't completely laugh my head off because I was in so much pain and trying hard to breathe.

How would she cope if Ethan was taken away and put in prison? How could I be the one to put Anna in that position? She would hate me forever.

I'd do anything for her. She was my life. My miracle. Anything I could do to protect her, I would do in a second. And wasn't that what Tom had been trying to tell me, too?

The questions chased each other round and round in my head as I curled into a ball. What had gone through Tom's head when he was covering up Katie's death? Did Ethan kill her? Was Chris involved or did Tom really do this all by himself? Were all three of them in it together? How could I expose myself and Anna to Ethan if he had been involved? How could I live with someone if he'd murdered my friend? Or so-called friend. How could I ever be sure he was really being honest with me again? There would always be that permanent doubt and mistrust, just like with infidelity. I almost found myself wishing I'd discovered Ethan was having an affair, instead of this. But then I nearly laughed. He had probably been having an affair all along. With Katie.

At first I felt numb. So frozen with shock and uncertainty that I couldn't even cry anymore. As if my blood had stopped flowing. I felt disconnected from reality, separate from my body as though I were looking down at myself from a great height. Then a gripping fear that I'd never experienced before crushed at my chest with such force it was hard to breathe.

But if Ethan wasn't guilty, had I ruined my marriage in my quest for the truth? A truth I was still no closer to finding out. A truth I wasn't even sure I wanted to know anymore. So far, it was buried deep beneath layers of lies and deceit.

My head buzzed with pressure, as if it was about to cave in, my brain riddled with dark thoughts. One minute I decided I should go to the police and let them handle it. I wasn't equipped to deal with another murder investigation. It wasn't my responsibility to shoulder this. If Ethan or Chris were involved, they had to pay the price. That was the law. It was what I would've believed before any of this happened. When Anna was asking me before about her death row project, I was adamant that people should be punished for their actions. If you can't do the time, then don't do the crime, and all that. But the next minute, I thought about Anna and what this would do to her. The long-term effects of having a father in prison. She wouldn't just be labelled as the granddaughter of a killer anymore: she'd jump up a branch on the murdering family tree stakes. Didn't I have a duty to shield her from harm? Could I take the risk of possibly ripping Ethan away from her and destroying her world? How could I be the one to break up the family? It would mean the end of everything we had left. Our lives would slide down a slippery slope into a black chasm. I'd always believed in the truth. Believed in being honest and not telling lies. But was that always best for everyone? It was my fault that our family was being eaten up from the inside out. I'd wrecked everything. If I'd kept quiet, none of this would've happened. How could I be the one responsible for causing further damage and hurting Anna so badly?

Anna let out a wavering sigh and her eyelids fluttered as if she was dreaming. I hoped it was a nice dream, rather than the nightmare reality closing in on me in the darkness.

I slipped out of bed and went downstairs. Sitting at the kitchen table, I sipped whisky, trying to think and trying not to think simultaneously. As the darkness crept slowly into dawn and the start of another summer's day, I still didn't have a clue what to do next.

———⌣———

When Anna woke a few hours later, she found me in the same position, feet perched on the edge of the chair, arms wrapped around myself, resting my chin on my knees and staring out into the woods beyond the barn.

'Hey, sweetheart.' I put my legs down and stretched, stiff from being in the same position for so long. 'Sleep all right?'

'Yeah.' She shrugged, looking sad.

'What do you want to do today?'

'I don't know. I don't really want to go out anywhere in the village where people are going to see us. But I'm sick of being stuck indoors all the time.'

'Why don't we drive out to Swanage? Let's take a picnic and sit on the beach, just the two of us. And Poppy.'

Poppy's ears pricked up from the corner of the room where she was curled in her doggy bed. Her tail swished from side to side on the floor.

'OK. When does Charlotte get the results of her bone marrow biopsy?'

'Hopefully soon.'

'That's horrible, isn't it, all the waiting?'

'Well, maybe she'll be up to seeing us in the meantime and we can try to take her mind off it.'

She nodded. 'Is Dad at work?'

'He's in York. Not sure when he'll be back.' I stood and turned away from her. 'Now, what do you fancy for breakfast?'

'The car boot sale at school is on Sunday, and I've decided not to do it, after all,' Anna said as we got into the car.

'Right,' I said, doing up my seatbelt.

'I don't really want to see any of the people from school there. Some of them live in the village, and they'll know what Granddad did.'

'We still don't know what . . . Granddad did, sweetheart.' I angled myself to face her. 'But you can't hide forever. When you go back to school next term, some people will know. There's no getting around that, and sometimes you just have to face your fears. Sometimes the fear of doing something is worse than actually doing it.' I reached out and rested a palm on her cheek. 'But what you have to remember always is that you haven't done anything wrong. What . . . um . . . Granddad did is nothing to do with you. You're not responsible for anyone else's actions except your own.'

And that's when it hit me. Katie's death was not our responsibility to take on and bury and keep in shame. These were not our lies to keep secret. Ethan or Chris or Tom had killed Katie. We shouldn't all be defined by the actions of others. It wasn't us who had murdered her. No matter what it would do to Anna and the rest of the family, and to me, I had a duty to let the police know what I'd found out about the necklace, and that's exactly what I'd do, even if it was going to rip our family into even smaller shreds. It wasn't up to me to be judge and jury alone. I wanted someone else to make the decisions for me.

I was jarred from thoughts burning a hole in my brain by Anna's voice.

'Mum, you're not listening, are you?'

'Sorry, what?'

'I said, maybe you're right. If Charlotte can beat leukaemia, I can beat the gossip. They're only words, anyway, aren't they? And I still really want to raise money for the animal charity. I want to feel like I'm doing something to help.'

I leaned over and held her close to me. My beautiful, clever, strong, brave girl. I knew then that we'd get through this together. Whatever happened, we'd survive. Eventually.

As I pulled back my phone rang.

I glanced at the screen and then at Anna. 'It's Aunty Nadia.'

Anna bit her lip and clutched my hand.

'What happened? Have you got the results?' I asked breathlessly

'Yes. The doctor was right. Charlotte has acute lymphoblastic leukaemia.'

So that was it. It was official. Any little ray of hope was now obliterated.

'I'm so sorry,' I said, knowing those words were totally inadequate but wanting to say them, anyway.

'Charlotte is being quite brave about the whole thing. She hasn't even cried once today, which is a marked improvement. She's asking to see Anna. Are you guys free to come round?'

The beach would have to wait until another day. This was much more important. 'You bet.'

'I called Ethan but he said he's busy in meetings all day and he won't get back until later.'

'Yeah,' I mumbled.

'I'm worried about him. He's taking all this really badly. I've never known him to be so . . . well, broody and silent.' She paused for a moment. 'Are you two all right?'

'Um . . .' A lump formed in my throat. I glanced out of the window, away from Anna so she wouldn't notice me blinking rapidly. 'How are you and Lucas holding up?' I went for a complete change of direction instead.

'He's been amazing. Really supportive and loving. This is going to sound really strange but I think it will actually bring us closer together. It's bizarre that a tragedy can heal some things, isn't it? I think he's broken it off with that woman at work.'

'Really?' I glanced at Anna, not wanting to say too much on my end because she'd hear. 'That's great. But how do you know?'

'He hasn't been getting any of the unusual texts on his phone.'

'Well, I hope that's the end of it, then.'

'It is. I'm positive it is. You're staying for dinner, OK?' Nadia insisted.

'Are you sure that's not extra work?'

'When has my family ever been extra work? Besides, it'll give me something to do.'

'OK, but I'll help while Anna keeps Charlotte occupied.'

I drove with Anna chatting on about how she was going to take Charlotte's mind off things by playing Conspiracy Clubs, whatever that was. I wasn't really listening. All I could think of was what I was going to say to DI Spencer about the necklace when I got a minute alone, rehearsing the lines silently in my head. Nothing sounded right. It all sounded wrong. Completely and utterly wrong.

Chapter Thirty-One

'M um, you have to go into the garage for me,' Anna said the next morning after we'd taken Poppy out for a long walk through the woods. She'd rolled in fox's poo and absolutely reeked – Poppy, not Anna. I had no option but to give her a bath, which she hated, and usually ended up with me wearing more water than her. I really was not in the mood for it. In fact, the only thing I was in the mood for was repeatedly banging my head against a wall, or screaming at the top of my lungs in the garden, or curling up into a ball and crying for weeks, but I was desperately trying to hold it all together for Anna's sake.

'Why?' I said, struggling to lift a heavy Poppy into the bath. Seeing that gaping hole in the ground again, Katie's grave, was more than I could handle today. I had barely enough courage to call DI Spencer as soon as my little Klingon gave me some privacy, let alone see that again.

She sat on the edge of the bath, waving a hand under her nose. 'She stinks. Gross.'

Poppy struggled to get out of the bath but her legs just slipped on the enamel and the water splashed up, soaking my arms and chest.

'Ew!' Anna jumped back and stood in the doorway.

'If you want to roll in crap, then take the consequences,' I said firmly to Poppy, who wouldn't take a blind bit of notice. She'd do it again as soon as she could. 'What do you want in the garage?' I sighed. 'I really don't want to go in there at the moment.'

'I've decided I'm definitely going to do the car boot sale, after all. If I don't do what I can to raise money then I'll feel like I'm being selfish and childish about the whole thing.'

'Well, having principles and sticking to them is a mark of growing up, so I'm very proud of you.' I gave her an encouraging smile as I lathered Poppy up with some doggy shampoo that smelled of . . . well, the label said honey, but it was really more like mouldy sprouts and something synthetic.

'So I want to go through the stuff I've already collected. You know, you told me to put the box in the garage, so I did.'

I rolled my eyes at her. Typical. The one time I wished she hadn't taken any notice of me and she bloody well had. I sighed again. 'Where did you put it in there?'

'On one of the shelves.'

'All right,' I said reluctantly.

Half an hour later, with a pissed-off wet dog, a pissed-off wet me and a tension headache boring behind my right eye, I confronted my own fears and went back into the garage. If I was going to talk the talk to my daughter about being brave, then I had to live by my own rules. Otherwise I was a hypocrite, and that idea didn't sit well with me. I might be a lot of things, but I didn't ever want to be one of those.

I spied the box on the first shelf and heaved it down. God, it was heavy. How had Anna managed to lift it up there by herself?

After closing the door again firmly, I prayed this was the last time I'd ever have to go back in there. When we sold the barn, I'd just employ a moving company to come in and pack everything up.

I dumped the box on the island in the kitchen and called Anna. She came in and sat down on one of the stools while I made a cup of chamomile tea to stop my hands shaking with, well, with a culmination of everything, really.

Anna pulled out two table tennis bats. 'I got these off Chris.'

I picked one up, a sudden memory of him and Ethan playing it together. 'Yeah, he had a craze on ping pong for a while. Used to try and rope us all into playing. Granddad set up a table in the back garden one summer. It's still in the garage, actually. Oh, where did you get that from?' I picked up an ornately carved elephant in dark wood. Inside its belly you could see a baby elephant.

'Nadia. She had loads of stuff in a box in the loft I went through. She said I could have whatever.'

'She must've got it when they went on safari for their honeymoon.'

'What's that?' I lifted out an old vinyl record of *Complete Madness* by Madness. It must've belonged to Lucas. He used to love them. Despite everything, I felt a smile overtake me, remembering us all dancing at Nadia and Lucas's house one day before the girls came along and we got a bit more sensible. All of us had arms and legs waving around, jumping up and down, Madness-style, and pogoing everywhere. I think Ethan actually got a black eye from Lucas's elbow, and I accidentally smashed one of Nadia's favourite glass vases that was a wedding present from a friend.

'What's funny?' Anna asked.

'Just us lot, being mad.' Would we ever have the chance to laugh and be crazy together again? Or would Ethan or Chris be locked up in a prison cell for the rest of their life?

I put it back then picked up another magic wooden box, smaller than the one Tom had made for Eve. It was made out of pine and had *21* carved into the top with flowers around it. I remembered Tom giving it to Nadia for her twenty-first birthday.

'Did you ask Nadia if she wanted to keep this? Granddad made it for her.'

She shrugged. 'Yeah, I asked her. She said anything in the box could go.'

'Do you really need to get everything out on the kitchen worktop?'

She peered into the bottom of the box. 'But I'm looking for the necklace that was in here. Did you see it?' She turned to look at me. 'It's silver but it looks kind of dirty, and it's got a pendant of a sun and a star on it with some writing on the back. It's not here anymore.'

Icy fingers of dread clamped over my scalp. 'Necklace?'

'Yeah. I think . . .' She scrunched up her face. 'I think it must've fallen out.'

'Fallen out,' I repeated, sounding like a parrot.

'I was stretching up, trying to put the box on the shelf above but it was too heavy and it tipped over. Some of the stuff fell onto the floor. I picked up everything I could see, but I must've missed it. It's probably still on the floor in there somewhere.'

I stared at her but I wasn't really listening.

'Mum?' She waved a hand in front of my face.

I snapped to attention, standing up and retrieving the necklace from the drawer. 'Do you mean this?'

She reached out for it. 'Hey, you found it! Thanks, Mum. I think I could get quite a bit for it if I clean it up. You've got some silver cleaner, haven't you?'

I enclosed it in my clenched hand. 'Where did you get it from?' I asked.

So she told me.

Chapter Thirty-Two

C hris opened his front door, looking even worse than
before, if that was possible. A waft of alcohol fumes
engulfed him. He smelled like Rose, and it made me want
to throw up all over him.

'Hi,' he said to me, then turned to Anna and ruffled her hair.
He stood back. 'Come in.'

I followed him into the kitchen. Lucas sat there nursing a coffee,
although judging by the half-empty whisky bottle on the table, it
was laced. We'd need shares in a distillery at this rate. His usually
tanned skin was pale and shiny, as if he was one of those lifeless wax
dummies at Madame Tussaud's.

'I'm so sorry about Charlotte,' I said to him.

He sighed. Ran a hand over the back of his neck. 'Yeah. We're
all sorry. Don't know if that's going to do her any good, though.'

'Is she OK?' Anna asked him.

He laughed. It sounded bitter. 'She's up in her room. She's
looking forward to seeing you.'

Anna galloped out of the room as fast as her legs would carry her.

'Where's Nadia?' I asked.

Lucas pointed through the open bi-fold glass doors out into the garden. At the end was a wooden bench overlooking their pond. Nadia sat with her back to us, smoking.

'She's started smoking again?'

'Me, too.' Lucas picked up a packet of cigarettes on the table and dropped them back down.

'That's not going to help.'

'Thank you, Nurse.' He shrugged.

'Want a drink?' Chris tilted his tumbler in my direction.

I looked at it. 'No. And you should give it a rest, too. How much are you drinking at the moment?'

He wouldn't meet my gaze. 'Who cares?'

'You just missed Ethan,' Lucas said.

My heart jolted in my chest. I'd accused my husband of murder. I hadn't trusted him. Hadn't believed his explanation. Automatically, I'd believed the worst of him. How could I ever have thought he was capable of something like that? I was a horrible person. Would we ever be able to get back from that? Jagged shards of remorse ripped at my heart.

There was no time to think about it now, though. I pushed the thoughts into a corner of my mind to deal with later and walked outside towards the pond. There was a swell of dark clouds moving in. The wind danced on my skin. A summer storm was on its way. The end of the heat wave.

I sat next to Nadia. She kept her eyes fixed on the water, blowing out a line of blue-grey smoke before throwing the butt on the grass and squashing it with her sandal.

I pulled the necklace out of my pocket and held it out to her in my palm. 'Do you remember this?'

She looked at it. Frowned. It took a while, maybe half a minute, for the light of something to spark behind her eyes. I thought it was recognition, but I couldn't be certain because her gaze whipped away from me.

She took another cigarette from a packet resting on the bench, even though she'd just put one out, and lit it with a shaky hand. She inhaled deeply. 'No, I don't recognise it. Why?'

'Don't lie to me, Nadia. Anna found it when she was going through your things for the car boot sale. She found it in the magic box Tom gave you for your twenty-first.'

'I don't know what you're talking about.' She flicked the ash off her cigarette a few times. 'Anna must be mistaken. There was nothing in that box. She must've got it from somewhere else.'

I leaned forward and gripped her arm. 'Chris said Katie was wearing this the day she ran away. How did you get it?'

I prayed to be wrong again. Wanted with all my heart to be wrong.

'I don't know anything about it.' She shook my hand off and laughed, but I knew that laugh. I'd heard it many times over the years. It was higher than usual, a tinkling sound she took on when she was nervous.

I gripped her arm again, harder this time. 'Nadia. Do. Not. Lie. To. Me.' I pronounced each word slowly, the tone of my voice letting her know I wasn't going to drop this. 'I want to hear it from you. You owe me the truth. Or do you want me to go inside and tell everyone else about what I've found?'

She looked down at my hand that held the necklace, then closed her eyes briefly, her blonde lashes fluttering against her cheeks. She inhaled on the cigarette. Exhaled slowly. Opened her eyes.

'If you don't tell me, I'm going in there right now to show them this.' I jabbed a finger towards the bi-fold doors into the kitchen beyond and stood up.

'Wait!' She grabbed hold of my arm. 'Wait.' She pulled me back down again. She took a deep breath and licked her lips. 'I'd forgotten all about it,' she said softly. 'All this time and I'd completely forgotten. It was . . .'

'What? It was what?'

'It was mine.'

'Yours? Then why—' And I suddenly knew. 'Katie stole it from your room, didn't she?'

She stood stiffly and glanced into the house. She smoothed her sundress down with her hands, threw the cigarette on the ground next to the last one and ground it into the grass. 'Let's go for a walk and I'll tell you everything. Not here, though. I don't want to do it here. Not with everyone around.'

We walked down the street, heading towards our usual dog-walking path along the side of the barn and into the woods. We didn't say a word. My heart felt heavy with adrenaline, anger, resignation and sadness. The sky was black over our heads now. In the distance I could hear thunder, see the spikes of lightning flashing on the horizon. The air was thick with electricity. When we got through the woods and came out into the sprawling fields that led over the hills to Abbotsbury, she finally spoke.

'Yes. Katie stole that necklace from me. Lucas had just bought it for me, and I couldn't believe she was wearing it that day.'

I grabbed her shoulder and spun her round to face me. 'How did you get it back, Nadia? What happened?'

Her anguished eyes stared into mine, glistening with tears. She folded her arms across her chest and gripped her elbows.

Thunder rumbled over our heads.

I clutched both her shoulders. 'Tell me what happened.'

She bit her trembling lip. 'Katie was sleeping with Lucas. I caught them at it one day. Over there, in the woods.' She pointed back to where we'd just emerged. 'Do you remember Sparky, our old dog? I was walking him. He was a bugger for running off when he wasn't on the lead. He'd caught sight of a squirrel or something in the distance and belted off through the trees, so I was off the beaten path looking for him. I heard them before I saw them. Lucas had his back to me, sitting on this fallen log. She was on top, facing my direction. I couldn't believe it. Couldn't believe he was cheating on me. I love him, Liv.' She sank to her knees, wiping her eyes with the back of her hands. 'Love him with all my heart.'

Rain started to pour down in fat pellets. A bolt of lightning lit up the sky.

'What, so you killed her to get her out of the way? How cold and callous can you be?' I shrieked.

'No,' she wailed. 'No, it wasn't like that. She . . . um . . . she looked up when she was fucking him. I don't know if she saw me through the trees but she had this weird smile on her face. Triumphant. Part of me wanted to run over there and punch both of them, but I didn't. I covered my mouth to stop myself screaming and ran home, trying to think of what to do.' Her head dropped back and she turned her face up to the sky, her tears mingling with the rain, and she groaned. 'I was hoping it was just a one-off. That it wasn't going to happen again. I could deal with that. I could forget about it.'

'So what did you do?' I sank down next to her, ignoring the water lashing down, soaking my hair and clothes, dreading the next words out of her mouth.

She didn't speak. Just stared in the distance.

'What did you do, Nadia?' I yelled over the thunder.

'I kept an eye on Lucas. When he wasn't with me, I followed him,' she said, head bowed.

'*What?*'

'I'm not proud of it, but I couldn't lose him. Not Lucas. He's the love of my life. My soul mate. He's everything to me. I couldn't lose him to *her.*' Her shoulders stiffened. 'But as far as I knew he never saw her again, so it was a shock when months later I was at his house and she put a letter through his door. Lucas never knew. He was in the shower and I was in the kitchen cooking dinner for us. His parents were away for the weekend so we were making the most of having their house to ourselves. I heard the letterbox go, and when I looked out the window she was going back down the path. So I opened the envelope and inside was a letter that said she had to meet him on Sunday at the barn. She knew there would be no one there on a Sunday, and it would be somewhere private they could talk. It said she had something of his and she wanted to make sure he paid for it. I thought she'd stolen something from him at first. I didn't think she could be pregnant.' Nadia let out an almighty sniff. 'So I went instead of Lucas and . . .' she trailed off, shaking her head.

'Go on,' I said stiffly, guts churning.

'We were in what would be the kitchen now at the back of the house. All the doors and windows were fitted so there was no chance we could be heard from the outside, but the place was still unlocked while the other contractors were coming in to do stuff. She was obviously pretty surprised I was there and not Lucas.' Nadia took a deep breath. Held it. 'Everything happened in a hazy blur of anger. I told her to leave him alone. She laughed at me and said it was too late for that. I noticed she had my necklace on. *My* necklace that Lucas had given me and she'd stolen. I tried to grab it but she darted away from me. She undid the chain and threw it at me, saying she'd let me have it back, seeing as she had something much more valuable now. I put the necklace in my pocket and asked her what the hell she was talking about. That's when she told me she was nearly six months pregnant. She'd waited all this time to tell anyone so no one could try and talk her into getting rid of it. She said she wanted money from Lucas to support her and the baby or she was going to say he'd raped her and get him put in prison.'

I cupped my hands around my mouth and sucked in a breath.

'I told you she was a liar. I think she did it on purpose, you know – got pregnant. She wanted one of the rich boys from the village so she could use him to get away from Rose and Jack. She didn't get anywhere with Chris so she tried it with Lucas. She used him to get herself knocked up, although obviously he didn't need much persuading.' She let out a laugh devoid of any humour.

'She was fucking pregnant, for God's sake! She was about to be a mother!' I wiped the hair now sticking to my forehead away from my face and shivered involuntarily.

'I wasn't thinking straight. I was screwed up with emotion. When she told me about the baby and the rape I just snapped. She was prepared to get Lucas sent to prison if he didn't go along with her blackmail. And she didn't give a toss about anyone she hurt in the process. So—' She stopped abruptly. Stared at the ground, tears splashing down her cheeks, mingling with the rain.

'They wouldn't have found Lucas guilty of rape! Especially not back then, when rape convictions were rare and there was no evidence. Was that worth killing her over?' I cried.

'I just lashed out and pushed her. It was one split second! I didn't realise how hard at first, but I was raging with anger and jealousy. She fell backwards and hit her head on a pile of quarry tiles.'

'Oh, no.' I closed my eyes and tried not to picture it, but an image of the scene flew into my head. I sucked in lungfuls of air, my head spinning.

'I thought she was pretending at first. I yelled at her to get up. I kicked her foot but nothing happened. That was when I noticed the blood pooling out onto the tiles beneath her head along with some kind of other fluid.'

I fought the urge to retch. We'd been walking over that floor for years and all that time it was where Katie had been killed. No matter how much scrubbing and cleaning you do, how can you ever get rid of that?

'We'd done a first aid course a few months before at college and I felt her pulse. There was nothing there. She was already dead and it was too late to do anything. It was an accident. A terrible accident. I didn't mean to kill her. I didn't know what to do next. I panicked. I panicked and ran home. I expected the police to knock on my door any second. But they didn't. No one came. No one said anything about Katie being dead.'

'Because everyone thought she'd run away,' I said bitterly.

'Yes.' Her hands trembled at her sides.

I stood up and walked a few paces, hands on hips, staring at the ground, fighting for breath. 'I can't believe it.' I thought about the scene in Tom's room when DI Spencer and DS Khan were questioning him. Nadia had said *Please, Dad*. At the time I'd thought she was pleading with him to tell the truth but it was the exact opposite. She was pleading with him to stay quiet.

'He was protecting me. Everything he did was to protect me.'

'So you just let Tom take the blame for it? How could you? How selfish could you be? What did he say to you afterwards? "Oh, hi, Nadia. I've just cleared up that little mess you left in the kitchen and buried her under the garage. Don't worry – it'll be our little secret! Oh, and can you pass the mashed potato, please? I'm starving"?' I screamed out. 'You let everyone think it was Tom! You let me think it was Ethan! You put us through all this and you had the bloody cheek to blame me for it all!' I slapped her hard across the face, my chest heaving with rage.

Her head jerked sideways and she put a hand to her cheek. Her shoulders sagged. 'I deserve that.'

'Did Ethan know?' I glared at her.

She dropped her hand and stared out in the distance.

'*Did he?*' I grabbed her chin between my forefinger and thumb and forced her to look at me.

'No. No one knew. It wasn't my decision in the end. When I came home Dad was working in the garden. I told him what had happened. I cried and cried and told him how it had been a horrible accident. He told me to stay where I was and not to tell anyone. Not a soul. Ever. Maybe if there had been a trial I would've been convicted of manslaughter, not murder, but in those days if you killed someone you were sent to prison for life, not the few years you get now. And what if the jury didn't believe it was really an accident?'

I shook my head, dropped my hand, unable to bear touching her anymore. I clenched my fists. 'I can't believe I'm hearing this.'

'Dad didn't want shame on the family. He didn't want us all to suffer. He disappeared and came back in the middle of the night. All he said was that he'd dealt with it, and I could never tell a soul. When the police didn't come knocking and everyone was saying Katie had left the village I thought that maybe I'd got it wrong. That she was still alive and really had got up from the floor after I left and just run away. That I hadn't really killed her, it was all just some horrendous nightmare. But then . . . I understood. Sometimes I'd catch Dad looking at me in a certain way. As if he was in agony. And I knew that if she was really alive she would've never left me and Lucas alone. She would've done everything she'd threatened to do and more. Lucas would be in prison for rape and I'd be right alongside him for attempted murder or something. Dad covered it up – buried her body, somewhere they'd never find her. So as the days went on I knew Dad had done what he had to do to protect me. He kept the secret until he couldn't remember not to anymore.'

I shook my head, my bones feeling too heavy to stand. Dizziness took over, and I sank back to the slippery, sodden ground again. 'You have to go to the police. Tell them now what happened.'

'I can't. Don't you understand? Not with Charlotte like this!'

'So we just carry on hiding this, do we?' I wanted to slap her again, then caught myself. I was letting my anger unleash itself, just like she'd done all those years ago with dire consequences. 'Can you live with this?' I let out a mirthless laugh. 'Oh, yeah, I forgot. You have been for twenty-five years!'

'It was an accident. A horrible, horrible accident. I never meant for it to happen. There hasn't been a single day that I didn't wish I'd done something differently. But I've tried to make up for what I did. Doing the volunteer work for children's charities, being a good wife and mother. Looking after my family. It was my redemption. I've tried to be a good person. Tried to pay for it all. To balance the good with the bad. And now I'm paying the worst kind of price. Charlotte. It's motherly karma, isn't it? Maybe she has to die for it all to be made right.'

The wind grated on my skin; the rain stung my eyes. A chill worked its way through my bones, like spiders crawling deep inside.

'What are you going to do?' she asked.

I stared down at Tate Barn in the distance, wanting to set the place on fire. 'I don't know.'

Epilogue

I used to think that everything was black and white. Crimes should be punished. People shouldn't tell lies. Not big ones, anyway. Not important I've-just-killed-someone lies. But then, I'd never been in this situation before.

Katie was a liar. She was manipulative; a thief; maybe even toxic. But she was also a desperate, vulnerable young woman to whom fate had dealt a horrible hand. I also know she could be kind and compassionate and warm. Maybe she went about things the wrong way, but unless you've lived her life, how do you know you'd do things any differently?

But what Nadia did was wrong. She should've admitted it at the time. Confessed that it was an argument that had gone horribly wrong. An awful accident. She didn't. Who knows what would have happened if she had? It's too late to speculate and too late to change the past. What's done is done. The only thing I'm thinking about now is the future.

And I have thought. Long and hard. For days I've tried to decide what to do. Should I keep the secret Tom made a decision to keep all those years ago? Should I let him go to his grave with people thinking he's a murderer? Should I respect his wishes, even if people think he's guilty of something he'd never done? Should I expose Nadia?

In the end it comes down to one thing.

Family.

Charlotte needs Nadia. She needs her family to stay together and support her through her illness. If she goes into remission it could take months of treatment, years, and she could still relapse and have to go through it all again. And if the treatment doesn't work, well . . . Either way, how can I tear Nadia away from Charlotte when she needs her the most? None of this is Charlotte's fault. How can I break up their family when they needed to cling on to each other tightly? Despite Lucas's affair, which thankfully now seems to be over, he needs Nadia to be there, as well, to help him get through this. They all need each other.

Anna also needs to believe her aunt is all the things she seems: kind, compassionate, caring; the foundation that holds the Tates together. Ethan and Chris need their sister, too. Should all these people have to pay their own price if Nadia is convicted?

Tom knew what he was doing when he buried Katie. I don't agree with it. Not any of it. But he knew. It was his choice. He lived by the code he'd always steadfastly believed in. He made that decision to cover up what Nadia did and stuck by it. It's what he wanted. His sacrifice to his family. He's paid the ultimate price to keep the truth from being discovered. He's given his life so he can never reveal what really happened. Parental love is like nothing on Earth. Immeasurable in its strength. The fierce, burning need to protect. To do anything it takes to keep them safe. Tom's love for Nadia. My love for Anna. Nadia's love for Charlotte. The fallout from the world believing Tom was responsible is far less for us than it would be if they knew the truth. The Tates have suffered enough devastation as it is. Do we need any more?

I'm weighing up opposite ends of the scale in my hands.

Truth and lies. Justice and complicity.

It's an impossible choice. Can I really let the truth go unpunished? Let a lie prevail?

I now believe there's a hazy line between right and wrong. Am I walking on the right side of the wrong line, or the wrong side of the right line?

Life is messy. There is no black and white, only blurred shades that intermingle and co-exist. How can I destroy the people who mean more to me than anything in the world?

Our Range Rover pulls up at the crematorium behind the funeral car and it disappears into a tunnel marked 'Private'.

Ethan parks and turns off the engine. He glances over at me and I'm lost in his eyes. My heart contracts with love. He isn't just my husband. He's my friend, my lover, my life. He means everything to me. I'd accused him of killing my childhood friend. Of killing his own father. Heinous crimes that I should've known he could never commit. I don't know if I deserve his forgiveness, but I pray for it with all my heart. We have a lifetime of history. A lifetime of love and memories. You can't just give that up. Things are far from perfect between us, but at least he's talking to me again. At least he can bear to have me near him, and that gives me hope. I'll work on that. Whatever it takes. Piece by piece, I'll do anything to rebuild the trust.

I touch his hand. He pauses for a moment and lets it rest there, his eyes fluttering closed before he gets out of the car.

I exit, too. Wrap an arm around Anna and kiss the top of her head.

So, yes, I'll do this. For my family, I'll do anything to keep them whole. Keep them safe. Just like Tom wanted. This time I can't go to the police.

Nadia, Charlotte and Lucas get out of Lucas's car and greet us solemnly. Chris has refused to come. In time I hope he forgives Tom. Forgives me, too, for what I'm about to do.

Nadia's gaze seeks out mine above Anna's head. There's a question in her eyes. I glance away.

'Shall we go in?' Ethan takes hold of Anna's hand.

'I'll be there in a minute,' I say.

I watch their retreating backs, their blackness making them look like a swarm of rooks.

Rose had made it clear to the police that she didn't want anyone from our family to go to Katie's service, but I still want to say my own goodbye to a friend I once loved.

I walk away from the building out into the gardens. I know which plot it is from DI Spencer, who attended her funeral. I head past engraved plaques and flowers and plastic toys and photos and balloons that people have left for their loved ones.

And there she is. Finally marked with a proper grave. A deserved resting place.

The brass plaque reads *Katie Quinn. 1972 – 1990. Beloved Daughter.*

I'm too busy biting back the tears to laugh at those words Rose has added. *Beloved Daughter?* I wonder again what Katie meant in her letter about them knowing what they did. Had Jack really sexually abused her, or had she been talking about the neglect? I suppose I will never know now. Some of the secrets Katie had have been buried with her.

I want to tell her something. Say a big speech that expresses everything I'm feeling, but I don't know how to say it all. And words are sorely inadequate. In the end, I crouch down in front of the plaque, touch my fingertips to my lips and then press them against the cool metal.

Goodbye, Katie. I'm sorry. So, so sorry.

I rise and go inside. There are no friends of Tom's sitting in the pews. He'd lost touch with some when the Alzheimer's began, and the few who were left have either died or probably want to distance themselves from what he's done. There are some employees of Tate Construction here, and I nod to them as they look at me with sympathy.

Anna starts crying. I hold her close to me, stroking her hair.

Ethan sits rigid on the other side of Anna. Nadia is on the opposite end of the pew. Tears stream silently down her face. One of Lucas's arms is around her, one protectively round Charlotte who is dry-eyed but pale. I wonder how long it will be before her hair begins falling out. Nadia has already bought her a selection of wigs.

I don't even hear the vicar's words as he speaks about Tom. I'm too busy wondering if I'm going to regret my decision. When I hear him call my name to give one of Tom's eulogies, I jump with a start.

I look at Ethan over the top of Anna's head. He looks back, eyes glistening. Finally, he gives me an encouraging half smile. I stand up and walk towards the lectern at the front of the room. I have it all written down on a folded-up piece of paper in my pocket, but in the end I don't need it. I've been over this so many times in my head that I know off by heart what I have to say

I take a calming breath, trying to release the flutters in my chest. Then I begin.

'Tom was an amazing man. He would do anything for anybody. Nothing was ever too much trouble. Even if he was rushed off his feet, he'd make time for you. He was compassionate and kind-hearted and lived to see us all happy and contented. He was loyal to a fault. If you told him a secret, it would never be repeated.' My gaze strays to Nadia. She fidgets with the neck of her black dress. 'He single-handedly raised his family with dedication and devotion. He was driven and focused but still knew how to have fun. Family meant everything to Tom. Like any parent, he would always do what was necessary to protect them from harm.'

Anna sniffs loudly. Ethan hands her a tissue.

'If he had to make a choice, he would even die for his own family.'

Nadia wipes her eyes with a soggy, balled-up tissue.

'Today we say goodbye to a loving, generous and kind man. A man who is probably looking down on us now and making sure we're taking care of each other. A man who takes his secrets to his grave.' I look up and meet Nadia's eyes. The message to her is clear.

Her lips curve slightly in a strained, grateful smile as her hand flutters towards her mouth.

'Goodbye, Tom. We love you, and you'll always be in our hearts.' I step down and take my place next to Anna and Ethan.

I will keep the secret Tom desperately wanted to hang on to. The one he thought would protect his family forever, until the Alzheimer's made it impossible to stay hidden. It's my final gift to him. My goodbye. I will hide the truth to save Nadia, and in turn save all of us. Some mistakes you just can't take back.

I have no idea if it's right or wrong. Tom's plan was flawed, just like all of us. I've learned that some people should have second chances and some secrets should be kept. I've also learned that I'm something I never wanted to be – a liar and a hypocrite.

But how far would *you* go to protect the ones you love?

Author's Note

Firstly, I'd like to say a huge thanks to my readers. Thank you so much from the bottom of my heart for buying my books, and I hope you enjoy them!

A massive thanks to my husband Brad for supporting me, being my chief beta reader, and fleshing out ideas with me. Also for giving me the premise for *Where the Memories Lie* from a dream he had about a guy with Alzheimer's who confessed to killing somebody. I love working with characters who are unreliable, and I knew immediately there were so many places to go with that idea. Without you, this book would never have been written!

Big hugs and thanks to my fabulous nieces Chantelle and Annice for all their advice on school lesson plans and inspiration for the character of Anna. It's been a long time since I was twelve, so your input was fantastic!

Thanks so much to D. P. Lyle, MD, for his advice and information on DNA in skeletal remains.

And finally, a huge thanks to Jenny Parrott for all her invaluable editing suggestions. And also to Emilie Marneur for her ongoing support and belief in me, along with all the rest of the Thomas & Mercer team.

About the Author

 Sibel Hodge is the author of the #1 bestseller *Look Behind You*. Her Amber Fox Mysteries and romantic comedies, *Fourteen Days Later* and *The Baby Trap*, are international bestsellers on Amazon, Barnes & Noble and iBooks. She writes in an eclectic mix of genres, and she's a passionate human and animal rights advocate.

Her work has been nominated and shortlisted for numerous prizes, including the Harry Bowling Prize, the Yeovil Literary Prize, the Chapter One Promotions Novel Competition, *The Romance Reviews*' prize for Best Novel with Romantic Elements, and Indie Book Bargains' Best Indie Books of 2012. She was the winner of Best Children's Book by eFestival of Words 2013, and winner of Crime, Thrillers & Mystery | Book from a Series in the SpaSpa Book Awards 2013. Her novella *Trafficked: The Diary of a Sex Slave* has been listed as one of the top 40 books about human rights by Accredited Online Colleges.

For Sibel's latest book releases, giveaways and gossip, sign up to her newsletter at: www.sibelhodge.com/contact-followme.php